BLOOD HUNT

Neil Miller Gunn was born in Dunbeath, Caithness, in 1891, the seventh son of nine children. His father, James Miller, was a fishing skipper, his mother, Isabella, a domestic servant. At the age of twelve Gunn went to live with his married sister in Kirkcudbrightshire, where he was privately educated in preparation for Civil Service exams which he passed in 1907. After brief spells in London and Edinburgh, where he became aware of new political and philosophical thinking, he was appointed Customs and Excise officer in Inverness in 1911. During the First World War he began to write but it was not until 1926 that his first novel, *Grey Coast*, was published. His first commercial success came with *Morning Tide* (1930).

In 1937 he became a full-time writer. The next twelve years were his most productive, including *Highland River* (1937), *The Silver Darlings* (1941), *Young Art and Old Hector* (1942), *The Green Isle of the Great Deep* (1943), *The Key of the Chest* (1945) and *The Silver Bough* (1948).

His writing also extended to journalism and he wrote articles for American and British publications, including *The Scots Magazine*, in which he argued for the preservation of the Highland way of life.

Later years were spent at Kincraig and Dalcraig on the Black Isle. He was heavily involved in Scottish Nationalism and grew increasingly fascinated by Zen Buddhism, discussed in his unconventional, spiritual autobiography, *The Atom of Delight* (1956). He died after a short illness in 1973.

Neil M. Gunn

Blood Hunt

Introduced by Frederic Lindsay

Polygon

First published in 1952 by Faber and Faber Ltd

This edition published in 2007 by
Polygon, an imprint of Birlinn Ltd
West Newington House
10 Newington Road
Edinburgh
EH9 1QS

www.birlinn.co.uk

ISBN 978 1 84697 024 5

The publishers acknowledge subsidy from the

 Scottish
Arts Council

towards the publication of this volume

British Library Cataloguing-in-Publication Data
A catalogue record for this book is
available on request from the British Library

Typeset by Palimpsest Book Production Ltd, Grangemouth, Stirlingshire
Printed and bound by Creative Print and Design, Ebbw Vale, Wales

For R.W.

Introduction

Born in 1891, by the time he came to compose *Blood Hunt*, his penultimate novel, Gunn had, like his protagonist Sandy, lived through the futile carnage of the First World War, the dark nightmare unleashed by the Nazis and the souring of hope for the future as the long enmity between West and East began under the shadow of the atomic bomb.

After a lifetime at sea, Sandy has come ashore to spend his last days on a croft not unlike the one on which he spent his childhood. Accompanied only by his dog Queenie, he spends his time on the round of chores which keep him self-sufficient. To an outsider, it might seem a narrow, even an impoverished, life. In such a place, however, each casual contact takes weight from the times of solitude which surround it.

As he follows his domestic routine and through the seasons, calling upon all he has experienced and pondered, he is increasingly preoccupied with the mystery of mortality. All the same, he is no churchgoer. His beliefs have to be earned and he wrestles against the certainties of Mr Davidson the minister, a contest drawing upon a deep common humanity which each draws out from the other. Is death the end of the spirit? By reading and reflection, he is preparing for the end and has a half-unacknowledged feeling that the ideal way to meet it would be on the same open hill where in a moment of epiphany he had felt that 'to pass out of his body was in the order of things, now revealed; not an end and not quite a translation, but precisely a passing on and away'.

This internal drama is interrupted by the policeman Nicol Menzies who comes to search the croft for a murderer on the run. When he names the fugitive, Sandy recognises Allan Innes as the brightest spirit of a group who have frequented the croft from boyhood, given freedom by him to use it as their base for poaching expeditions undertaken out of a youthful longing for adventure.

The motive of the killing, suggests Nicol, has had something to do with a woman. The policeman has cut off Allan's escape into the nearby hills and believes that he has gone to ground somewhere nearby, perhaps somewhere on the croft itself. Asked for his permission to undertake a search of the barn as a first step, Sandy takes the decision which will determine the course of the novel. Taking an old key, he makes a pretence of unlocking the barn and keeps silent about the obstruction he has felt between door and wall as he pushed his way inside. As the policeman's steps echo in the loft above, a stolen glance shows the face of Allan Innes: 'The eyes were on Sandy not with fear but with a strange glistening smile as though guilt were looking at him through a window.'

This momentous decision of Sandy's is not the product of reason but of a complex of instinctive sympathies. If he had heard of the murder from a different source and been given time to reflect on the life that has been taken, his reaction might have been different. From that instant, however, Sandy learns that the murder victim is Nicol Menzies' brother, killed in a quarrel over a woman, and he senses that the policeman's hunt for the killer has in it something driven and remorseless, with an avidity which is too personal to be about justice in any simple sense. In addition, since this is still in the time when a convicted murderer will face sentence of death, there is the revulsion the old man feels at the ending of one young life even in payment for another. For the reader, this is perhaps the most powerful motive of sympathy with Sandy's actions. After all, the impulse which leads us to identify with the hunted creature comes from the better part of our nature and is, unless brutalised by passion or perverted by ideology, almost universal.

This initial deceit of the old man's thrusts him back into the stream of life from which he has been preparing a quiet leave-taking. It is a distraction which he resents. 'All the time anxious not to be involved himself, anxious to get rid of Allan, to get rid of them all, to be left alone – to find the precious way, the last brightness, that fond illusion.' A burden then and one he would willingly lay down but never attempts to evade. He supplies Allan with food, oatcakes smeared with butter, boiled eggs, salt in a screw of paper, not much to withstand the hardships of a winter reluctant to surrender its grip to spring. His dearest wish is that the boy will make his own way from this part of the world altogether. To this end, he lays aside for him a bundle of clothing which may act as some kind of disguise, and prepares to go to town to lift money to provide for his escape.

At this point an unexpected but wonderfully appropriate *deus ex machina* intervenes. Nancy is no tamed domestic creature, but a Highland cow with shaggy coat, hair over her face to hide the glint in her eye, and a pair of curved horns sharp enough to put out a man's eye. Come into season and on the way to keep her appointment with the neighbouring bull, she runs off in her eagerness, dragging Sandy with her, the lead rope wrapped around his body.

Taken out of the action, the old man is confined to his bed for some days, hoping that the fugitive may have evaded the searchers and succeeded in fleeing over the hills. Meanwhile, from the croft over the hill, the Widow Macleay bustles in to care for him, a woman of wit and sharp kind-liness, who all the same carries for him something of menacing comedy inherent in her spinsterhood. They would make a fine match for one another. There is the nurse who comes in and washes his wounds, another good-hearted woman, joining in what he feels as the feminine conspiracy around an old bachelor. The doctor who visits, with a typical touch of narrative economy, has been a ship's doctor, sharing an understanding of death and adventure with his patient.

It is in this enforced waiting period that a young woman turns up, offering as explanation only, 'I heard you were ill and needed someone.' Allan Innes' sweetheart, Liz Murison, seduced after a lovers' quarrel by the policeman Nicol's brother, is carrying the dead man's child. Although her pres-ence complicates his task of at once protecting Allan and being free of him, there is no hesitation in Sandy's courage or compassion and the rightness of tone and delicacy in delin-eating the relationship between the old man and the fright-ened girl rejected by her family is one of the book's strengths.

At this point all the elements of the tragedy are in place, and from it the book moves swiftly to a denouement which has from the beginning seemed likely yet never certain as we experience it through Sandy's dour struggle to affect a better outcome. It is an ending which involves a death but one which comes in the company of renewed life.

In 1931, Neil Gunn wrote in answer to an attack on the 'lethargy and slackness' of the Gael: 'In the midst of plenty (called over-production), we suffer the grisly spectacle of famine. Against the tyranny of the machine and the preda-tory instincts of the go-getter, new conceptions of life and work are needed.' There is nothing dated about that insight. It informs the novel, which like *The Green Isle of the Great Deep* is in part an attempt by Gunn to come to terms with the violence and terror of the last century.

Introduction

If there is some final victory recorded here, it is not an easy or glib victory. Sandy's epiphany that 'death did not matter' given to him in the hills is hard to hold on to and there are times when he feels death will be no more than an end of all things, the natural issue of a violence inherent in nature itself, that violence which is at once the most terrible of all things and the most tiresome since 'it empties life to the dead dregs'.

The bleakness of that pessimism is not to be easily overcome. Gunn answers it by his assertion that the basic goodness of people is to be held on to in spite of all. Again this is no mere image of rural values. If Gunn had ever held too much to that image, here in his penultimate book it has been modified by the knowledge of the depths to which humanity can sink. The assertion of life and the value inherent in it is achieved in the end after a full accounting with the forces of darkness.

Frederic Lindsay
January 2007

ONE

As the collie whined again, the old man quietened her and listened, wondering if some of the lads had turned up for a night's poaching. It wasn't the season of the year to borrow the dog, but the spring salmon were on the run. Someone was pushing at the barn door. He slipped the braces back over his shoulders, for he had been on the point of getting into bed. Footsteps were coming now, quietly. The latch of the outside door rattled and Queenie growled.

Old Sandy buttoned his trouser-band and, going to the door, called, 'Who's there?'

'Police. Nicol Menzies.'

The boys had used the barn to hide a salmon net often enough. Sandy pulled open the door and peering into the darkness said with astonishment, 'God bless me, what's taking you here at this time of night?'

'Anyone been around in the last hour or so?'

'No. I was just going to bed.'

'Do you usually lock your barn door?'

'Lock it? No . . . I got some hay in yesterday for the cow and may have – but what's wrong?'

'My brother Robert was murdered two hours ago outside the public hall in Hilton.'

'Your brother – murdered!' So great was the shock that Sandy's understanding seemed blinded by the darkness. 'I can't see you. Come in.'

'I want to have a look in the barn first. Give me the key.'

'The key? Wait till I get my boots on.'

'Just give me the key.'

But Sandy had turned back and as he pulled on his boots
wondered where on earth the key was. Certainly he had
not locked the barn door that day, or yesterday, or any day
his fumbling mind could think of. The menace of the
policeman was about him, about the lads he had known
so long, and he could not gather his wits.

Groping along the top shelf of the kitchen dresser, his
hand encountered a rusty iron key. Relieved to have a key
of some kind, he called, 'I've got it. Will I light the lantern?'

'No. I have a torch.' The policeman had not come in
and his voice was guarded. He was obviously keeping
watch on the long croft building, of which the barn was
the lower end. There were no doors on the other side.

'This is terrible news,' said Sandy outside. 'What happened?'

'Not so loud. A dance at Hilton. Allan Innes attacked
my brother.'

'Allan Innes!' Sandy's voice was no more than a whisper
now. 'You don't mean Allan Innes – killed your brother?'

'Yes.'

'Dear God!' breathed Sandy. 'Allan!'

The policeman did not switch on his torch. Touching
the wall now and then, Sandy arrived at the barn door.

'Where's that keyhole?' he said, a sudden strong compulsion on him to speak loudly as though to warn Allan. The
key rattled going in, but when Sandy tried to turn it in
the lock it wouldn't turn. All at once, however, the door
yielded. As Sandy staggered forward his mind went blank.
He could not let himself believe that the door had been
opened from the inside, though his ear had caught the
faint scrape of a wooden bar as his key had squeaked.

The policeman pushed past him and a circle of light shot
onto the opposite wall. It began to travel slowly. A scythe

hanging from its blade, coils of grass rope, a broken-toothed rake, a bunch of old rabbit snares, a wooden bin – across junk and cobwebs the light moved until it rested on a load of hay in the off corner with a two-pronged fork stuck upright in it. Now it was up on the ceiling of rough boards, sweeping towards the dark opening in the loft above the hay. A wooden ladder stood against the back wall, near the opening, yet not quite under it. The barn was small and clearly anyone hiding must either be under the hay or up in the loft.

As the policeman crossed to the hay, Queenie whined, not a loud sound but high-pitched, and Sandy, knowing every word the brute could utter, realised she was welcoming someone. He was harshly clearing his throat before his eyes quite picked out her dark body in the deep shadow. Her tail was wagging for someone behind the door.

'What are you doing here? Get out!' As his leg thrust her away his shoulder pushed the door still nearer the wall. At once the beam of light was round on them. Queenie slunk out and Sandy explained, 'She sometimes gets between my feet.'

'Hsh!' said the policeman.

They both listened, but outside there was no sound. The policeman pulled up the fork and began prodding. Not satisfied, he laid the torch on the floor and with both hands forked the hay over until a cat couldn't have escaped the prongs.

That left the loft. The ladder could hardly have been used – it was just too far away from the opening. But part of what had once been a horse crib was still fixed to the wall and with its help a young fellow could have heaved himself up. Sandy watched the beam of light working it out.

The policeman moved the ladder into position beneath

Blood Hunt

the opening, had another look around the barn, then with the torch inverted, as though he would still keep its beam below, he began mounting the rungs. The light swung as his hand moved up and Sandy wondered how far it might reach behind the door, for the door hadn't gone as far round as it should when he had shouldered it; it had crushed against something that yielded like a straw-stuffed bag.

Sandy took a couple of paces away from the door as the policeman's head rose above the boarding. The beam of light went up the front wall on its slow swing to the loft. The wall had once been white-washed and was still pale enough to reflect the light sufficiently for Sandy to see Allan's face with a blood smear on the left cheek. But the eyes – the eyes were on Sandy not with fear but with a strange glistening smile as though guilt were looking at him through a window. It was an instant of revelation so intimate, so blood warm, that it lingered in the darkness as the torch went in over the edge of the loft.

Sandy took a few clattering steps over the stone cobbles towards the ladder and called, 'What's up there I don't know, for I haven't been up for years.'

The policeman did not answer. Slits of light shone between the loose boards.

'I think the flooring will be strong enough, but watch your footing when you go in over.' The compulsion on Sandy to keep on making covering noises was stronger than ever.

The policeman was examining something close at hand, his feet still on the ladder, his body slewed round, chest against the edge of the flooring. Sandy heard his fingers scraping the boards as if he were writing on them. Presently he came down and said thoughtfully, more to himself than to Sandy, 'There's been no one up there. The dust is not marked.'

This left Sandy without a word, for he had not thought

of such powers of detection. Everything was a menace, even the stillness in which the policeman stood. Now a queasiness began invading his stomach for at any moment the torch might shine behind the door and he was not absolutely certain if Allan had gone.

The light flashed across the space where Allan had been and in a few moments they were outside. When Sandy tried to turn the key in the lock it wouldn't turn, but it rattled. Withdrawing it, he put it in his pocket. They were standing in the dark once again.

'You don't usually lock it?'

'No,' replied Sandy. 'But it's been a long winter and hay is hay just now.'

'There was some trouble over at Achdunie. Robieson says he has missed two or three bales.'

'I heard something like that. Anything in it?'

'Where did you hear it?'

'I heard it at Milton, where I bought my own load.'

The policeman's voice had remained menacingly impersonal. His slowness was a deadly deception. 'I'll have a look in the hen-house and that will finish it.'

'You think he came this way?'

'I know he did.'

There was no moon but some stars were in the sky and Sandy could now see the vague outline of the hen-house, a rough wooden hut which stood over from the barn. Under the still night as they stood listening, his mouth went dry. He had not been gripped by such direct physical emotion for a very long time. He was seventy-four years old.

Quiet-footed the policeman crossed to the hen-house and pulled the protesting door open. As his torch flashed on more than a score of fowls they set up a cackling. But plainly he had been prepared for this for he did not hurry. He shoved the door shut.

'You've been in all night?' he asked.

'Yes. I went out to milk the cow as usual about seven o'clock and gave her her feed. Since then I have been in the house alone.'

'You heard nothing?'

'No. What makes you think he would come here?'

'He was in no condition to go farther.'

It was not the complete answer, as Sandy knew. Doubtless it was the man's duty to search the premises, locked or unlocked, but there was much more to it than that. Then in a thoughtful tone, Nicol suggested, 'He might have gone into the house when we were in the barn.'

And for a wild moment Sandy wondered if Allan, believing the house to have been searched, just might have gone in. It was the bold stroke he was capable of in a desperate emergency, particularly as he now knew that his old friend was not going to give him away. Sandy's toe hit a dry hump in the ground and he staggered.

'The ground is hard,' he muttered. 'It's thirsty.' When his hand found the latch, he pushed the door open. 'Go right in.' He saw the wariness in Nicol's body as it stooped slightly on entering the living room.

The glass of the lamp funnel was clean and bright on the small kitchen table. Two books lay on the table, a pair of spectacles and a weekly newspaper. The fire in the iron grate had died down. Washed dishes were stacked on a corner of the dresser which stood against the back wall, with shelves above holding more dishes, two or three pieces of old lustre ware, and a short row of books. There was no trace of recent haste, of company. The very position of the armchair suggested an evening spent in reading, and the seaman's black jersey, sprawling over the chair, told of the sudden call to the door when he was preparing for bed. He lived all alone.

The policeman's eyes went round to the inner wall, against which stood the old-fashioned box-bed, with its wooden walls and roof. The light shone right into the bed and the policeman as he approached it could see there was no one there. He hesitated for a moment before stepping on a deal chair by the head of the bed and taking a quick glance in over the roof. On the floor again, he wiped the spot he had stood on with his hand. Stooping, he lifted the valance and shot a beam of light under the bed.

As he was doing this, Queenie came in, looked at her master and gave a small close-mouthed whine, her eyes shining against the light. At once Sandy beckoned her sternly to the fireside, and with head and tail down she went to the mat and crouched. As her eyes came round to him, he brought his fist down with an angry silent gesture, then turned to the policeman's back and said:

'If you're satisfied here, we can go through to the other room.'

The policeman looked about the kitchen as if somewhere there should be something that would give him a sign. His eyes rested on the dog.

Queenie's eyes turned on him from her lowered head. She moved restlessly but did not growl.

Sandy lifted the lamp and ushered the policeman into the only other room. It held an iron bed with brass knobs, a large mahogany chest of drawers, a seaman's chest, a silent black marble clock on the mantelshelf flanked by gilt ornaments, a round claw-legged table, black horse-hair chairs, and a thick stuffy smell. The policeman's eyes and nostrils missed nothing.

'You have an upstairs?'

'There's a loft, but you can get to it with a ladder.'

'Where's the ladder?'

'The only ladder I have is the one in the barn.'

The policeman remained silent.

'No one has been up there for a very long time,' said Sandy.

'I may as well fetch it and finish the job.'

'But no one could get up without the ladder, and the ladder was in the barn as you saw.'

'Still, I may as well have a look. Where's the opening to the loft?'

While Sandy led him back into the kitchen and round the head of the bed, he was wondering desperately how he could stop the policeman from fetching the ladder, for if the policeman demanded the key of the barn, he would find that it did not turn the lock, and that therefore the barn door had not been fastened from the outside. Someone's presence in the barn and Sandy's collusion would then be obvious.

The policeman brought his beam to play on the rectangular wooden hatch in the roof.

'I'll get the ladder for you if you like,' Sandy offered.

'It's all right,' said the policeman, moving towards the front door. 'I won't trouble you.'

'It's no trouble,' said Sandy.

But the policeman went on until he stood outside. 'Give me the key.'

'No,' said Sandy. 'If you thought someone came into the house when we were in the barn, the same person could come out of it when you're in the barn. You stand here and make certain this time.'

'Do you want the torch?'

'I'll manage,' replied Sandy in a voice firm enough to show that at last he was becoming aware of the suspicion cast on himself and his house and was going to have no more of it.

Presently the key grated loudly in the lock, and Sandy

found little difficulty in going straight to the ladder; its fore end rammed the door as he was coming out and almost put him on his back. This so lightened his spirit that he muttered.

But the ladder was too long to negotiate the short narrow passage to the kitchen, though the policeman tried it all ways. 'How was it done before?' he asked.

'I remember now. Through the window.'

'Perhaps we needn't bother.'

'Yes, you'll bother,' said Sandy. 'I'll go inside and lift the window and you can push it through from the outside. I told you no one came in, but that's only my word.'

It was a stiff window but at last Sandy raised it and kept it up with the slat of wood which lay on the window shelf for the purpose. Catching the ladder as it came through the opening, he had it in position under the hatch by the time Nicol the policeman entered.

Nicol stood looking up at the hatch. 'I'm not disputing your word.' He turned his head and stared at Sandy, whose name at that moment suited him well, for his short beard and eyebrows and hair were all sandy-coloured, except for a greying over the ears, and had a shine, like his blue eyes, in the soft lamp-light. His cheeks were rounded and ruddy. There was a roundness in the slope of his shoulders, too, as if time and thought had rounded off his whole person into something final and matured. He was like a fruit that had grown ripe after its kind, like a gathered apple that keeps a long time.

He looked back at the policeman, who stood half a head taller, lean, dark, thirty years of age and of a persistence that no imagination troubles.

'You're doing your duty,' replied Sandy and the shine in his eyes carried its own smile.

'He had a good start on me, so I did not follow him

straight here. I headed him off and then came back this way. He has gone to earth somewhere hereabouts. That's how I worked it out and why I'm searching your place now.'

'I see.'

'He might crawl in somewhere without you knowing.'

'He could hardly crawl up there without me knowing.'

'The only certain way is to make sure. Then we write that off.'

Sandy nodded. 'You can go up now.'

As the policeman mounted the ladder, Sandy thought. What if Allan actually is up there? He couldn't be; yet what if, somehow, he was? The magical touched him.

Nicol lifted the hatch on the flat of his hands and pushed it to one side, then mounted until his head and neck were through the opening. Sandy's hearing was good enough to catch the click of the small torch as the light was turned on.

In the magical is a touch of the old primeval fear. Beyond belief, something is there or is not there. Looked at from underneath, the policeman's features were also of that realm of fear and strangeness, foreshortened, bony, with the nose prominent and ominous as any hound's.

Without a word, the policeman mounted three more rungs and swung himself in over. Now the ceiling was creaking under his heavy tread. Sandy's lips fell apart, his breathing short and shallow as he listened. The squeak of dry hinges brought up the image of his old American trunk. The fellow was missing nothing. Sandy breathed deeply twice, filling his chest full, but did not sit down, though his legs were trembling.

The footsteps were coming back to the hatch, and now there was the boot, with its iron toe-cap reaching down for a rung. As the leg of the blue trousers got hitched up a thick grey woollen sock showed and a white strip of skin.

Standing once more before Sandy, the policeman dusted himself and kicked his legs. 'I'll put the ladder back in the barn for you.'

'No need,' said Sandy. 'It's high time I had a look at some things up there myself.'

'You've been here a good while now?'

'Fourteen years.'

'Thanks for letting me look around. It'll go in my report that you assisted me.'

'I wish the assistance hadn't been necessary. I can hardly believe it yet.'

'You knew Allan Innes well?'

'Indeed I did; as nice a lad as anyone could meet – though he's been away for some time. I didn't know he had come back. How did it happen?'

'Something between him and my brother,' replied Nicol from his dark reticence. Already Sandy had noticed that Nicol never looked at him unless he wanted to read his face, not from training but from instinct.

'Had they been drinking or what?'

'Hardly at all, I believe.'

'You don't know what started it?'

'A girl, they say.'

Something in Nicol's look, the twist of his lip, the concentration of feeling and purpose, made Sandy realise sharply that the man whom Allan had killed was the policeman's brother. Not only duty but blood. The blood hunt.

'A girl!' was all Sandy could mutter.

'So they say.'

'Not Liz Murison?'

'What do you know about Liz Murison?' Nicol looked at him.

'Nothing, except that some of the lads were pulling his leg about her – but that must be a year or more ago.'

Nicol began to walk towards the door. Outside he stood quite still for a moment, then said, 'Good night' and quietly disappeared.

Sandy shut the door and wandered back into the kitchen, where he stood staring at things he did not see. The force of the policeman's concentration, behind the cool talk, the restrained manner, kept him from being able to think. It was as pure a human force as he had met. The lack of haste had something terrifying about it.

His legs tremored and brought him into the armchair. He leaned forward and with the long poker stirred the fire slowly, shedding the ash from the red embers. He shook the iron kettle. There was enough water in it for a cup of tea and he pushed it solidly down on the embers, then he looked around him like one listening.

Everything was very quiet and still, the bed, the dresser, the backs of the books on the second shelf.

The kettle sounded a low note and he got lost completely. He came back thinking there was nothing in the books which could deal with this kind of moment; nothing at all to dispel what came out of it, the awfulness of the human act.

More than that and deeper: nothing to explain why he himself had, beyond thought, before its grip could get him, so instinctively shielded the murderer. All the time the policeman had been with him, he had refused to look beneath the surface, to ask himself what he was doing. Why? he asked himself now and out of his bleak misery answered, Goodness knows.

His thought became confused; brought up images from his past that swirled and vanished; a figure running along a quay in a foreign port, a revolver shot . . .

What had possessed Allan?

Allan, of all the young men who had come about the

place, the laughing face, the bright one. Sun on the grass. They said he could go through a pool like an otter. He had seen him grow from the age of fourteen, when he had left school. Good hands on him. He had worked in a garage in Hilton and done a repair for a passing motorist that got him a foreman's job in a garage in Perth – about a year ago. He could hardly be twenty-five.

Allan would never have had a knife on him. Just his hands.

Sandy stirred and heard the high pitch of the kettle's note. Tea was his stand-by at all times, cold or hungry, weary or wide-awake. Sometimes he would get up in the night and make himself a cup of tea, for it hardly mattered when he slept. Occasionally he would have the lightsome feeling of inhabiting a small dawn-grey oasis.

Now he lifted the kettle off the fire for he suddenly had no stomach for tea. As he stood on the floor his body gave a small spasmodic shudder. The night was chill.

Tomorrow in the daylight that policeman would sniff Allan out as Queenie a rabbit. To lie up in a loft was his only hope.

The old man sat down again with misery in his eyes. He realised that he was thinking as much of himself as of Allan. He had not wanted Allan to be caught on his premises. It would be like handing him over.

Going to the door, he found it locked. Quietly he turned the bolt back, then went to bed.

TWO

Allan did not come in the night, and earlier than usual Sandy carried an armful of hay from the barn to his small cow. A hardy cross from a Highland mother and a Shorthorn bull, she had developed in his company a strong conscience which helped her to steal when she could with cunning. There were occasions when this brought from Sandy a flow of talk, and as she was much nimbler on her feet than he, his talk could be heard at a distance. Farm hands in an outfield of Milton would hold their laughter to listen. Only in extreme moments would he call her a wanton bitch, for he never swore. This temperance was an added peculiarity, an extra 'queerness', to the farm men who could swear at beasts with a potency rich and warm as mature manure.

'Get over, will you?' and he shoved at her solidly, then dropped the hay. Down came her head into the fragrant armful, caught a mouthful, and tossed it up, carrying wisps about her horns and ears.

He removed the wisps, clapped her strongly and went over to the hen-house. As he pulled its door open, the fowls came out with a rush like bairns from school, looking about the ground for something unexpected and wonderful. Not finding it they began to follow him. Queenie was sniffing the off corner of the barn. Sandy's eyes travelled, but far as they could see there was no sign of life and their sight was still very good. As he walked back to his door he saw that the hard ground would leave no signs.

After stirring the porridge he picked up his milk pail and

a fistful of grain. He threw the grain wide and the fowls raced every way. As he milked the cow, his head was turned sideways, his left eye on the door.

All morning he was haunted by the feeling that Allan would suddenly appear before him or be found in some unexpected corner. The expression on Allan's face, behind the barn door, had remained vividly with him in the night. The transparent eye, the warm blood guilt: the memory of it moved him beyond reason.

But no one came near his small croft, and in the afternoon he had a strong urge to get news.

The croft lay in a shallow scoop of the hillside which rose westwards into rough heather country, hollows and hills, with concealed lochs and birches, an intricate country full of surprise and, in its very wildness, an intimate beauty. Sandy liked to get 'lost' here, indeed this was the secret country of his mind.

The land sloped to the south, an easy slope that flattened into boggy ground before it reached the wide belt of trees that ran with and concealed the river. Also among trees but on the other side of the river went the main road to the west. Beyond the road rose a steep conical hill, its base rusty with old bracken; then more hills, to far mountain tops.

Sandy turned eastward over the low shoulder of his own ground and presently saw before him and to his left the farm steading of Milton on the western slope of a wide strath. Three miles down this strath lay the town of Hilton and with luck a bus would overtake him some time, though for that matter he often got a lift, for no farmer would fail to offer him one. In fact only in the last year or two had he realised that he was regarded as a 'character'. Folk repeated his 'sayings', and occasionally made them up. This had come as a great surprise to him.

He had not gone far along the road when a small car

drew up so closely that Sandy stepped into the ditch and fell over.

'Well, well,' cried the minister out of his grey dried face, 'did I give you a surprise?'

'A pleasant surprise, thank you,' said Sandy recovering his old hat.

'Come in! Come in! I'm sorry if I upset you.'

'I upset myself – which is not unusual,' Sandy replied as he got in.

'If man attributed his fall to himself as clearly as that – and as generously – there would be some hope for him.'

'Ay, indeed. It's not the Devil that sits at his wheel, it's himself.'

The minister was an erratic driver at the best of times; he now dispensed with any particular preference for either side of the road and drove as fast as the defective timing of the old rattle would let him. For man's fall was a noble subject, of great scope.

When it reached the murder, Mr Davidson with a mighty swerve saved the car from the ditch, then drove flat out until the brakes abruptly squealed on a new thought. He turned to Sandy. 'You knew Allan Innes?'

'And liked him,' replied Sandy.

'Terrible.' The car stopped. 'The spirit of the age, the picture houses. And the girl, Liz Murison – I would have said she was as sensible a girl as ever sat in a pew. Her father is a deacon in my own church.'

'How did it happen?'

'They quarrelled over Liz, and when Allan got Robert down it seems he caught him by the throat and bashed his head and choked him.'

'But,' said Sandy, his brows gathering over strained eyes, 'I don't understand. Had Robert been trying to take Liz Murison from Allan or what?'

'Liz Murison is in child, far gone.'

Sandy looked at the minister, his lips fallen apart. 'To—?'

'To Robert.'

Sandy kept on looking at him. 'My God,' he said; his body sagged and his eyes turned away to the windscreen.

The minister talked of the three families involved, the three mothers, the horror and the stigma, but Sandy hardly heard him. In the night he had worried over what could have driven Allan to the fatal act, and no passion from any love rivalry, he felt, could excuse him, no hot blood, no spite, no anger. But *this* – this in a moment took all questioning from Sandy and left him sitting dumb and still.

Presently he asked, 'Have they caught Allan?'

'No, not yet. But they say it can only be a matter of time.'

Sandy nodded slowly.

'Within an hour of the news of the murder reaching the police station in Hilton, cars and lorries were being stopped between Inverton and Achnabeen. Some said he would take to the hills he knows so well. They have probably caught him by this time, for I have been from home since ten o'clock this morning.'

'Why didn't Robert marry the girl?'

'Some say that he wouldn't marry her and some say that she wouldn't marry him – though that last is surely unlikely in view of her condition and the familiar relationship it implies.'

'She wouldn't marry him? Why not?'

'Exactly. That's what I asked.'

But Sandy wasn't sure that the minister and himself meant the same thing. He had got a knock and was sitting far within himself where the figures of ordinary life took on their tragic shapes.

The minister's voice went on and on and concluded, 'It's the materialism of the age.'

Sandy nodded, staring far through the windscreen.

'And where you and I differ is in the application of the only force which can counter that materialism: the spirit. Spiritual power to be effective needs a vessel, it needs an institution, it needs the Church.'

Sandy nodded through the echoes of what was now an old controversy between them.

The minister triumphed for a little while, then drove on. His manse stood on the outskirts of Hilton, among some trees, and he stopped before the short drive that led to it. Sandy got out and thanked him.

The dry old face with the dark eyes looked at him. 'You will think on these things.'

Sandy looked back and between them flickered a humour old as dried peat.

'Words,' said Sandy.

'Ay,' said the minister.

The main street was busy for it was market day. Cars and lorries seemed to be increasing in number every time he visited the town. Cattle droves got divided, beasts went up side streets and with yells and whacks were brought back. The small square in front of the Town House was so congested that the Town Clerk had to dodge his way to the front door. A policeman was on point duty at the principal crossing. Knots of country people stood on the pavement.

He was turning in at the ironmonger's for a hoe-blade and some mending wire when the police inspector, coming towards him, raised his hand.

'Any news?'

'No. None yourself?' asked Sandy.

'Not yet. He *may* have taken to the hills for the time being. You'll have to keep a sharp look-out.'

'But if he has taken to the hills—'

'He'll need food.'

'Yes,' said Sandy. 'He'll need food.'

'We may be doing a search up your way and we'll expect your help.' He looked at some idlers and they moved on.

'I'm afraid my mountaineering days—'

'Any sign or suspicion, let us know,' said the inspector. 'You have been helpful already.'

Sandy went into the shop but had to wait his turn to get served. Those also waiting were discussing the murder. 'Not for nearly a hundred years has there been anything of the kind,' said an elderly lawyer with the nice tone of a connoisseur, 'and that was when one of the tinker clan killed the horse-dealer at the old hill market.'

Sandy left the shop with his hoe-blade but without the wire, which he had forgotten. At the street crossing where the policeman was on duty, he stopped beside four men in rough tweeds and heavy boots arguing hotly, with fists knotted on their staffs and dogs about their feet. They had obviously had a few drinks.

'He'll swing for it, that's sure.'

'It's not sure. If he was attacked first, then it was self-defence, and that makes a difference.'

'Attacked first be damned. Why should Robert Menzies attack him? The same lad, in the circumstances, would keep out of his way.'

'Robert Menzies was a bloody weed, dead though he is,' said a third wet mouth before it spat.

'That's not the point, and it's not a weed he was either.'

'The point is—'

'The point is that no one actually saw the first blow.'

'Do you mean to tell me that anyone acting in self-defence would when he got his man down throttle the life out of him? You tell the judge that. Allan is for it, and I'm bloody sorry about it.'

The policeman shifted his point and the argument drifted across the street.

Sandy followed, but when the men stood again to have their argument out, he went on. He was beginning to wonder if his legs would carry him to the bus stance there was such a lassitude in his flesh. By the town clock he saw it was four minutes to five. A bus left the stance at five. Many looked at his bushy face and old half-trotting body and laughed as at something that had come out of a croft bog in its Sunday clothes.

The bus went up the broad valley but the town remained in his mind, the voices and motor engines, the human swarm, the cattle and sheep, the shops, the cobbled street. As he stared through the glass, the throng of life threw out a quay wall from New York, steamer funnels, smoke puffs, a siren blast. He moved his head lifting it from all scenes, and saw some older school children looking at him. At once they turned their eyes away but one boy secretively nudged another.

He got off the bus on the crest of the rise and as he stood for a moment looking after it all faces stared at him, two or three of the boys on the off side standing up.

Along the footpath by the drystone dyke he wondered over their curiosity, then smiled thoughtfully at some comical aspect of himself which he hardly quite caught but understood.

Here was Queenie coming to meet him, the low flagging of the tail, the beginning of the welcoming twist in the body. Because she was well received she forgot herself a little and with a small jump licked his hand.

THREE

That afternoon and evening the croft had an extra quietness. No one came his way. He found the key of the barn and got the lock to work. Small tasks long awaiting his attention were seen to. He could not stay inside lest something came too suddenly upon him.

When he had eaten his evening meal, he sat down and polished his spectacles. But his attention wandered. What an ancient sage had achieved in the way of aphorism did not hold the insistence, the urgency, of a human life wandering in the dark, hiding and hunted. Hunted by other humans, after him like dogs.

Allan could not live without food, the inspector had said. So he would have to get food somewhere; he would have to come *back* for food.

He saw his croft, not as an oasis of grey light in darkness, as he sometimes saw it when he got up to make an early cup of tea, but as a trap with the jaws flattened out and covered over.

Beyond resentment there is a vacancy through which the eyes stare at the fire. He began to nod for he was tired, worn out; the old frame had served him well enough and now needed sleep. That's what things came to in the end. Some day someone would find him dead in his bed. Though that was not how he had meant to die. He wanted death to come to him in a way which he would arrange, his own secret way. He might arrange that yet, only a little sooner now, perhaps—

Queenie whined. The footfall came on his ear, the hand on the door. Allan! He was coming in. Sandy got up.

The policeman, Nicol Menzies, entered, looked about the kitchen and nodded to Sandy, 'Good evening. No sign of anything?'

'No one has come near the place.'

'I heard you were in Hilton.'

'Yes. Sit down there.'

'I'm not going to stop.' He sat down. 'I want the key of the barn. Have you locked the barn door?' He was given the key and asked, 'When do you go to bed as a rule?'

'It varies, for time is a thing I sometimes forget.' Sandy's voice had taken a low note to match the policeman's. 'Why?'

'If he's hiding out this side of Carn a Choire, yours is the only place he would risk coming to, because it's the most outlying, because he knows you, knows you're here alone.'

Sandy nodded.

'Milk from your cow – eggs – potatoes – what he could pick up without telling you, if he felt he couldn't risk that.'

'I see,' said Sandy, aware of the significance of that 'if', but only asking, 'Have you no word at all?'

'Word has come in that someone did get a lift on the main road down there, going to Inverton; a young fellow, near enough the description of Allan Innes. But I have checked the times and I am far from satisfied.'

'Haven't you found this fellow?'

'Not yet. But we will.'

'You yourself think Allan is still hereabouts?'

'My brother was no weakling. Allan took some punishment. I have worked it out. The driver who gave the fellow a lift found no signs of injuries. Besides, however, I am going to watch here through the night and the barn will be handy.'

'There's no search going on?'

'Yes. But not from here.'

So it was the trap all right. Allan would be headed this way. Sandy nodded, as he had a habit of doing when there was no more to be said.

'At the earliest he wouldn't come in until some time after your light is out. If he's in the hills, it's now twenty-nine hours since he had food.'

However wary, a time came when the wild animal took a risk on the trap. This man knew. The bones of his face were clear and regular, moulded with a clean thumb. The eyebrows were black, strongly defined on the bone ridges, but not really heavy. The hair was black and strong. A good-looking face but without something, without light.

'Are you all alone?' Sandy asked.

'If he should come to your door, let him in,' replied Nicol.

'I'm going to my bed. I'm tired.'

Nicol got up. 'You'll put your light out. So long just now.' He went out quietly, closing the doors behind him.

Sandy sat on for a little while. If Allan came to the front door he was to invite him into the trap. Then the policeman would enter behind his back.

He had seen the spirit in Allan's face behind the barn door. It still haunted him. It would always do so, because it was the spirit, the last thing. It shone through the eyes.

It had been one of Sandy's hopes that before the end he would find out if the spirit was immortal. Already he had had a remarkable experience about this.

The country of the spirit had been gradually taking shape, gathering a feature here, a snapshot there, a certain light, a vague climate; but mostly when he wanted to catch a whole glimpse of it and enter its mood, he only saw the hills, the lochs, the bracken, the birches, the long tongue of water lilies where the trout fed and set their circles on the still water . . . This was the land he had come to from the sea, the bit of earth that held his heart, the beautiful country . . . where Allan, having committed his murder, was now hiding.

If Allan came to the door, he would not let him in. With this decision, Sandy undressed and blew the light out.

If Allan had been watching the light in the window he would think all was clear now.

Allan had always been very good at thoughts of that kind. It was he who knew when the gamekeeper had had a heavy day on the hill or drinks in Hilton. The three lads – Allan, Davie and Willie – had come about his croft for many years, turning and gathering his hay in the long summer evenings or giving most of a Saturday to hoeing or digging up his potatoes, odd jobs that needed more than one pair of hands. They came with a breeze about them, laughing, hurrying into their land of freedom. Sometimes it was impossible to get them to stop working. 'The rain is coming, Sandy,' Allan would say. On a fine autumn night they would 'borrow' Queenie and, under the moon, hunt rabbits into openings they netted under drystone dykes. Queenie was quiet, she never barked, and she would quarter a field like a setter, putting the rabbits on the run towards the nets. The river and the rabbits, salmon and game: their pay and their compensation, their delight. Until over a year ago when Willie went away from Hilton first, then Allan, and Davie suddenly got married.

Sandy turned over in his bed. All he could do was wait for the boy to come. For at twenty-five Allan was no more than a boy to Sandy.

He saw Nicol leaning against the jamb of the open barn door, listening, and realised how thoroughly he had worked things out. The fellow might appear slow in speech, humourless, but in this matter he had gathered information about Allan's visits in past years and come to conclusions that now gauged the hunted mind of the human animal with a ruthless insight.

The trap was set.

Sandy got very tired and restless. There were calm stretches of living when a philosophy worked; but when the mind got properly upset, trivial feelings, futile idiotic thoughts, would keep on invading it, let will and reason do what they liked.

When sleep did come it was so deep that Queenie's growl seemed to follow his last waking moment. Morning was in the window. A slow, low knocking on the door . . .

'Who's there?'

'Me,' said the policeman.

Nicol followed Sandy back to the fire, rubbing his hands. 'It's cold.'

'I'll make a cup of tea for you.'

Nicol made way for Sandy before the fireplace. The skin on his face was frost-grey.

'It was a quiet night,' said Sandy as though speaking of the weather.

'It was,' said Nicol and he began to cough as a puff of fine ash from the poker got him in the throat.

FOUR

The policeman left immediately he had his tea and Sandy sat quite still for a long time, then he put on the porridge pot.

He always made sufficient porridge for himself and the hens, for he ran the croft in his own way. Indeed it had surprised him, when he had first come back from the sea, how much he could remember of his mother's ways with hens and cows, sour milk and butter-making. The memories returned in the form of vivid pictures. He could not see his mother, for example, actually giving porridge to the hens, but he could see the hens pecking at the cold grey wobbly lumps. In the matter of the left-over potatoes, however, what he saw was her hand with the warm potatoes spewing out between the fingers as they closed. In this way the oatmeal which she had first spread over the potatoes got thoroughly mixed into the mess.

That hand he could see at any time, three or four yards away. It brought two lifetimes together, making of time a curious kind of illusion.

In the early afternoon he made a sandwich of bread and cheese and put it in his pocket. The hens followed him a few yards. Queenie walked beside him, giving him a look now and then.

'We'll go as far as the lily loch,' he said, and though she was pleased to hear the normal friendly voice, she did not lose her subdued air. Now and then he stopped to look about him. Growth was stirring from the root though nearly a month behind. Nothing discouraged new life like a persistent withering east wind. He stopped to look at a Blackface ewe with a heavy sag to her lean body. She wouldn't have a big drop of milk but she would manage, short of a bad lambing storm, and it might be bad enough before it could take the hard core out of the weather. A peewit dived at them and brought a smile to his eyes. After all, many a walk he took like this when the birds were setting up house and bringing to the old earth a singing glory.

If Allan was about, he wouldn't last much longer without food. He might give in in his hole and die there. The death feeling might come over him and take him to itself. As Sandy's legs began to drag he thought with a touch of humour that dying was not such a long way from himself. The policeman and lack of sleep, between them, had squeezed the vitality out of him in a way he would hardly have believed possible.

At last from a crest of thick old heather he saw the loch of the water lilies down in its hollow. It was a beautiful spot, sheltered and nearly always calm in the long summer evenings, but now dark-skinned from a small searching wind. The sky was a pale cold blue, clear of cloud. He stood for a little on the crest, looking beyond the loch along a slope that rose to a higher ridge with the left shoulder of Ben More against the sky far beyond. In between lay every kind of country, with birches following the hill streams, both growing smaller as they pushed up towards the corries, and pines here and there, solitary or in little groups, like watchers or conventicles left behind from the ancient Caledonian Forest. Here stags roared in the autumn and a roe deer could be startled at any time.

Over the crest and a few yards down Sandy came on his resting place that was like a winged armchair with its back to the north. It was Allan who had called it Sandy's Chair. As he lay down he was completely sheltered from the wind and the strength of the sun surprised him. Presently, as he sank, the familiar feeling of being freed had not its usual ease, did not rise upon the air and drift away; and he was conscious of this . . . just conscious of the thought that finally there might be no drifting away, only a total sinking down.

His mouth fell open and his breath came out in gusty lumps. The felt hat tilted off his head. The bone of the skull, his hair, the skin on the hands, were old like the lichen, the moss, the runtled heath stalks.

After ten minutes he was awakened by Queenie. His mouth opened wider as he looked and wondered, then found himself back on the earth again, his wits about him and cunning in his eye. He put his hand on Queenie's neck to keep her down.

Through the long heather, he saw a man and a dog disappearing into the dip beyond the loch of the lilies; up the slope above the dip another man was also moving sou'westwards. Had the time been autumn, he would at once have thought that a hunting party was taking the ground before them. For five minutes he lay against the heather slope; then satisfied that the drive had swept past him, he crawled up over the ridge and started for home.

As his hand hit against the sandwich in his pocket he smiled with a weary humour, for he hadn't put the food there for himself. Nor had he intended to sleep in the Chair. But perhaps it was as well he had or otherwise he would have been seen.

After forking some old straw about the cow's legs, he cleaned a pot of potatoes and put them on the fire, then started skimming his basins of milk. There was nothing he liked better than freshly churned butter on a boiled potato from which the skin had burst away in flavoured goodness.

How many would be engaged in the drive heaven alone knew, but if he in a chance moment had seen two men and a dog so low down, then the really likely spots were being combed like a boy's head. He turned the handle of his glass churn, thinking that the fellow who had got the lift to Inverton had either come forward and was not Allan or he had not come forward. Allan might have given them the slip after all. It was the price of a fellow like Nicol anyhow.

But after ten o'clock that night, when the printed words went no deeper than the surface of the page and he was about to turn in, he fell into a state of lassitude and half trance.

Queenie wakened him from so clear a vision of Allan that when he heard the hand on the outside door he was certain that at last the lad had come. The outside door was quietly shut and now the door into the kitchen was swinging open. But for the third time the man who entered his home was Nicol the policeman.

For a few moments Sandy could not move. Then he got up. 'Come in,' he said. 'I was nearly asleep.'

Nicol crossed over to the fire with his slow deliberate movement, his shoulders straightening after their slight stoop at entering, like the figure of dread in a traditional story.

'Chilly outside,' he said, extending his hands to the dying fire.

'No sign of a change in the weather,' Sandy replied, stooping for the poker.

Nicol said nothing.

'No new developments?' Sandy resented having to speak, having to draw words out of the fellow.

'No, nothing much.'

Sandy decided to ask nothing more and sat looking into the fire.

'Seen nothing yourself?' asked Nicol.

'No.'

'You were up the hill?'

Sandy looked at him. 'The dog and myself went as far as the lily loch. Why, did you see us?'

'There's been a search,' said Nicol. 'Working in from the other side.'

'No trace of him?'

'Not even a footprint.'

'The weather has been a bit hard for footprints.'

'There's always the soft spot on a hill track.'

How true that was! An imprint on a damp skin of peat came before Sandy's inner eye. Following any kind of track at any time, in the very height of summer a man could not fail at some spot to leave his footmark. For the first time Sandy realised that Allan must have left the district. That bright lad, with his instinct for action, had promptly cleared out, got away.

'You said something about a fellow who got a lift to Inverton.'

'Yes,' replied Nicol. 'We haven't been able to trace him.'

Sandy looked at Nicol, who was staring at the fire with a slight puckering of the muscles about his eyes. The greyness in his skin from too much concentration, lack of sleep, brought out the rather high bones of the cheeks, the clean cut of the jaw. Then Sandy caught a glisten in the dark eye, where the fireflame danced, and was shocked by something remorseless in the man, and once again he thought: it's not just a policeman doing his job, it's the dark hunt of the blood, beyond the tribal blood, the blood of the brother.

'I haven't had much sleep for the last two days, so I think I'll get home.'

The word 'home' arrested Sandy. He looked at Nicol again.

'I don't expect you'll be troubled tonight,' added Nicol, but whether he meant by Allan or some police watcher he did not say.

'They'll be troubled at home,' Sandy remarked solemnly. 'My mother is . . . badly.'

Sandy nodded. 'I do not know your family.'

'There were just the three of us. Robert . . . was younger than me.'

'Your mother is taking it badly?'

'She is.' Nicol got up.

'A terrible business,' said Sandy, rising also.

'We'll get him all right,' said Nicol. He filled his chest slowly. 'We're relying on you to pass on anything suspicious.'

'Do you think he'll try to leave the country?'

'They went through his belongings in Perth. But—' Nicol stopped. He was giving nothing away.

'I'll confess I'm feeling tired myself,' Sandy admitted. 'I went for a breath of air this afternoon and fell asleep in the heather. By the look of you, you could do with a sleep too.'

'I could.' At the door, as they paused, looking into the night, Nicol added, 'It's his third night without food. He may be in a hole that he'll never come out of.'

'It's possible.'

Sandy came back to his chair. Even that hole the policeman would find. He would hunt the body, alive or dead, until he got it.

It was perhaps one of the penalties of living alone and thinking about life and what has been thought about it by wise men in other ages, that division of time and place grew thin, sometimes quite transparent, and a sentence spoken today became the echo of one from down the ages.

Robert was 'younger than me', Nicol had said, after mentioning his mother. His pauses, the look in his face, the brooding air about him . . . Possibly Robert had been his mother's pet and Nicol was now getting the backlash. He would hold his own against her, wouldn't say much, but . . .

Into his wonder about Nicol's mother came the performance of an old Greek play in Buenos Aires. Two or three of the crew had gone, and though the play had looked highbrow and the whole affair a bit posh, still the company was English and they would see a bit of stuff from home. The girl who had played the part of Medea had let herself go. Terrific. Sandy himself had felt uncomfortable, and when his mates, afterwards, turned on him and jeered at him for having inveigled them into going to the show, he had defended himself by saying that at least they had seen what a woman could do in the way of murder and slaughter when the lid was off. The talk after that! The confessions!

Nicol's mother might be the brooding kind of mother, who couldn't sleep, who couldn't rest. Her face turning to Nicol as he went in: Have you found him? The still-brooding woman, with harsh thrusts of passion, and Nicol wouldn't know what to make of her, yet knowing something that he could put no words to.

I'm probably fancying things, thought Sandy, drawing away for his own comfort, and yet seeing, as he drew away, the dark figures move on the plane of vision, that nether plane which went back so far.

Queenie lifted her head, turned her nose to the door. Her nostrils twitched but caught nothing. Then she whined and got up. The difference between the whine that went back to the edge of the growl and the high whine of expectation that lit the eyes was something that Sandy could recognise when he bothered about it. A weakening touched his whole frame. And now the sensitive bitch twined upon herself. 'Quiet!' he muttered and heard a scratching at the door.

He got up and, after pulling the kitchen door behind him to shut in the light, went slowly to the outer door. He knew he hadn't locked it because he had wanted to lock it but his hand wouldn't let him. Nor did he call now, Who's there? Very carefully he turned the knob and pulled the door open, but against his eyes no darkness of a human body loomed. There was something at his feet. Queenie pushed out between his legs.

The whisper came up, 'It's me, Allan.'

Sandy did not look down but stood staring away into the night, hearkening beyond what he could see; then carefully he thrust a foot forward and followed it over the threshold. For a few moments he stood again with his back to the house, then with a quiet 'Sst!' to Queenie went down towards the barn. It was the sound he made, the sound the three boys had made, when they wanted the dog to hunt. If there was anyone about, Queenie would growl now. Allan must have been on all fours.

At the corner of the barn Sandy stood casually in the exercise of nature while Queenie ran sniffing around. As he began to see better he felt more confident and moved quietly back to the house. There was just the chance that Queenie might not growl at Nicol, seeing he had been in the house so often lately, but she would make some sign. She had sensed the lack of friendliness in the man and would be storing it up. When she took a dislike to a person she never got over it.

As he stood on the doorstep she brushed in past his legs. This time he locked the door; kept his hands out until they touched the inner door and pushed it open. There was no one by the fire, no one in the kitchen as far as he could see. He went round the top end of the bed, stood mid-floor and listened, then went and sat in his chair.

Queenie looked at him and looked at the door, she whined restlessly, she told him Allan was out there.

He sat on.

The night was quiet. If Nicol or any other watcher came in now he would find things normal enough. Sandy would not be involved. The house would still be his old quiet dwelling.

Sandy did not think of Allan, he was so aware of the night, of the paths that came to the house, the gable ends, the ear below the window.

He got up. Queenie hit the leg of the table so strongly that it protested. Sandy quietly pulled the door open and looked into the dim passage. Some old coats hung there. He felt them as he passed to the second or ben room. It's door was ajar. 'Are you there?'

'Yes,' the whisper rose from the floor.

'Are you hurt?'

'No.' There was a slow scrambling.

'Policeman was here. Just gone.'

No answer.

'Don't know whether it's safe to take you into the kitchen or not.'

'Something to eat.'

'Yes,' said Sandy. 'Will you wait here till I get the kettle boiling? If anyone comes in, you could slip out.'

Sandy went back into the kitchen, felt the weight of the kettle, attended to the fire, began to lay out food as for his own supper, one cup and saucer, one knife, then paused to wonder whether it wouldn't be safer to give Allan a parcel of food at once and send him away. Safer for them both. But he could not solve this problem, so he took the fresh butter from the dresser, oatcakes from a tin, a brown loaf.

An old-fashioned wicker basket held the eggs which once a week he delivered to the vanman who brought his rations and other groceries.

When he had made the tea, he had a final bout of listening, looked at Queenie, then went to the other room. 'Come in,' he whispered. If anyone came knocking at the door, he might have time to hide Allan.

He heard the slither and brush of the groping body behind him then turned and saw Allan against the light.

'God, boy!' said Sandy, going to his help.

FIVE

Allan sat slumped in Sandy's chair, the table before him. There was a faint smile on his face, a sort of embarrassed smile, but his eyes were hunted. He could not control the shake in his hand.

'Easy, now! Queenie will listen by the door; it's all right.'

But Allan had to get to the floor to stretch himself out. There he breathed gustily.

Sandy stirred a teaspoonful of whisky and a little hot water into a cup of new milk. Lifting up Allan's head he made him drink slowly then got a pillow from his bed.

At first Allan seemed to fall into a stertorous sleep, but after a few minutes he grew restless and Sandy got him back into the chair.

'He nearly fell over me,' said Allan.

'Who?'

'Nicol, was it?'

'Yes.'

His eyes now came on the oatcakes and butter.

Sandy saw the famished look. 'When did you eat last?'

'Forget.'

'You'll start slowly then; chew a bit of that until it runs between your teeth.'

The business of feeding Allan took up Sandy's attention. Clearly no one had been following him or seen him come in. There was that respite anyhow. He did not let Allan eat much and would have put him back into the other room for safety had he not seen the tremble in the lad's flesh.

Then suddenly Allan was sick, and once more Sandy got him stretched out on the floor.

When he had made him comfortable before the fire, with the bed-quilt over him, and cleared the table, Sandy carefully unlocked the front door and with a whisper to Queenie they both went out. For a long time he stood at the end of the house, then entering after Queenie, he re-locked the door and, once more in the kitchen, blew out the lamp, leaving only the fire-glow.

Allan was breathing heavily but regularly. The lad's spirit was broken, but not altogether, not utterly. The trap had been set for him, but before going into it he had out-lasted Nicol, if only just. It was possibly the nervous reaction that had thrown the food up. Next time a small quantity might stay down. But it was going to take time to get him on his legs.

Even now Sandy could not set his mind to work, make it overcome the strange reluctance he had experienced all along to think out the awful problem, with its tail-end of court trial and hanging. Extraordinary thing was that in the moment of emergency he acted with incredible cunning in order to mislead the law and shield Allan. This was done without any thought at all.

But he wanted to get rid of Allan. Before the morning broke the lad must be on his way back to his hiding place. Where that hiding place was he did not particularly want to know.

Sandy wondered in a bleak moment if he was just being selfish, if he was too old to be troubled, if he resented – and here something touched the quick – the interference with the quiet ways, the quiet place or country, he had been preparing for the end of his days.

But he knew, too, it was more than all that, though in what way it was more he did not know.

Allan was plainly in a deep sleep. After a time Sandy's head began to nod for the last two nights had drained him; soon his mouth was open and his breathing harsh.

Queenie pushed the door open and came in and looked at them, first at Sandy then at Allan. Clearly this state of affairs was not what she had expected; it was not only unnatural, it was dull. She gave a quick sniff at Allan's face, but her tongue did not appear in a vacant lick till she had turned her head away. Once she stood quite still, as her master had done, listening to the night, then threw the night away and the breath sharpened in her nostrils. She wanted to whine but didn't, not quite. When she got as near the fire as she could she flattened with an audible thump.

It was a queer way of passing an evening; however, she shut her eyes. Presently her eyes opened and her ears stirred, but she did not lift her head. Her eyes shut and her nose nuzzled into its own warm breath. In a couple of seconds her eyes were wide again and this time she got up, listened, then padded across the floor, went through the half-open inner door and sniffed the cool wind that sifted beneath the outer door.

She lifted her head and looked at the dark barrier as if it might miraculously open to let her out. Then she sniffed again. But if it was one of those hares down from the mountains, she could not do much about it. She padded back to her place by the fire without even looking at the two human effigies and flopped.

But deeper than her attitude to the impudence of a wandering hare lay an anxiety that had her instantly on her feet when at long last her master stirred and began rubbing the crick in his neck before he had quite opened his eyes.

Sandy's astonishment as he saw Allan was ludicrous. He

looked at Queenie. She was on the alert. Had she wakened him? He got down on his knees and began to shake Allan gently. Allan stirred sluggishly, then all at once he was fighting away from Sandy in a frenzy. The next few moments were a terrible revelation of Allan's state of mind.

'Hush! for God's sake,' whispered Sandy desperately.

At last Allan, sitting up, let his head droop, his mouth wide for his panting breath. His hand came up to wipe his forehead and his eyes. He was trembling all over. Sandy saw he was not far from going to bits.

Second after second passed and Sandy listened. He motioned Queenie to the outside door and she went, but in no time was back on the threshold looking at them as if she expected them to follow. Sandy studied her expression and let out a long breath. She had her own world, too, and he understood it. He motioned her back to the door.

'I think it's all right,' whispered Sandy. 'We were both asleep. We'll give it a minute.'

Presently he was preparing a warm milk drink for Allan, and this time he did not add whisky. 'Take it slowly,' he said. 'Chew it.'

Allan did not want anything, but after he had finished the drink he was quieter, more resigned, and had to get support for his back and head.

'We're doing fine,' said Sandy. 'When I get some more food in you, you'll pick up. But no hurry. Nicol is off home to his bed.'

The last sentence had a visible effect on Allan; it brought the glisten back into his eyes. The root in him stirred alive at that moment, as Sandy saw.

'Keep a calm sough,' Sandy added. 'I'll make up some food for you.'

Allan's tongue came between his lips and his eyes shot

here and there. It was a sensitive face, but with strength in the fineness of the bone, the face of one who might indeed go through a pool like an otter. In the dim light from the fire his hazel eyes and dark-brown hair looked black. His skin was fair and the growth of stubble on the chin left it less dark than Nicol's clean-shaven jaw. His dark-blue suit was rumpled and soiled but not torn. The yellow stud showed in the neckband of a blue-striped pale shirt. The collar and tie were gone. For the dance at Hilton he had plainly got into his best clothes.

He watched Sandy going quietly about his business of gathering food. Presently as he was chewing a small bit of oatcake with a thin skin of butter the flavour came about his palate with an incredible freshness. Saliva rose into his mouth. His boyhood rose in him and hunger.

Sandy boiled two eggs hard and put salt in a screw of paper. On the corner of the table he was collecting what Allan could stuff into his pockets.

'How are you feeling now?' whispered Sandy.

'Better.'

'You can rest for a while. Only trouble is they might come back any time. I'm going to make some tea for you, with plenty sugar in it. How's the stomach?'

'Fine.'

'Good! Keep your mind easy. We're all right.'

Sandy saw to it that Allan ate slowly and sparingly; his manner to him was now calm and natural, partly because the lad was coming back into his affection, but more because he knew it was the best way to help him keep his food down.

'I'm wondering if this is the best place to let you rest. I would never feel sure of that fellow Nicol.'

Allan's breathing began to quicken. He glanced and listened. 'I'll be going,' he said. But he was no sooner on his feet than he had to lunge at the chair for support; he rolled away and would have fallen if Sandy hadn't gripped him. Sandy had no sooner set him in the chair than Allan's body convulsed as if about to throw the food up. Sandy caught his hands.

Allan's hands broke loose and gripped the old man's arms.

'Easy now, Allan,' said Sandy, his breath and his heart warm.

The top of Allan's head came against Sandy and his whole body shook and quivered.

The boy was at his breast; my God, he was clinging, poor lad; he was keeping his head down to hide his emotion. I ought to have had more sense, thought Sandy, than to weaken him with kindness.

Presently the surge left Allan, but at least it had diverted his body's concern with the food, which stayed down.

'I'm damn weak,' he muttered, repudiating the moment.

He was game always, thought Sandy, setting him square in the hard armchair.

'Of course you are. I don't know if it would be safe even to put you in the other room. We'll wait a while.'

Allan said nothing, and did not wipe his eyes until Sandy had turned away.

Clearly the lad was in no state to tackle the night and the mountains. It was a difficult problem. If he put him in the next room and anyone came in, Allan would never be able to walk out quietly enough; while a cough, a creak from the old iron bed . . .

The only place for him was the barn, the loft. And perhaps the sooner the better. He could stay there for three or four hours and slip away when he felt fit enough. The house was a trap. At any moment the jaws might spring shut.

'I'm not hurrying you. I'm only thinking of what next,' said Sandy.

Allan nodded, gathering his resources.

'I was thinking they won't look in the barn again. If we got you up in the loft, you could lie there for a while.'

Allan glanced at Sandy; anxiety was coming back.

'Don't move. When you feel like it, I'll first have a look at the night and make sure the way is clear. Wait!'

But Allan was swaying on his feet. 'I'll wait in other room.'

Fear was back in him, and cunning. Sandy helped him into the next room, then very quietly unlocked the door and with Queenie went right round the long building. If anyone had been left on watch he was bound by this time to have given some sign. As he stood for a minute, his heart was stirred in him towards Allan. The death hunt was after him. In his nostrils he smelt the night and for a moment its small shiver took him beyond thought.

Back in the house, he had a quick look about the kitchen table, lifted the food and stowed it in his pockets, then went through to Allan. In the darkness they groped a little and fumbled, but soon Allan was walking slowly down to the barn with no more than Sandy's arm to guide him.

Sandy got the ladder into position. 'I'll go up first.' And he went. Soon he was pulling Allan in over the edge of the loft. It was pitch black. 'You'll be cold here.' And down the old man went for hay.

'You'll be all right now and I'll tidy up in the first of the daylight.'

'Thanks.'

'Queenie is worth three watchers,' added Sandy with some of the old humour in his voice.

Allan stirred and Sandy felt that human movement.

'Have you far to go?'

'Loch Deoch,' answered Allan.

'Loch Deoch!' Sandy's mind groped through its astonishment. 'Where?'

'The island – Crannock.'

'But how?'

'Swam.'

'You swam?' Sandy's hands felt Allan's dry body.

'Took my clothes off. Found bits of old beams and pushed them in front of me.'

'Well I'm blest!' said Sandy. 'You thought of that!'

'By time I reached Loch Deoch it was daylight. Couldn't go farther. Saw bits of grey beam washed up; made a heather rope and lashed them and put my clothes on top. Easier to swim naked. I just made the island.'

'And you've been lying there ever since?'

'Yes. Couldn't move next day. But tonight – I had to get something or would never come out of it.'

The words came from Allan without stress; they dripped from him like water.

'My God,' said Sandy. 'You did well. Anything wrong, boy, anything broken?'

'No. Have a bit of pain on left side, but – nothing. It'll go.'

'You'll never reach Loch Deoch tonight.'

'I'll try.'

'No, you won't. You'll stop here. I'll lock the barn door. If anyone comes, I'll lift my voice or give you some sign. There's a risk whatever you do. But at least this place has been searched by Nicol, and the hills are still being searched. Did you see anyone today?'

'I saw someone on the horizon, but no one came down to the lochside.'

'Is the boat there?'

'No. I made sure of that first.'

'Good! They'll have taken her away for repairs before the fishing starts. She was in need of it two years ago and more. If they're doing a systematic search, Loch Deoch and the Crannock might well enough be down for tomorrow. Others can swim as well as you. So all in all, you should be fine here for a day and I'll feed you; you need it. Make as little noise as you can.'

'Very well.'

'And now I'll be off, boy. That fellow Nicol won't rest much. Are you sure you're all right?'

'Yes.'

'I'll move the ladder back a yard to where it was. Nicol is a great fellow for signs. He couldn't find a footprint.'

'I thought of that.'

'One of the searchers I saw had a dog.'

'Had he?' The tone sharpened.

Sandy realised he needn't have said that, but he had been thinking of Loch Deoch. 'Queenie and myself will cover everything. Don't worry.' He could not see Allan and in the silence the darkness was suddenly charged with a deep human intimacy. 'So long just now.' As Sandy got over the edge and searched for a footing on the ladder, he felt Allan's hand gripping at his shoulder to steady him. When his own hand hit the food in his pocket, he made a small joke about his forgetfulness and pushed the food in over the edge.

Down below he shifted the ladder away and with feet and hands raked back invisible wisps of hay. He took his time going to the house for the key, then returned and locked the door.

If someone turned up and wanted to search the barn and found Allan that would pin Sandy down as an accomplice. Yes, that was so, for no one else could have locked Allan in. No way out of that. He stood for a time before his own door. Then the idea came to him: Allan might have stolen into the barn without his knowing and then at night he had locked the door in all innocence.

I'm taking care of myself, he thought, as he sat down in his own chair. I am not going to be involved.

There was something pitiful in that. There was indeed. The thin bubble that was man's own self, nursing itself to the end, sheltering itself still from the near burst.

But that wasn't the whole of it. Not quite.

The lad was going to bits. Getting jumpy. That quick glance of the eye; fear like a sudden needle in his heart. The shake in the hand. He was further through even than he looked. Yet the life-thrust was there, too. He would go through the pool till he was hit, rolled over and sank. That would be the best way, the natural way. Not the hanging. Not that. God no, not that.

Sandy's head lifted.

He had better go to bed. He was worn out. The fire had died down to a red glow and the old willow-pattern soup tureen, with its broad brow and narrow chin, looked at him obscurely. He saw Chinese faces . . . though it was in Calcutta that he had first known the phrase 'life is cheap'. One dead body – hunger – then another, on the street, and no one paying any attention, as though even the scavengers had gone on strike. He saw the scene very vividly and himself as a young man – about Allan's age.

He had not thought of the Crannock. Then he realised that though he had not deliberately gone over all the possible hiding places, had not wanted to, yet some part of his mind had done this but had missed the Crannock.

Only a few old people knew it by that name; to others it was just the island in Loch Deoch. And few enough would ever have seen it anyway, for it was over four miles away. In the wilds were many lochs with islands. But Professor Sandieman had told him that this was not a natural island, it was an artificial one, a hut-dwelling or crannog made by man in the remote past.

He had spent many afternoons on the island with the professor while the work of excavation was going on, for one day, under a hydro-electric project, the island would be completely submerged, and archaeologists had decided it might be interesting to find out first just how the island had been constructed and then to ask why.

Fascinating it had been, for it had linked life up in a continued story. Mention of the crannog under various Gaelic names by old bards, telling some epic tale of personal adventure, made it clear that there had been a house or human shelter of some kind there in the sixteenth century. Not only had the present bare slopes about Loch Deoch been covered by forests then, but from analysis of soil, with its pollens, the professor had a fair picture of the kind of trees. Wolves roamed the forests in hungry packs, and it was a fair conjecture that in the beginning at least the main, if not the whole, reason for building the crannog was to provide shelter from the wolves. Travellers would use it at night, going out to it by boat.

Shelter from the wolves! Once – on a Sunday – the three lads had turned up and from the eastern slope above Loch Deoch had looked through Sandy's old sea telescope at the trenches which had already been dug into the crannog. They could see the exposed beams of solid wood and Sandy told them how they had been tied. But what had brought the astonished smile, a wild laughing glint to their eyes, was the story of hiding from wolves. In the Highlands of Scotland, even well into the seventeenth century! It was hardly credible. They had to laugh in sheer astonishment.

Allan would find good enough shelter there if he took care not to move about in the daylight. And at least he knew what a telescope could pick up.

He had spent only one whole night there. It would have

been a long night, with what was on his mind. The old kind of wolves would have seemed simple enough then!

Sandy stirred and looked blindly about him.

The story, life's continued story, as the professor had told it, as they had worked it out, with Sandy giving the Gaelic pronunciation of a word now and then, had brought a certain warmth about his heart, a happiness, a feeling of sitting at an old fire, of belonging to a community that had endured a long time, long enough to bring vague notions of time and of eternity into some sort of conjunction. Near enough to help him, anyway; to make him feel that he was part of something bigger, of what endured, in realms beyond the human word. Vague it was, like the feeling that moved one in the old bard's times, but very pleasant.

It hadn't been vague tonight. When the top of Allan's head had come against his chest and his hands had gripped him, the living warmth had flooded his whole being. Again, the long silent moment in the dark of the loft, the hand helping him down the ladder . . .

It was not a thing of learning, of knowledge, that gripped at the heart. But the heart liked the learning and the knowledge because the grip was hidden in them.

He saw the inscrutable smile on the face of the soup tureen, and now remembered the old Chinaman in Rangoon. The Chinese knew about death, whatever else.

He got up and listened to the night. Queenie lifted her head. She would not rise now unless he took a deliberate step towards the door. When she saw him shedding his jacket, her head went down, but her near eye watched him until his right knee pressed on the bed.

SIX

As Sandy went over his doorstep in the morning he looked slowly about him and up at the sky like a seaman. His house faced a few points south of west and the prospect was wide. It was a dull morning and the weather might be making for a change, but not quite yet. The wind was in the same airt, if he was not mistaken, and as if to make sure he went round the corner of the house where he stood taking his ease. He now commanded the ground behind his steading. All the time he had Queenie under his eye. She had wakened him during the night and he felt certain that someone had come round the house but had not stayed long.

Anyone watching the house would have seen the blue smoke going up for the morning tea, and now here was the old man going calmly about his early chores. He let out the hens and scattered a fistful of oats; then he went to the barn but found the door locked, returned to the house, and emerged with the key in his hand. Once in the barn he moved quickly to the ladder; set it under the opening, climbed up, and from his poacher's pocket drew out a bottle of hot tea and richly buttered oatcakes.

'Here you are,' he whispered, pushing them over the edge.

Allan came to the opening on all fours.

'Heard anything?' Sandy asked.

'No. Slept solid.'

'Queenie was disturbed once but it may have been

nothing. Lie close. You can't get away before the dark. But you'll hear me if anyone's about.'

In no time the ladder was back in its original position and Sandy was going out of the barn with an armful of hay. Into the byre he went and back to the house for the milk pail. The cow had calved early in the year, but he had sold the bull calf. He had stopped keeping an extra beast or two and had now a working arrangement with the farmer of Milton who put down his small crop and used his considerable outrun of rough grazing. The cow hadn't a great flow of milk but the quality was good. Until a week ago, when her own cow had calved, he had supplied Widow Macleay whose small holding lay over a quarter of a mile away on the east side of the main road before it dipped down towards Darroch. Sandy hadn't any near crofting neighbours, but the poorest in the district had good reason to know him, and when Sandy's own cow was dry he never lacked for milk.

All forenoon he was quietly busy with the tasks that never get done, and when he was carrying water from the well for his midday meal the sun came through. No one called on him, no one came within sight, and he found something new in the loneliness that troubled him.

After eating, he went to the barn and gave Allan his share of the meal.

'I'm going for a walk and I'll lock up the place. Anyone coming will think I've gone away for the afternoon. Lie close and you'll be all right.'

'Right,' echoed Allan.

From the ladder Sandy gave him a glance. He had quietened and from the dim light his eyes looked down for a moment with what seemed a reddish gleam.

The cow gave a roar; she was wanting out. After he had driven her down to the low ground, he returned and brought some hay from the barn; then he locked the barn door, fixed a stone that kept the byre door open for the cow, and presently locked his own front door and with Queenie and his telescope set off in the direction of the lily loch.

What Allan had done was coming back on him. Now that he had rested and the pains of the body were eased, now that he had not to face action's next moment, the lad had time to think.

The loneliness around was like a watched loneliness. That's what was troubling about it. The invisible eye. The eye of the human enemy, the eye of the wild beast, the eye of the demon . . . the eye of the demon-god, the god, the eye of God.

That's probably the history of it, thought Sandy lightly, using his thought like a veil, casting it between him and the eye. For the awful thing was the eye. And in Allan's case the eye was the reality.

From a head that turned slowly and naturally, Sandy's eyes focused sharply here and there, looking for a movement, a sign, for a figure standing by a tree. He knew exactly how Nicol would stand.

Sometimes as he paused to get his breath and gazed around, he saw nature in the freedom of being unwatched. The buds on the birch were crammed with life, with folded green leaves waiting to burst – slowly, so slowly, in the kind of delight man did not know. They opened into the bright emptiness, into the small soft rain; they came out, they unfolded; but man's eye saw only the burst of green fire.

His breathing hardly troubled him, as if he were in a fitter condition than he had been for a long time, but this did not astonish him, for he had noticed more than once before how after an exhausting spell his body had seemed to get lighter, less solid or gross. Sleep then came in a natural way, at once as a sinking into the earth and as a floating away upon the air.

He was heading for the Chair, instinctively escaping from Allan and the police, from murder and the eye. He had to escape or otherwise he would get bogged and lose his way. As a man grew old and became half conscious of his way, he did not like it to be interfered with too much.

It had been his intention, once in the Chair, to use his telescope on the slopes and hills beyond, to quarter the near and the far with its magnifying eye, so that he would be in a position to advise Allan when it came to his departure in the night. Yet when he did sit down such a physical relief came over him that he saw the loch of the lilies waiting for him.

Then in a moment it all came back. He had never forgotten the experience; it had remained like a memory of a bright air, a perfect climate.

There had been nothing at all dramatic about the experience. Some time after he had come to the croft and got properly settled in, he set out for the mountains determined to make a day of it and see the hills and the hollows, the lochs and the trees, the country that was around and beyond him and was now his country. From this country he would make one more journey only, the final one.

He had walked and climbed, feeling more fit and free the farther he went. Indeed a sort of gluttony of exercise had come upon him as if he could neither have enough of what he saw nor tire himself too much; a sort of debauch that set his legs swinging and his mind remembering old jokes. Once or twice he caught himself laughing with an old shipmate. Nothing could have been more natural, more health-giving, and altogether he had got the notion that he was going to live for a long time. Occasionally a view brought an exclamation. By God, it was wonderful; and God's name held the view for a moment and got lost in it.

The sun and the air, the roll of the hills, the ups and downs, perhaps brought back something of the sea. Anyway, he could hardly have enough of it, and when at last he saw his croft in the distance he sat down, reluctant to end his day, to lose this happiness, with the sun and the wind warming and blowing past him, knitting him into them and into everything with a sense of wellbeing throughout his utterly tired body that was rare beyond telling.

And then, as simply as a thought might come to him when taking his porridge, he saw that to pass out of his body was in the order of things, now revealed; not an end and not quite a translation, but precisely a passing on and away. At that moment it would have been easy and pleasant to die. He could have gone.

Not only had death no sting, *it did not matter*.

Something of that day's bright air could readily be recaptured afterwards; indeed most of the experience could in some measure be evoked. What eluded him was the assurance that death *did not matter*. He never again quite got that.

But he could get enough of it never to ask himself: *Why* did it not matter? For the actual experience was not concerned with what happened afterwards to the spirit. Even a momentary speculation about immortality did not arise: there had been no need for it.

And now as old Sandy settled in the horse-shoe scoop that Allan had once called Sandy's Chair, something of this 'no need' came back upon him.

His breath went from him, that breath which some of the ancients fancied was the spirit itself, and he looked away over the loch of the water lilies. Then his eyes were on the heather beside him, stalks, tiny ashen buds, moss, lichen, each a thing in itself and all in their world, their own order. Orders and worlds; aspects. There followed a pause of understanding that was pure freedom.

He lay over on his right side, and his body, the old ship, slipped its moorings.

His eyes opened and saw the heather stalks with an extraordinary clarity. 'What is it?' he asked, answering Queenie's growl which he had heard in his sleep. He pushed himself up and screwed his head round and saw Nicol against the sky. A tall menacing figure he was, his blue uniform very dark-looking.

Nicol came down and sat beside him with a confidential air that had no suggestion of a smile about it. 'Seen anything at all?'

'No.' Sandy followed Nicol's glance to the telescope. 'To tell the truth, I was going to have a spy but fell asleep.' His body gave a shudder. 'It's cold.'

'It's not that cold. But, it's dangerous going to sleep in the open.'

'I suppose so.'

'Lumbago is the least you might get.'

'Ay. I should have more sense. Sleep came over me.'

'You're lucky.'

'You haven't my years.' Sandy smiled, and saw a dryness in the policeman's skin, a sleepless tension.

'You have seen nothing at all?'

'Take the glass yourself,' answered Sandy, picking up the telescope. 'That's my mark – but move it to suit yourself.'

Nicol spied for a long time. 'It's very clear.'

'It's a good glass.'

'I might borrow it from you for a day or two.'

'Surely,' said Sandy. 'Only I don't like to be separated from it for long. Old sea habits.'

'You don't know of any place where he could hide out?'

'I should think you and your people have seen more of this country now than I have myself. This is about the farthest I go. You haven't any trace of him at all?'

'Nothing definite.'

'What about that fellow you spoke of who got the lift to Inverton? Has he come forward?'

'No.'

After a while Nicol said, 'There are rumours. One is that Allan has been seen going to your place.'

Sandy looked at him – and met his eyes, brown, with dark motes in them. They had a steady intensity and for a moment washed out everything else, even thought. The sheer menace of the eye.

'My place?' echoed Sandy, glancing away, as if Nicol and himself had just met in an unhallowed spot. 'You mean the night that – it happened?'

'Since then.'

'When?' Sandy looked at Nicol again and his own eye was steady.

Now Nicol's eyes shifted. 'I traced the rumour to its source, or as near as I could get. The time suggested was wrong because your place was under observation. But – I found out a few things.'

Sandy nodded. It was the policeman's business.

'You know Davie Urquhart and Willie Fraser?'

'I knew them well.'

'They used to come poaching here with Allan Innes?'

'Well,' said Sandy, 'as to poaching—'

'You needn't be afraid to admit it. They have been questioned.'

'In that case,' said Sandy, 'you'll have their answers.'

'You admit it?'

'Look now, officer,' replied Sandy reasonably. 'These lads came around my place at odd times for years. They helped me with the croft. Many a hard hour they put in on it. If they had their own ploys, that was their concern. I'm saying nothing about it.'

'Do you mean you refuse?'

'It's not a question of refusing,' replied Sandy and his brows gathered. 'I never went with them, so I can't tell you at first hand what they did or where they went. And that's all I'll say about that, except that I'm not sure why you're asking.'

'It's nothing against you.'

'I wasn't thinking of myself.'

'We're trying to establish habits. It's not exactly a credit to us that he got away as he did.'

'That's different. I can understand that. So long as you are not asking me to give the lads away over a bit of fun that's now long past. Hang it, man, there's hardly a young fellow of spirit in the Highlands who hasn't at one time or another poached something for a lark. Foo! I'm cold.'

'You should watch yourself at your age.'

'I'm fine. A cup of tea is my medicine.'

'I could do with a cup myself.'

'Weren't you home for your dinner?'

'No.'

Sandy's heart rumbled in his breast at the thought of Nicol coming back to the house for tea with Allan in the barn. He could not speak.

'I had not meant to come near your place until it was dark,' said Nicol, concerned only with his own slow thoughts.

'If you don't want to be seen there, I can take you out a bottle of tea easily enough – and something with it. Will you wait here?'

Nicol's head turned in the direction of some small birches and broken ground nearer the croft and well above it. Sandy had suspected the spot.

'I don't know,' said Nicol. 'It's not that long till the dark anyway.'

'Just as you like,' said Sandy. 'It's no bother to me to bring it to you.'

'I want to spend the night in the barn, like before.'

Sandy waited but Nicol said no more. 'You think he's still about?'

'Couldn't we go back, keeping higher up?'

'We could,' said Sandy. 'Only I'm not so young as I was. If you take the high road and I take the low road, you could drop in when I have the kettle singing.' He smiled.

Nicol looked slowly about the landscape without any smile. 'If we're seen, we're seen,' he said at last. 'It would look more natural if we went back together, as if nothing doing.' His mind was now made up and they started for the croft, Queenie keeping close behind her master.

For some distance they walked in silence and Sandy's thought was desperately engaged working out how Allan could have got into the barn without his knowing, when Nicol said, 'The case against him on the capital charge is complete.'

Sandy staggered as he turned his head. 'Is it?'

'Yes. He's for it.'

'You have it complete?'

'He searched for my brother, hunted him until he got him. Then he murdered him.'

'Ah,' said Sandy on his sea legs.

'Either he's dead in a hole,' said Nicol, 'or he's got food from someone. And anyone who has been deliberately shielding him—' Nicol's voice just stopped. He had not raised it. He was actually being confidential.

There was something more deadly in this than Sandy had yet encountered. Then he remembered the bottles of tea he had given Allan. Anyone finding Allan in the loft

would also find the two bottles . . . the crumbs . . . the signs
that Nicol would look for so inevitably.

To his surprise, this final incrimination relieved Sandy.
It committed him. There was no way of getting round this;
nor would he try when challenged.

He looked at the homestead as they drew near and saw
it very clearly, not in its familiar details so much as in something enduring in its waiting stillness. It had the patience
of God.

The path forked at a hundred yards and Sandy took the
prong that brought them in between the hen-house and the
barn. As he was passing the barn door he stopped and tried
the door.

'I was sure I had locked it,' he said, in a carrying voice,
over his shoulder.

'You always lock it?'

'When there's anything in it, I do as a rule.'

'Don't you trust your neighbours?'

Sandy looked at Nicol to see if he were joking. 'As a
policeman you must never think that,' he answered very
clearly indeed, then threw a glance at the hens. 'If you make
a habit of locking it, hens won't get in for one thing. But
more particularly the cow. Not to speak of a neighbour
who might come to look for me and leave the door open—
So she's back!' he concluded, for at that moment the cow
mooed from the byre. 'I'll just tie her up.' As he came out
of the byre and shut the door, he said, 'She won't stop out
long if she thinks there's more to be had at home; but things
are beginning to grow at last, though late.'

'All the farmers are complaining.'

'They say they're of a complaining kind but we have
our trials. I didn't expect to have to buy that hay for one
thing.' He took the key of the house from behind an old
quern stone that leant against the wall. 'I'll go in front of

you,' he said politely, like one who might have to clear the way.

As he entered his living-room, Sandy's eyes ran here and there though he knew he had left everything normally tidied up. 'Sit down. I'll soon have the fire going.'

Sandy was glad to get to his knees.

Nicol looked at him as he blew into the fire trying to kindle the sticks. 'Let me,' he said, and getting to his knees soon had a flame running up. 'You still use peat?'

'The dry hard clods catch easy, and with a core of coal you can have a lasty fire. But I don't cut many peats, for I have to carry them on my back. Wait now.' And with the tongs Sandy soon built a good-going fire.

'Don't you find it lonely, living here alone?'

'Lonely is the one thing I never feel.'

'What if anything happened to you?'

'Time and chance happens to us all.'

'You're a bit of a philosopher.'

'It's a big word. How do you like your eggs?'

'Almost hard.'

'Well, you can time them yourself. I'll set the table.'

As they ate, Nicol had to pursue his questioning of Sandy's 'philosophy', but his manner never became warm or intimate yet it was clearly natural to him as to a man who must see how the bits and pieces make the machine. Once an idea got into his head, he could not lightly forsake it.

When Sandy produced a well-worn saying or an echo from the Bible, Nicol looked at him as though he were an interesting old fellow, one who had seen a lot and thought a bit. 'Where was that, did you say?'

Sandy finished his story of extreme violence in an East Indian port.

'Life is cheap there.'

'I got that impression more than once,' Sandy agreed. 'Violence – well—'

'What?'

'Violence is the most terrible of all things, and – in the end – the most tiresome.'

'Tiresome?'

'Ay. It leaves nothing. It empties life to the dead dregs.'

Nicol had nothing to say to that, but he looked at the old man, whose faint smile seemed to come through arid leagues to his face.

'Did it ever happen to yourself?'

Sandy was silent, remembering Maria, the Italian girl whom he had loved. 'It would have been easier if it had happened to myself,' he said at last. 'Try some of the crowdie, it's fresh.'

'You were never married?'

'Never actually married,' replied Sandy.

'I see,' said Nicol, who would have liked to have seen precisely. 'It makes a difference when violence comes near yourself.'

'So much of a difference,' replied Sandy, 'that I had forgotten.'

Nicol spread crowdie thickly on his buttered oatcake. 'I'll get him in the end.'

'You'll want to.'

'Didn't *you*?'

'There's a violence you can do nothing against.'

'How so?'

'Because it's too big for you and crushes you like a fly.'

The old man seemed to have changed in a curious way. Kindliness was still in his expression but it came from the lines on his face as from a mask. He looked older and harder, but with a hardness from an earlier manhood of action. Nicol began to understand him better. He had probably been a tough customer.

'You can understand my position,' Nicol said.

'I understand it.'

'If this country isn't to go like yon countries out East, law and justice will have to be looked after.'

'It's as old as the first tribe,' said Sandy.

'What tribe?'

'Any tribe. When a man broke the law of the tribe he had to be brought to justice. It was the only way to keep the tribe intact and strong.'

The clarity of this so arrested Nicol that he lifted the shell of the first egg, crushed it, and pushed it into the egg-cup. 'That's right,' he said. There was a hard assurance in his voice. He looked about the kitchen then at the old man. 'You haven't eaten much.'

'It's a little early for me; but I never take much at the best of times.'

Nicol thanked him for the good tea and Sandy set about clearing the table and washing the dishes in a tin basin. He moved around slowly and when Nicol approved his tidy habits 'for a man', Sandy referred to the sea.

But Nicol had no idea of light talk and Sandy did not seem to bother, which was unlike him. He fed Queenie and gathered scraps for the hens. He scrubbed potatoes, went to the well for water and found Nicol in the doorway on his return.

'The sun is down,' Nicol said.

'In an hour or less it will be dark enough,' Sandy replied. 'I'll see to the hens and milk the cow; then I'll be through.'

'Just go about things in your ordinary way. Where did you put the telescope?'

When Sandy came with the milk, Nicol was by the door jamb. The dusk was deepening.

Nicol went back into the kitchen and laid the telescope on the table.

'Did you say you were going to watch in the barn?' Sandy asked.

'Yes.'

'It would be warmer here. But just as you like.'

'No,' said Nicol. 'The one thing he would be likely to do first is creep to this window and listen.'

'You have thought it out.'

'The barn is the place to get him from behind.'

They stood for a little while without speaking, then Sandy said, 'Well, I better do my last chore for the day and that is feed the cow.' He went to the dresser for the key of the barn. 'I won't be long,' he said, going out.

Sandy went along to the barn, unlocked the door and entered unhurriedly, without looking back. As he scraped the cobbles with his feet, he lifted his face to the opening in the loft and in a high thin whisper from the back of his throat called, 'Are you there?'

He heard the slithering movement of Allan's body and continued to scrape outlying wisps of hay back into the main bundle, then stooped and caught an armful.

'Get out in the next few minutes. Nicol is here; he's going to watch in the barn all night.' He coughed the strain of whispering from his throat and went out with the armful of hay and gave it to the cow. Then he returned, shut the barn door, but did not lock it. As he went back to the house he looked around. It was not so very dark. Movement could be seen at a fair distance. Queenie came along and looked up at him. They went in.

'I thought we were in for a change this morning,' he said, 'but it's holding off.' He could not see Nicol and for a moment stood cramped in the deathly stillness. Then he saw him by the head of the bed.

'I may as well go,' Nicol said.

'It's not very dark yet,' Sandy answered.

'Seems dark enough from here. I saw the fire's reflection in the window.'

'You'd better give it a few minutes. I'll light the lamp and draw the blind. That would make it look natural.'

'It would.'

But Sandy could not find his matches and then he could not even find a piece of paper. It was dark in the corners and he trod on the dog. 'What on earth!' he said as she yelped. He burnt his fingers with the first piece of paper and had to drop it. 'I'll soon be needing my spectacles to light the lamp.' But he got it lit in the end, left the wick low to warm the funnel while he pulled down the brownish-yellow blind, then returned to the table and slowly screwed up the wick. Lifting the lamp in one hand, he pulled the table nearer his armchair. The legs protested and the cutlery rattled in the drawer. 'Now I'm set,' he said.

'I can see you have fixed habits.'

'Ah well, living alone, I suppose, gets a man into a rut. And I must confess I don't like my habits disturbed too much.'

'I have been disturbing them lately.'

Sandy looked at him, but there was no trace of any kind of smile on Nicol's face.

'You have, I suppose,' Sandy allowed. 'But maybe I'm none the worse of that.'

As Nicol moved off, Sandy said, 'Would you like something to eat with you?'

'No.'

'It's no trouble. Wait a bit and I'll put a couple of oatcakes together.' And Sandy got busy.

'It's good of you.'

'It will be a poor day when hospitality dies,' said Sandy. Then he paused. 'There's a bit of cheese somewhere.' And though Nicol protested, Sandy would insist on finding the cheese.

As Nicol was going to the door, Sandy asked, 'Will I put an extra bit of fire on? You could come in for a warm. It will be cold enough in the small hours.' His voice was normally loud and friendly.

'No,' said Nicol.

'As you like,' said Sandy. 'It will be a long night.'

'You're not expecting me to find much?'

'Are you expecting it yourself?'

Then Sandy saw the hardness in the man's face. His eye sockets were in darkness. 'I'll make sure anyway.'

For the moment something elaborate and futile in his position had got the better of Nicol and brought out the unyielding bitterness. As they stood in the silence that followed the remark, the dark forces came around. The silence was an ear that Sandy trod on with his boots, for in that moment it seemed to him that even the smallest sound Allan made would travel a mile.

He followed Nicol out. 'I'll leave the door open.'

'Don't lock it.'

'I left the key in the barn door. Here, come in!' Sandy called harshly to Queenie.

Nicol moved away quietly. Sandy watched him for a moment then closed the door. His flat-open hands against the wood, he leaned there heavily with lowered head trying to hear beyond his heavy breathing and the thump of his heart.

A full minute passed and nothing disturbed the night. Sandy staggered slowly back to his chair.

He should have made certain that Allan came down. The lad may not have understood the whispering. He may have been hit by fear, decided he would have a better chance lying close.

Even a rat running along the loft would sound like a trotting horse to an ear below. The slither of an elbow, a heavy breath . . . The floor of the loft was like the skin on a drum.

What if Nicol climbed up to have a look at the loft? Even if Allan were gone, Nicol would find the empty bottles, the bed of hay . . .

This new thought knocked the bottom out of Sandy's mind. There could be no explaining it . . . Still, if Allan was gone, he could deny all knowledge of the bottles. Someone may have come when he himself was away – say, at Hilton – found the key of the house behind the quern stone, cooked some food, taken it to the loft, and lain there for a day or two. He could not swear on oath that the door was locked or unlocked at any particular time . . .

Excuses, to cover himself! How many different persons there were in a man!

He had gone on speaking and stamping around to drown any sounds Allan might make, to give him time to get away and so avoid the tribal law, escape with the violence unpaid for, unredeemed . . .

And all the time anxious not to be involved himself, anxious to get rid of Allan, to get rid of them all, to be left alone – to find the precious way, the last brightness, that fond illusion.

In the early hours, after many bouts of listening following odd sounds, his mental exhaustion produced a grey indifference and he fell asleep.

When he awoke the light was in the window, a strong light. He looked for a figure at the fire. He hearkened. Then he got up.

Though late, he set the fire going and put the kettle on. Outside, Queenie ran before him down towards the barn. The door was shut, locked. He turned the key and entered, saw the hay, the ladder in the same old place. At once he came out and shut the door and looked around. Anyone watching him would understand he was wondering where Nicol had gone. He opened the hen-house door and went into the byre. He was now going about his usual tasks. Certain there was no one close at hand, he returned to the barn. The fowls were clucking behind him as he lifted his high whisper, 'Are you there?' There was no answer. Allan was gone. He came out with an armful of hay for the cow.

Extraordinary that Nicol had not come back, had not come in with the daylight to say his words, to get his tea.

After he had milked the cow and drunk a cup of tea, he found his gradual way back to the barn and climbed the ladder. He peered about the flooring for the bottles but could not find them. They would be under the hay . . . but they were not under the hay. For several seconds Sandy stood, wondering what had happened.

Could Nicol actually have got Allan? In the small hours, had Allan betrayed himself by a movement, a sound? Had he, when challenged, just given himself up? There was no suggestion of a struggle, no trace of haste.

On all fours, he went over the loft looking for the bottles. The light was dim but clear enough for him to make certain they were not there.

He climbed down the ladder and put it back in its old place, then went about his business. Surely if Nicol had found Allan there would have been sufficient disturbance, noise, to waken him? Bound to have been, surely? But if he had not found Allan, why hadn't he come back to the house?

Then a new question hit Sandy: Had Nicol found the bottles? Had he, for something to do, out of his bitterness and feeling of futility, as hour had followed hour, climbed to the loft and found the bottles? Taken the bottles away with him – as evidence – for finger prints? When he had previously inspected the loft there had been no bottles, no hay. With his torch Nicol would have made a very thorough examination of the loft. Then he would have replaced the ladder, locked the door, and gone away as if nothing had happened.

But why, in that case, had he not returned to the kitchen if only to allay suspicion, to say he was giving up the search?

It might depend on when he had found the bottles; if long before daylight, the very wakening of Sandy would rouse suspicion. In any case, he would want to waste no time in getting a watch set on the trap, particularly when he could leave everything, including the ladder and the locked door, as he had found them.

SEVEN

The thin-drawn cunning of his brain finally wearied Sandy, and when, after his midday meal, he was taking the cow down to the lower pasture and caught a glimpse of a figure on all fours crawling behind a salley bush, an arid smile came about his eyes. The trap was being watched!

His inclination was to pretend he had seen nothing, but something hardened in him and his feet took him past the bush. Then he stopped in astonishment, for crouching before him was a boy of eleven or twelve.

The boy looked at the ground in a queer confusion. His clothes were soiled, his legs dirty, one of them streaked with blood from the knee. But what startled Sandy was the look of Allan in the boy's face. Then he remembered . . . there had been some sort of joke about so late a birth in the family. Allan's brother.

As Sandy sent Queenie out to direct the cow, he looked about the landscape, then he sat down beside the boy.

'What are you doing here?' he asked in a kindly voice.

The boy glared at him, then looked away. His face was quite solemn, had even a sort of withdrawn expression. He brought his look back to the ground below the bush and poked it with a finger.

'Won't you tell me?'

'Nothing,' said the boy.

'What's your name?'

The boy did not answer.

'You're Allan's brother, aren't you?'

'Yes,' mumbled the boy, poking harder at the bank.

'If you tell me your name, I'll know what to call you.'

'Bill.'

'So you're Bill. And you're looking for Allan?'

Bill glared at him again but did not answer. Sandy had forgotten how fresh the skin of a boy was, how clear his eyes.

'Who told you Allan was here?'

'I heard it.'

'So you heard it? I suppose it's all over the place.'

Bill glanced at Sandy again. He was giving nothing away.

Sandy smiled. 'You can trust me. Allan is an old friend of mine. Were you wanting to see him about something in particular?'

The young clear eyes were now on Sandy's own, searching. But they were not disposed to trust anyone yet and it took Sandy a little while to find out that Bill was hoping to give his brother something.

'You'll never be able to find him yourself. But if he ever comes my way, I might be able to hand it to him. What is it?'

'Money.'

'Money!' Sandy was genuinely astonished. 'Is it all your savings?' Then his look narrowed. 'Did someone send you?'

Bill did not answer.

'Look,' said Sandy gently. 'We'll go up to the house and have something to eat. Money is the one thing I never thought of. Come. You know who'll be watching us here.'

On their way Sandy increased the confidential note in his voice and by the time the flame was under the kettle, the boy was half won and admitted, 'It was Davie. He said Allan would need money to get out of the country.'

'I see. Of course.' Sandy's tone was that of one who would never have thought of such a thing; as indeed he hadn't. 'So Davie sent you?'

'Yes.' But he did not look at Sandy.

'Did he send you to me or just to find Allan?' As the question was obviously difficult, Sandy added, 'How much have you?'

Bill was looking at the window and took a few moments. Then he said, 'Twenty pounds.'

Sandy controlled his astonishment and remarked quietly, 'Davie gave you all that?'

'Yes.'

But Sandy took his eyes off his face. The boy was lying.

'Well, we'll do our best. But you'll never find Allan yourself. And the police are about. Did Davie send any message to me?'

But the boy was no good at lying. He did not answer.

'Do you know who I am?'

'Davie said you can trust old Sandy.' But the calm in his face was growing taut; he did not seem to be breathing.

'I'm old Sandy and you can trust me. Tell me where you got the money.'

But it took another minute for the storm in the boy to break; then he became excitable and cried, 'He did! He did!' his eyes glancing, his limbs jerking. But even when the tears came, he cried, 'He did!' And Sandy knew he meant: Davie did give me the money. For that was the story he had made up.

Never had Sandy seen such innocence and guilt conjoined in a face so flower-fresh and passionate and terrified. It moved him deeply.

The old had sinned and the boy was bearing the sin, with all the terrifying apprehension of sin that the old had lost; crying out against the shame of breaking down, full at once of horror and the high will to save; fighting for his brother.

Sandy took his time, but not too much time. It was easy

to break down Bill step by step if he went about it logi-
cally for logic is something that a boy understands while
emotion merely makes a mess of him. Allan needed the
money to get out of the country as Davie had said. But if
it were found out that Bill had got the money from somewhere, that would at once raise suspicion because Bill was
Allan's brother, and by following Bill the police might find
Allan and what would be the good of the money then?
Now if he, Sandy, could put the money back in time, and
no one found out, the whole thing would be easy. Why?
Because Sandy had twenty pounds in his own chest which
no one knew about and which he could give to Allan. 'So
tell me everything and we'll see how to go about it at once.'

But the story was more involved than Sandy had expected.
Clearly the atmosphere of his home had got the boy down,
for his father was dour and terrible as one who himself
might commit a crime, while his mother said little, was
always under fear, and sometimes could be heard weeping
in corners. Sandy had met her several times and knew her
as an intelligent warm-hearted woman, fond of cheerful
company and very hospitable. For years their potatoes had
come from Sandy's croft – a poor enough recognition, as
he always said, for Allan's help. He knew the father, too;
an active hard-working man who would now, in his frustration, be stalking around like silent thunder.

The boy crept into or out of his home. He had played
truant from school and no one had challenged him. Then,
concealed, he had overheard Davie and two other men
talking of Allan, the need for money to get out of the
country, 'the chances' – and so on. Plainly Davie himself
had wanted to go to see Sandy but did not dare, and
anyway, 'you can trust old Sandy'.

Sandy got the whole picture quite clearly in his own
mind, often a word from the boy, a broken phrase, being

more than enough. The atmosphere of the home in particular came very strongly upon him; and the father's dark face, with the conflict behind it, had the force of a face in a boy's nightmare.

Emotion got the better of Bill again when he began on the church bazaar. But Sandy had known of the bazaar to raise funds for the church hall, and he made confession easy for Bill by saying that if he did take money it was not for himself but for his brother. He would never take money for himself. Naturally. The bazaar had been held yesterday, the money counted, and the whole sum left at the manse. Bill had got into the manse during the night by simply raising an unlatched window and had found the pound notes in a black tin box in the sideboard. The key had actually been left in the money box; but this did not surprise Sandy, for he knew the minister. What astonished him was the boy's cunning and spying, once he had found a place where money was being gathered in heaps. He had crawled through the manse garden, climbed an apple tree that grew against its high wall, and seen the minister and others in a room. Women came in and out. There were sheets of paper and men counting piles of coins. Even after the lights were switched on, it was some time before anyone drew the blinds.

'How did you manage in the dark?'

'I had a torch. Allan gave it me – when he came – in a present.'

The notes had been counted in bundles of twenty. He had taken one bundle.

Sitting in thought, Sandy knew that the minister or the church treasurer would have taken the cash to the bank that morning. The total would be twenty pounds short – exactly. Could a mistake have been made in the manse count? There would at least be that initial doubt.

Blood Hunt

Bill took the notes from a trouser's pocket and Sandy, with many wettings of his finger, counted them. Twenty exactly.

Sandy sent Bill off with food and wise counsel, dressed himself, and on the way to Hilton got a lift in a building contractor's lorry. The driver immediately started talking of the murder and told Sandy of the rumours about Allan being seen near the croft. 'I'm only warning you,' added the driver.

'I'm wanting off at the manse drive,' said Sandy. 'I'm putting up the banns for my wedding. I'm only warning you.'

As Sandy was going along the drive he met the inspector of police, accompanied by a sergeant.

'Ay, Sandy,' the inspector greeted him, 'and what's doing?' Two pair of eyes, behind easy expressions, were watching him closely.

'I didn't manage down yesterday to make my small contribution,' Sandy explained.

'I didn't know you were a supporter of the church.'

'I'm a friend of the minister,' replied Sandy, 'and in the course of nature I may need his ministrations before you. Though one never knows. Is he about?'

'He's at home, yes.'

As Sandy continued on his way the smile remained on his face but his heart was full of dismay. No meeting could have been more unfortunate for his present purpose.

The old housekeeper conducted him to the dining room where the inspector had left the minister, and soon Sandy was hearing from Mr Davidson all about the missing twenty pounds. The police had made a very thorough inspection of the house but could find nothing beyond an unlatched window and that did not help much because of the number of people who had come and gone the night before.

'The police have worried me because they wanted the

names of all who were here. But surely, surely it couldn't have been anyone who helped with the bazaar?'

'The police have to suspect everyone.'

'Terrible. Terrible. An awful reflection on our human state.' Mr Davidson's normal pallor had gone a trifle grey and the bones in his face looked hard and vindictive, but his eyes were worried. 'Faces will keep coming before me, since I had to name them.'

'Especially one or two.'

'Yes,' said the minister and he looked at Sandy with surprise.

Sandy smiled. 'I've come with my own contribution.'

'What!'

'You look surprised as if I'd found the twenty pounds.'

'More,' replied the minister and a wry humour began seeping back into his face.

'It's a thing I have never been able to understand, why there should be more joy over one sinner than the ninety and nine.'

'The one sinner that repenteth,' emphasised the minister.

'I admit,' said Sandy, 'the Word always has the word. Its wisdom was distilled over a long time.'

'It has matured well.'

'It had the spirit in it to begin with.'

'How true indeed,' murmured the minister, turning his good ear to the door. Then he opened the sideboard. 'She hasn't put the glasses back yet.' He thought for a moment, then gathering his independence and his calm, he excused himself and left the room.

Sandy looked into the sideboard and in an off corner, behind cases of knives, saw the top of a tissue-wrapped bottle. Before taking it out, he hearkened also.

The minister returned, making low unconcerned humming sounds, and produced two small tumblers.

'At this time of day it's tea you should be offered,' he said gravely, 'but you haven't a housekeeper.'

'No,' replied Sandy, 'and tea I have always with me.'

'You're lucky,' said the minister. 'I know of no more refreshing drink.'

'We are in agreement there.'

'However,' said the minister, 'in view of the upset in which you have found me—'

'And in view of the one that repenteth—'

'Yea, verily,' arose the response from inside the sideboard as the minister thrust his hand beyond the cased cutlery and lifted out the bottle of whisky.

Then there was very nearly an accident, for inside the tissue paper were further wrappings which so astonished the minister that but for Sandy the bottle would have slipped through his hands. Only the bank notes slipped – and fluttered – to the floor where they lay with folds in their spines like leaves from a teller's till.

Hitherto Mr Davidson, the Auld Kirk minister, had only read of miracles. Now even the word was taken from him.

Looking at him, Sandy saw his open mouth.

'The lost money.' Sandy's voice was not without a touch of quiet awe.

'Eh?' But the minister's eyes were vacant.

'Now how on earth could that have happened?' Sandy wondered.

But the minister wrestled in silence.

'Some foolish person,' said Sandy, 'must have been playing a joke.' As he stooped, he placed the bottle on the floor and in the same moment they both began picking up the notes. They picked and they counted and Sandy broke the silence.

'How many have you?' he asked.

'Nine.'

'I have eleven.' In silence they added the two numbers and arrived at the same total.

'Well!' The minister blew a deep breath.

'At least it's good to have found them.'

'What a strange idea of a joke,' said the minister as his eyes grew smaller in a hardening face.

'Who is your treasurer?'

'Mr Mackay, the bank manager.'

'A very nice man, very exact.'

'Exact, is it? When I wondered, before him, this morning, if a mistake had been made, he said, "I checked the amounts." That was all he said. I confess I was driven to reply, "Man is only mortal." Whereupon he smiled at me. There came upon me,' added Mr Davidson, 'a memory of a very small boy about to hold out his hand for the first time for the strap.'

Sandy laughed softly.

'And now I'll have to confess,' said the minister bitterly, 'and I'll have to confess, moreover, that the notes were found wrapped round a bottle of whisky. Mrs Mackay, the banker's wife, takes a great interest in the Temperance Guild. She and my housekeeper—' He paused and added, 'Both very estimable women.'

'If only,' said Sandy regretfully, 'we had found the money in a tea caddy.' And he looked about the room. The minister looked also. It was a deep sideboard but they searched its recesses. As the minister backed away he upset the bottle on the floor.

'A near thing,' he said breathlessly.

'If I hadn't caught it when it slipped from your fingers the bank notes themselves would have been sodden and the floor awash,' said Sandy.

The minister's hand shook as he placed the bottle on the sideboard. 'What a mercy! And I'm not just thinking of the loss of the spirit.'

'Think of the banker smelling the notes.'

'Counting them with his nose,' said Mr Davidson grimly. 'Not but that the same man, when his wife isn't about—'

'Quite, quite,' said Sandy.

There was a *snick!* and Mr Davidson exclaimed, 'I have broken my nail next!' But he had got the metal cap off the bottle. After hearkening to the body of the house with his good ear he poured two handsome noggins.

They toasted each other and drank. They sat down.

'That's one thing I insist on: having a drop in the house for an emergency. Not only that but where I was born and brought up in the wild but beautiful country of Wester Ross, my parents always had hospitality for the stranger. No man ever had better parents than I. You have come to me from a distance, and through the instrumentality of your presence what was lost has been found. I think I'll have a smoke.'

'Many an old custom was beautiful,' said Sandy, 'and goodness knows but I sometimes think it's a pity an old custom should be frowned upon because there are those who have forgotten how to observe it properly.'

'I agree. But the flesh is weak and we have to exercise responsibility for those who cannot exercise it for themselves.'

'Perhaps you're right.'

'But you have qualifications?' The light was coming back into the minister's eye.

'If in the exercising of responsibility you do away with the custom – in this case, the custom of hospitality – you may also do away with the kindliness, the fellowship, the – the warmth of the spirit which was the background to that custom.'

'I smell a suggestion of ambiguity in your use of the word "spirit".'

'In profound matters, as I have heard you say, it is often possible to talk only in parables. But there is a real point in what I would be at. I have seen too much goodness and kindliness wither away under some fancied notion that restriction and denial and regulation would cure the world of its evils. Unfortunately it's never the evils that get swept away in the process, it's the goodness and kindliness of the human spirit. And if the world today isn't a witness to that, I'll – I'll leave the rest of the dram in my glass.'

'That would be going to extremes indeed,' said the minister, taking up his glass. He nodded brusquely to Sandy and they finished their drinks simultaneously.

It was clear from the minister's eye that the argument was going his way and that in a move or two he would have Sandy where he wanted him. For goodness could not appear magically in a human vessel any more than whisky in a bottle. 'Just as the inspector of police, aided by the sergeant, searched this room and turned over a bundle of sermons that had strayed into the sideboard, and even took them out and shook them, ay, and, now that I remember, took out the very bottle of whisky itself so that I wondered—' but then he stopped. His mouth remained open, pursed slightly, the skin around it crinkled like dry sheepskin, so great was the astonishment he now turned on Sandy. 'The bank notes,' he said at last, 'were not round the bottle then.'

'They didn't see them?'

'They weren't there – half an hour ago.'

'Did *you* handle the bottle then?'

'No, but they did.'

'So all you could swear to is that when you did handle the bottle the notes were there.'

But this kind of talk had little meaning for the minister now. One might talk lightly of a miracle, but here was sorcery. 'I have not been out of this room.'

Sandy regarded him thoughtfully, then he said, 'You went out for the glasses even since I came in. Memory is a weak instrument.'

'So I did,' murmured the minister vaguely.

'You have called me a pagan before now; so maybe you would not consider a pagan's advice.'

'What?'

'You have now got the missing money. Let that be an end of it.'

'But – the police, the banker—'

'You can just tell them you have found the money. You need not tell them any more.'

'But—'

'You can say a joke was played on you and you think it so poor a joke you're not going to say any more about it.'

'But the police handled the bottle. The money wasn't there.'

'Why mention the bottle at all?'

The minister stared at Sandy. 'How did the money – get round the bottle?'

'You're looking at me in a peculiar way.'

'I am.'

Sandy smiled. 'A pagan and his sorcery, you think?'

'I'm beginning – to wonder.' And the wonder was clearly not unmixed with something darker, harder.

'I have never presumed to offer you advice before. Leave well alone.'

'You know—?'

'Even if I knew a lot, why should you trouble your mind with it? Not, anyway, until you are finished with the police – and the banker.'

The minister's eyes left Sandy and roved strangely. 'You would treat me like a child.'

'You are a wise man, one of the very few I have known.'

'I cannot accept that, if it implies avoidance of my responsibility.'

'Responsibility to the police and the banker?'

'Even them.'

Sandy nodded. 'In that case, Mr Davidson, I have nothing more to say.'

'Oh yes, you have. You cannot stop now.'

Sandy smiled and said nothing.

'You put the money there yourself? You are shielding someone?'

Sandy got up. 'You will be thinking it's my contribution next!'

'Your own money!' breathed the minister.

Sandy shook his head, but whether in denial or at the general credulity of the human mind it might be difficult to say. 'I'll be going now.'

The minister sat on for a minute, letting the strangeness of what had happened become familiar to his mind.

Sandy stood staring out of the window at the wall of the manse garden. Above the wall thrust tips of an apple tree. He thought of the boy, the boy's mother weeping in a corner; the inside of their home was charged like the father's face. The boy's visit to the croft would undoubtedly be known to the police, as was his own visit to the minister immediately afterwards. If only he had been a few minutes later in arriving he would not have met the inspector and sergeant. But he had met them. The minister would now go to the police and inevitably tell how the notes were discovered. The police would not then question Sandy first, they would question the boy, and, by pretending they knew all, they would break him down in two minutes. Theft would be added to that dark home.

Sandy felt like one who moved in a futile way from point

to point, without guidance, dealing with each as it arose. Yet he felt prompted, too, by some obscure element in himself that he dared not look at too closely lest his intelligence, his moral sense, should disown it utterly.

Even now, at this moment, when he suddenly decided to tell the minister the whole story about the money, he realised that what prompted him was the same obscure element, which had now calculated that on the whole telling might be better for the boy.

So he told Bill's story, quietly, missing nothing, as he stood there before the window.

'Sit down,' said the minister, and Sandy sat down.

'That puts a new complexion on it.' The minister sat staring in front of him.

'What made me tell you was a sudden vision of the boy's home where his mother cried to herself and the father goes about with the look of death. The innocence of the boy is something I had forgotten.'

'Ay,' said the minister on a harsh breath, stirring.

'To save the boy himself would, I thought, be something.'

'I see well enough what you have done. You think it would save the boy?'

'I think so.'

'Hm.' It was a harsh satiric sound. 'You think you can take the law in your own hands?'

Sandy remained silent.

'What?' probed the minister. 'Eh?'

'I don't know,' said Sandy and his face looked tired and old. 'I am lost.'

'So it's coming home to you at last?'

Sandy's head shook the smile from it. He was tired. 'I told the boy he could trust me.'

'And you know now that no man can be trusted?'

'Perhaps you're right.'

'Unless man's trust can be measured against a greater trust, what can it mean? Will you never see that?' There was more than satire in the minister's tone: there was pugnacity. He was going to sweep the decks.

Sandy hardened. 'You are lucky to have a measuring rod handy.'

'Luck, you call it?'

'It is not given to everyone.'

'If only you could see that that is its universal merit. It *is* given to everyone.'

'It is offered.'

'Hm. You would find a qualification that didn't matter with both your feet in the grave. You'll take a small drop for the road.'

'No then, thank you. It's in my head already.'

'As long as it's not in your feet,' said the minister, pouring out two small drams. Then he added, 'You should pray.'

'Will you pray yourself before you do anything?'

'No fear,' said the minister. 'I'll see the banker first, and he can telephone to the police or do what he likes. For the great thing is: what was lost has been found. Shouldn't that be enough for them? They'll get no change out of me.' In his vigour he laughed. 'Slainte!' He took off his small drop in one draught and cleared his throat appreciatively. 'There's something stubborn in both of us. It's the old Adam.' He looked at his glass. 'I can't say when I have appreciated a dram more.' He put the glass on the sideboard, not reluctantly so much perhaps as carefully. 'When Mr Mackay, the banker – an excellent man notwithstanding his great accuracy – asks me where I found the money, I'll answer, "I came on the money myself, Mr Mackay, and in a place it would embarrass me to tell you. I must leave it at that".'

On his way home, Sandy found himself sitting in the ditch by the roadside smiling. Beyond the trials and sins of the world, beyond police and dogma, beyond prayer and innocence – but no, not beyond innocence, for it was rare as innocence, this sitting in a ditch smiling, with the spirit rising on the air. If I can rise from the ditch myself, he thought, for the dram had rather gone to his feet, but just then he heard something coming, got up and took off his hat in so courteous a manner that the strange automobile, though gleaming with wealth, drew up to give the simple old countryman a lift.

EIGHT

Sandy got off his bed, where he had fallen asleep for an hour after coming back from the town. His face turned to the window and stared at the daylight, which had gone silent and grey, waiting on the night.

The night . . . this night, things would close in.

He had the feeling of beasts coming by different tracks to a pool, great cats to a kill.

A house had the patience of God. It endured. Life and death, joy and sorrow, all happened to it. It waited.

And the house was a trap . . .

He made a strong cup of tea and sucked it noisily from the saucer, for it was hot. He ate and his mouth sounded as though the bread were sterile. Despondency is uniform, like a twilight.

As he went towards the barn he glanced at the scattered birches and wondered if Nicol was watching, 'You'll get your potatoes and meal if you'll wait,' he said to the hens. Until it grew dark, he pottered about doing odd jobs. When the wind changed and the rain came, weeds would shoot up quickly enough. He had to get ready for the ploughing. As he locked the barn door he thought of the inspector and sergeant who had looked at him with a certain watchful humour, the kind of humour that conceals knowledge. The last thing they would want to do was make him suspicious. Clearly they hadn't caught Allan, but they might have the bottles and the finger-prints . . .

Perhaps Loch Deoch was surrounded, waiting for

Allan to swim from the Crannock, to come back for food.

The case against him was complete. The capture, the trial and the hanging.

As he sat before his fire, his book and spectacles by the lamp on the table lest anyone came in, he caught something vindictive in the pursuit of justice, and stirred uneasily. The fact was he could not look at Allan's crime, did not want to judge it. That's the position, he thought, and had hardly thought it when something vindictive stirred in himself.

Nicol had first stirred vindictiveness in him last night, had brought it to an edge. Sandy had seen the face of the Italian girl he had loved, the dark eyes whose depths of kindness he had never exhausted, the movement of her body against the Italian scene. During the First World War, his ship had got blown up; a few of them made the shore and separated. Refuge in Maria's home and then, as the hunt had closed in, Maria had guided him, on the run with him. Her beauty – her beauty seeped into her, and the way she walked, the grace of it, walked in on his heart.

Before her image, an upsurge of feeling blinded him now.

Kind people, the Italians. Like the Highland people of an earlier generation, full of warmth.

The awful night in the hut, the separation, the news that she had been killed.

He had done some human hunting himself after that.

Sandy stirred out of the surge of his feelings. It was not just the memory of their love, but an ultimate inexhaustible quality of loving kindness in Maria that affected him now. Her movements, her small acts, the way she remained still and looked at him.

Queenie lifted her head, but she did not whine.

He saw her looking at him, the bright reflections in her

black eyes, and with a sensation of waiting, waiting for Nicol, he had a short but quite clear vision of Nicol coming in, his own vindictive reaction, the strong feeling that he had had enough of Nicol's pryings . . . a challenge . . . a quarrel . . . and he killed Nicol with the poker.

This reflex of madness from the Italian scene suddenly wearied him very much, made a mockery of him.

Queenie quietly got up and padded to the door, which he had left a little open the better to hear, pawed it open farther and went to the front door. Sandy listened. After a time Queenie came back, turned up her eyes at him in the way that always suggested guilt and lay down.

Dogs were not human. They had their own affairs. No good pretending you could always understand them.

No one came and, after locking his door, Sandy went to bed. Let them all be shut out beyond the ring of his dwelling, beyond its foundation line. Allan had to carry his own burden.

He turned over on his right side, turning away from Allan. The fellow had to meet his fate on his own feet. Let him meet it. But he had locked the door so that Allan could not enter – and be taken from behind.

Awake early, he arose and put his smoke up. There was no sign of anyone about, but instead of feeling the place deserted, lonely, he felt he had it to himself. The air was clean and his nostrils got a fresh smell from the earth.

Around eleven o'clock he wondered what day it was. The wet battery of his wireless set had run down two or three years ago and he had shifted the whole box of tricks to the other or ben room where it now sat on the floor in the dark corner to the left of the fireplace, and the world's radio waves did not disturb its dust. The one day in the week he had to remember was the day Danny the vanman passed along the highway from Hilton.

He set off as he was and saw the stationary van when he topped the rise.

From a distance Danny yelled at him: 'Mind the eggs in the basket if not your heart.'

Sandy's shambling trot eased up. 'Man, Danny, don't tell me I have kept you waiting again?'

'Didn't you hear me hooting?'

'I thought I heard something. Have you got a new whistle on her?'

'I have,' said Danny. 'I would need something to waken most of you. Back in the shop they think I should do the round in half the time.'

'It's not the time that troubles me, it's the day.'

'You're as bad as Mr Davidson, the minister. Did you hear the latest?'

'No.'

As Danny took the eggs from the basket and put them in his crate, he was voluble about the twenty pounds alleged to have been stolen from the bazaar funds. 'Oh, a great shimozzle, police in and all, searching the manse. Not a trace. But there was one place they forgot to search.'

'Where was that?'

'The water closet.'

'What?'

'The WC. The bazaar was a great success. They're saying that because of – you know, the murder – some people gave more than – well, they're saying we all have a conscience, and some people who should have given more to the Income Tax gave some of it to the church bazaar.'

'A redistribution not without merit, perhaps.'

'Wait till I get that!' cried Danny, with bright eyes. 'That's something to add to what Duncan-the-garage said, for he's having a fight with the Income Tax people. "That's all they're worth, anyway," he said: "taking to the water closet".'

'The Income Tax people?'

'No, the bank notes.' In his laughter, Danny waved both hands, an egg in each.

'That would be a reference to the recent considerable increases in the price of commodities,' said Sandy.

'Oh, be quiet, for God's sake!' cried Danny.

'Found them in the water closet?'

'Yes. The old minister is that absent-minded!' Danny gathered himself. 'There were that many banknotes about that Mr Davidson who needed a bit of paper took the bundle!' He rocked again and cried, 'Tough paper!'

'An expensive occasion,' Sandy nodded.

After a few more passages, Danny wiped his eyes. 'I've gone wrong in the count.'

'Four dozen exactly,' said Sandy, 'unless you want a dozen for your mother.'

'No, no, not today. What's this?'

'I churned. For your tea.'

'For one taste of your butter my mother would give all the margarine that was ever spawned. It's too much.'

'She belongs to the old days when we were all poor and only had butter,' said Sandy. 'It's just a taste.'

'And crowdie,' added Danny. 'She'll sit over it and wonder who mends your socks.' There was colour in his face as he looked quickly about the landscape from between the doors of his van. 'There's Widow Macleay. See her coming nearer, bit by bit. Wouldn't she like to know what we're laughing at, the same lady?'

'She enjoys a joke.'

'Enjoy it? When she hears about the water closet – oh boy!'

'What's this?'

'The knuckle end of a ham. They can't slice it. Now—'

'Now, Danny, you'll charge me for it—'

'Well now, let's get all your messages. Then we can add up and see where we are.'

Sandy had a much bigger load than usual, including two extra loaves.

'You won't have anyone staying with you?' said Danny, with a humoured glint.

'No, then. But a few come round about wondering if I have. I don't mind the bread for them, but the tea is hard on me, kind as you have been.'

'I can hardly keep my old mother in it, but let me see—'

'You'll not see,' said Sandy.

'Here,' said Danny. 'I have got some tins of meat, good stuff, from Denmark. No coupons.'

'I'm not great on the tins—'

'But the rabbits are no use just now.'

'They're breeding, that's true. Well, put in a couple.'

'And I can ask Nicol the policeman what they taste like, eh?'

'You haven't been hearing anything, have you?'

'What! Hearing, is it? There are enough rumours to float a battleship. As if Allan Innes was the sort of fellow to hang about, waiting to be taken! Whatever else, he was never stupid. Besides, as Mathieson the lawyer said no later than last night, don't hundreds desert from the armed forces every month and are never found?'

'Is that so, now?'

'It is. Thousands. It astonished myself. But it shows you that people are getting sick of wars, fair sick of—'

'There's not much sign of sickness here that I can see,' said Widow Macleay, casting an eye at the great bulges the extra loaves made in Sandy's pillow-case. Sandy never forgot to bring the pillow-case because he always spread it over the bottom of his basket before putting the eggs in.

'What do you feed your own cow on,' he asked her, 'now that the turnips are finished.'

The false teeth which gave her no trouble showed when she laughed and the wisps of grey hair had an untidy witchery.

'Cake,' she said. 'The currants keep her loose.'

Danny doubled up.

'Have they found out,' she asked, 'who stole the minister's twenty pounds?' Her voice was sharp, her eyes warm with the humours of the flesh which she had to handle so often and knew so well.

Danny threw his eyes aloft, praying to be delivered, then switched them on Sandy.

'He'll settle with me first,' said Sandy, 'then he'll tell you.'

'Very well,' she said, turning her back politely and taking a step away. For she had her manners and nursed her most caustic comments for the ignorant who had lost them.

At a little distance an outburst of Danny's laughter made Sandy turn round. Widow Macleay was giving Danny the push of modesty with a hand that did not push very hard. Then he heard her high skirl.

He began to laugh himself as he went on and the loaves on his back nudged him. The bread of life, he thought.

At the end of everything, there was something good in life and ordinary folk knew it well. Sandy suddenly had a vision of a beautiful sparkling morning sea. The deep sea of generation had risen up and in a moment was the sea he had sailed on.

His eye glimmered speculatively. Could the minister actually have mentioned the water closet? But he knew he hadn't. He would have said that he had found the money in a place he need not mention and stuck to that. For he had the reputation of being a disputatious, pugnacious man on a committee or in the Session. Once he had set a course he would sweep obstruction aside with the combined force of the law and the prophets. Nor did he reserve the combined force for church affairs only, as many of his fellow members on public bodies, particularly Education, knew. Even the banker or police inspector would know better than to probe him. Woe betide them if they made it a moral issue!

Then Sandy had his vision of the police inspector and the banker laughing together as one of them first thought of the lavatory. The higher up business and professional men and public servants got the sterner they had to be; so richer therefore became the private joke, more juicy its flavour.

Sandy topped the rise, saw his croft, and suddenly liked that quiet place very much.

NINE

As he was undressing for bed that night, Queenie called to him. When he heard the scratching on the door his mouth opened and he hearkened far away into the night. Then on his socks he went through the first door, pulled it tight behind him and groped for the key in the outside lock.

'Who's there?' he whispered.

'Me,' whispered Allan.

'It's not safe.' Sandy could vaguely see Allan's body flat against the wall.

'I have been round the house.'

'They're watching.'

'Can you give me some food?'

'Wait there.'

Sandy closed the door noiselessly and got back into the kitchen. There was no hesitation now in any of his movements. The part of his mind that was concerned for Allan had foreseen this possibility. Into the brown canvas sack he put two loaves, a carton of oatcakes, a jar of raspberry jam, butter and crowdie. He filled a bottle with that night's milk. An old tin opener hacked its way round the top of a tin of meat and he flattened the top back on the meat. Egg after egg he wrapped rapidly in scraps of newspaper and put the lot in a brown paper bag. Then he went back to the door.

'Here,' whispered Sandy. 'You can take that on your back,' and he handed him the sack, 'and that in your hand – eggs.'

'Thanks.'

Then there was the silence, and the intimacy.

'How are you doing?' Sandy asked.

'All right.'

'Did Nicol – when did you get away from the barn?'

'Just after you left me.'

'The bottles I gave you are gone.'

'I hid them.'

'Where?'

'In far corner, under the roof, beside beams, covered up.'

'I thought Nicol—'

'Thought he might, so tried to leave nothing that would point to you. I'd deny that to the last.'

There was a pause.

'I would like to ask you in.'

'I'm off. Did you miss some potato bags?'

'No.'

'Cold at night.'

'Sst!' whispered Sandy to Queenie, letting her past his legs. 'She growls at Nicol now. I'll give you an old blanket. Wait.'

'No more just now. I'll lie low for a while. Then if I could get an old suit and a little money—'

Down by the barn Queenie growled and in a moment Allan was gone so noiselessly that he couldn't have been wearing shoes.

Sandy's heart gave a few weakening thumps and, listening acutely, he heard Queenie's scraping paws. Though a bitch, she sometimes when scents or emotions were conflicting had a habit of growling and scraping the ground like a dog. She was getting up in years. Thinking she might have gone after Allan, he gave her a 'Sst!' Nothing happened and the feeling he usually got of night's immense distance, distance that could calm him like a benediction, was all at once charged with boyhood's old fear of the dark, of an invisible hand from the awful peril that was shapeless.

He turned back to the door and called Queenie again, the sound coming low and sharp off his tongue. When at last she brushed in past him, he closed and locked the door quietly. In the light, he gloomed at her and whispered angrily.

She looked very guilty.

He did nothing but listen for a little while, then the tension eased off.

'Growling like that!' he growled at her.

He had thought there was nothing she could do or say but he understood at once. Growling like a stupid bitch, like a half-grown dog with jutting legs.

Unless Nicol had left his personal scent about . . .

Her eye was on him and dropped as he looked at her and lifted again, while her body gave a sleek twist so purely feminine that he hoped she wasn't going on heat or all the damn dogs from the countryside would be around, including that brindled mongrel from Achdunie with the different coloured eyes and the hair that stood straight on the neck, wading from one battle to another as though they were picnics, even if Sandy had given him one real good crack last time.

She had her world. The scent of Allan must have stirred memories. Those nights with the moon, and a half-moon was enough. How she had loved it, how the coming of the boys had excited her! Then off into the night . . . her quartering of the ground . . . the hunt. Sex might bowl her over in its season, but the hunt was for ever. It was in her paws when she slept. Man and dog: it was a long partnership, and the hunt was clean and swift.

Laughing they came back from the hunt, and never did they forget to praise her. Allan had his own way of fondling her left ear with his left hand. Not that they made too much of her, though they made a lot.

In that world of hers Allan's crime could not exist. In a long moment the feeling of all this passed over Sandy, its swiftness, its innocence, the brightness going back into the moonlight, the silence in the moonlight, the running, the eagerness that, in the end, only laughter could express. Laying hold of her ear. 'She misses nothing.'

All the time Sandy was listening to the night and to its distance.

The young moon had set, but the sky was clear enough for eyes watching outside to get used to the darkness in some measure. Anyone coming down from the birches . . . might be tracking Allan now.

After all, Nicol, single-handed, was taking a chance, even if he had a weapon, even if he had a revolver.

Nicol's confidence was something that all in a moment arrested even Sandy's listening. For it was not a stupid confidence. It was something very different. In an instant the dark thought was about his heart: any difficulty, any resistance, and Nicol would kill Allan. Followed the darker thought of Nicol's satisfaction in the kill. Nicol's blood brother had been slain.

Sandy sat and stared at that nether region where acts complete themselves with an awful inevitability. When he turned his eyes away and looked about the kitchen he was breathing heavily.

He called reason to help him sweep the vision away, for he could never think on that nether plane, only see. Bodies move, the hand rises, the deed is done.

Reason helped him like a hand that cleared his eyes. For surely the real satisfaction for Nicol would lie in apprehending Allan and watching him going through the slow process of trial, step by step, leading to conviction, the driving in of the nails one by one, by this witness and by that, until condemnation had him transfixed. Then the rope, the public executioner.

Nicol could stand aside, his work, his actual job, well done. Satisfaction would reach beyond the personal, it would go tribal deep.

Yet if reason was all, Allan would never have done the deed.

Sandy stood uneasily. In these last years he had been getting away from violence, and now its impact weakened him, made his old muscles shaky, sickened him a little.

He had never even thought out what Allan would need. His mind had avoided wondering where or how he slept. He had wanted to slip by it all, to be left in peace, because for peace he had a small concern, with it he had a certain appointment, not an urgent one, but yet possibly a real one. A last adventure that might come off in some measure, if certain intimations meant anything . . .

In bed he could not sleep. If Allan got back safe to the Crannock, he wouldn't return for two or three days. If he got an old suit – and money – he would depart for good.

Sandy now gave his mind fully to the physical aspect of Allan's position for the first time.

There was a suit in his trunk, a grey-brown tweed with a herringbone pattern, which he had bought shortly after he had made his statement to the notary public on the total loss of the ss *Endeavour*. He had worn it once or twice, but then had put it away, for it had been a bit tight for him and, anyway, he had got used to a darker cloth, had been too long at sea to break into country tweeds. Its length would be right enough, but it might be a bit wide. As a sailor, he could use a needle . . . His legs were actually out of bed, before he restrained himself. To look at the suit now would mean lighting the lamp and carrying it to the chest in the next room where it would shine through the window. Plenty of time.

Money . . . he would have six or seven pounds in actual cash. It would mean withdrawing twenty or thirty pounds from a deposit receipt. It would mean a visit to the bank, Mr Mackay's bank.

Would that be awkward? It was an expensive time of the year. The price of grass seed alone had grown beyond a joke. He would deal with the bank all right. Say, twenty-five. Anything more might look suspicious. If he could give Allan thirty pounds, that would get him wherever he wanted, with a good bit in hand.

The ports would be watched. But that would be up to him. He could always do a job on the land down south for a time. The thousands who deserted from the Forces must find jobs somewhere.

Ah, yes, but this was different. Somewhere he had seen that many famous scientists and poets read detective stories. Now he knew why. They were after the murderer. They were on the old blood hunt. The satisfaction of the final kill.

More and more . . . nearer and nearer . . . violence upon violence, increasing violence . . . until the teeth champed and the juices ran about the gums . . . Then satisfaction, the satisfaction after the orgy . . . until the hunt did not need a murderer, could substitute something else, an *ism* or *ology* that stood for the murderer, providing a wider hunt, a greater kill, more blood . . . Smash the bastards, torture them, disrupt the core of matter and turn it on them, until their eyes burst and run down their faces . . .

Sandy turned away from that clarity of vision which

could come in the small hours and tried to wonder why Nicol hadn't come back.

But he couldn't wonder, and not until the desire for sleep was like a desire for death did he doze off.

TEN

The following forenoon the postman twitted Sandy about having to plough up more land. 'They're after you, boy.'

'They won't have to run hard,' said Sandy, accepting the agricultural form.

'Talk about being on the run—' and the postman got onto the murder. 'It's dying down in the newspapers, but the police won't let it die down. As you'll know,' and he gave Sandy an expectant look.

Later, Sandy went towards Milton and fell in with the foreman or grieve, a taciturn man but a hard worker. Sandy liked him well enough, though he always had the feeling that he resented having to plough up the croft.

'Is the boss about? It's a form I've got.'

'Ay, he was about the steading a little while ago.'

The farmer was a florid man with small eyes in a face plump as a Swedish turnip. 'More forms, eh?' Then on a low confidential note, he asked. 'Did you hear what the minister did with the bank notes?'

'I did.'

'For real satisfaction try an official form.' The farmer nodded solemnly. 'As for your bit of land, don't worry. The Executive know I'm looking after it and balancing it in with my own. What's this I hear about the police worrying you?'

'They're not worrying me.'

'No?' His look was acute. 'Let them do their own work.'

'I could hardly stop them.'

'Did you ever have anyone interfering with your girl?'

'I did.'

'Did you hit him on the jaw – or run and tell the police?'

Sandy smiled.

'What did you do?' persisted Milton.

'They brought me round in hospital. About this marginal land—'

'In hospital!'

'You have never had foreigners beat you up?'

Milton's astonishment froze his face and left only his small eyes to rove over Sandy. A car drove up, the vet got out, and Sandy took his leave.

In the afternoon, he was coming up from the low ground when he heard a distant whistle and saw the shepherd away towards the lily loch. He hadn't seen him for a week or two and realised he would now be concerned about the lambing. The ewes would keep to the low ground for feeding, though again some of them took odd enough notions at lambing time. The shepherd might never actually get in sight of Loch Deoch, but he would be around from now on, early or late.

Sandy looked about him, began to walk slowly in the shepherd's direction, then stopped. There was no one in the district with whom he liked better to have a talk, but somehow at the moment, no. There was a friendliness about wee Manson, a sunny quickness, that he could not guard against.

He began to wonder what the shepherd would do if he saw Allan or found a trace of him. Then a thought struck him: Danny the vanman, the postman, the farmer – they all spoke of police visits to the croft. Had someone seen Nicol arriving or leaving?

The shepherd's dogs would sniff Nicol out of any hide.

And then it dawned on Sandy: Nicol would have primed wee Manson to look out for signs; and not only Manson, but the shepherd of the four or five thousand acres beyond, and shepherds beyond that, far to the other side of Loch Deoch, and not only the shepherds but the keepers and stalkers, the real hillmen, whose eyes were as good as telescopes and who had telescopes as well. You could wander over the hills for days and never see one of them, then suddenly come on a pair of eyes looking at you.

Allan could not live among them and not be discovered. It was far easier to hide on a street.

In a little while the shepherd disappeared and Sandy felt relieved. His outrun was no more than the western corner of Manson's beat and for all his friendliness the shepherd was a shy mortal. Only if Sandy had gone on to do a bit of the endless mending his outer fence needed would the shepherd have dropped down for a talk.

Presently, with a feeling of stealth and haste, Sandy took the tweed suit from his chest, looked it over and measured it against himself. Immediately he saw the hopelessness of trying to alter anything. Allan had good hands. And it would be something for him to do in the long daylight hours. He would put a needle and thread in the pocket . . . Then he thought of a shirt, socks . . . finally he tied the complete bundle with a stout string and left it ready in the chest.

Back in the barn, he got up into the loft, and after groping around in the dim light found the two bottles hidden under old lime and rubble on top of the stone wall, put them into his poacher's pocket, and was soon outside again. Back in the kitchen he swilled out the bottles and stuck them out of sight in the dresser.

Allan would not come tonight, but he would come tomorrow night, and certainly not later than the following night. He was probably far more nervous than even his voice showed. Lying out there alone mightn't be so bad in the daytime, but at night, with his thoughts – he would want to get away from them, and he needed food. A trip to the croft would put in the night. In the daylight, with the sun's warmth on a sheltered spot, he probably slept or dozed.

If I go to the bank in the morning, thought Sandy, and lift the money, then I could give him the clothes and the money, a bit of food, and that would be the end of it.

Down towards the river Nancy his cow bellowed at some cattle on the other side. She's wanting company, is she? thought Sandy.

For the first time this year he had to fetch her home and she went in front hurriedly, throwing her head at Queenie, even giving a small dance, the old fool, with a slaver at the mouth. Queenie was so astonished that she in turn came alive, and together they cut a few capers, while Sandy, quickening his own pace, roared at them. When he was tying her up she twisted and backed away as if she would be off again. 'You just cool your heat!' And he gave her a flat-handed wallop on the haunch.

When he came back with an armful of hay she wantonly tossed it, crowning herself like a queen of the May.

'You have other things on your mind,' he allowed.

She didn't deny it.

The following morning she gave a bellow that shook his bed. Her power astonished him and brought some of the old natural humours to his face. Leaving the porridge pot to simmer he went out to meet the morning. The sky was overcast, the air was softer, the change was coming. By night the rain would be on them.

Nancy hadn't a great deal of time for him and their interchanges were short and pithy. In the barn he uncoiled the old tether and tested it, then fixed the halter for her head.

After he had eaten his porridge, he sat in thought. The visit to Milton with Nancy would take a fair while but if he went at once he should certainly be back in plenty of time to change and catch the bus which would land him in Hilton by two o'clock. It might help if he got his best suit ready now and put the deposit receipt in the inside pocket.

Sandy had two deposit receipts, one for no less a sum than £850, and the other for £132. He would take £32 out of the smaller one.

The sight of his fortune, which he was inclined to forget (though even in forgetfulness it had a comfort) increased his confidence. No one had come near him during the night. Nicol must have given the croft up. His bosses would have decided that it was no use wasting manpower on what had already been searched so thoroughly.

To take out more than £32 might give rise to comment. And £30 was enough for Allan. If he was caught – more than enough. Though Allan, of course, would say it was his own money. Allan would suffer rather than incriminate his old friend. Sandy had been touched by the thought Allan had already given to this.

After feeding the hens, he locked the barn door, then his own door, and with the rope over his arm called on Nancy.

'Ay, ay, you're for your nuptials,' he told her, fixing the halter on her head before he took the chain off her neck.

He was watching for her head as she swung round, and was braking her with the rope before she was out of the door. But she had a power in her neck that brought his heels clattering over the cobbles and before he could quite regain his balance he came with a thump against the door jamb. It both hurt and angered him, and he swore at her for a rudderless craft. Mistaking his anger, Queenie did anything but help by dancing at the brute's head. And once outside Nancy knew where she was going. She had been there before many times, and though Sandy stuck his heels in, she took him at a trot.

By the time he got her down to a fast walk, with Queenie at heel, he was breathing heavily and feeling light-headed. The thump had shaken him. He was getting old – though not so old but that, if he hadn't dropped his stick, he would have walloped some sense into her, even if it wasn't the lack of it that was bothering her now.

He tried to remember if he had seen the Milton cattle yesterday, but could only recall where he hadn't seen them. Were they out at all? The least obstructed way would be by the main road and then up to the steading. But motorists, used to biddable engines, would have no notion of Nancy's incalculable nature when she was in top gear. Not to mention comments by such possible observers as Widow Macleay if Nancy led him a dance. He headed for the five-barred gate in the drystone dyke that gave on an outlying field of pasture. From there he could work his way along the slope, keep an eye lifting for the cattle – the bull would be among them – and, through one opening or another, come down on the steading from above.

Nancy was still pulling him along, but not so ardently, and he knew he had her under control. When they reached the gate he lifted the iron latch and pushed the gate open. He had shortened the rope and had folds of it over his left arm, ready to check her. But he also had to shut the gate and now Nancy did not want to come through. She was not in the habit of going this way on such an occasion. Sandy knew it from her glistering eyes. 'Oh, come on!' he cried impatiently, for the gate had slowly swung back on him. As he thrust it away with his right hand a cow bellowed wildly along the slope towards Milton. Nancy charged through the gate. With his right hand Sandy grabbed the wrong loop of the loose tether, and while he was pulling at it the rope tightened fiercely on his left arm and yanked him forward with such force that he was swung off his balance and brought violently to the ground. Nancy, slanting down the slope, dragged him ten yards before she got the last coil free of his body.

Sandy did not lose consciousness, but when at last he sat up he decided that his left arm must be out at the shoulder. Nancy disappeared through a gap in the thorn hedge at the low off corner of the field.

His instinct was all for following her but as he got up the world heaved and the horizon swung. Holding grimly to his feet he reached the gate and hung on it with closed eyes.

But he had to sit down and with the stone wall against his back thrust his feet out and his head back.

It took Sandy a long time to get home and at first he was vaguely worried lest anyone saw him staggering on like a drunk man, but once over the rise such vanity left him. The threshold nearly beat him, but he rounded the bends and came at the bed, got a knee up, fell in and lay, relieved at last to let the sickening world go.

He came back to full consciousness before a figure in the kitchen. It was Angie, the cattleman from Milton.

'God, boy, what's wrong with you, eh?'

'That wild brute.'

'Did she tumble you up?'

'Ay, going through the gate.'

'We wondered, but waited, thinking you would turn up. You're not badly hurt, are you?'

'Is she all right?'

'Never better – nor quicker. I took her back myself and she's in the byre now. By God, you're grey in the face. Are your bones all right? Let me have a feel of you.'

'I'll tell you what you can do.' And Sandy told him where to find the bottle of whisky. It was more than half full and Angie had to pour out two good drams. Sandy's right hand so shook, however, that Angie caught the glass only just in time. After he had given the old man the whisky, he got the story of what had happened out of him, and went over the left arm but could not find anything broken. At last he said, 'By God, I think you're out at the shoulder. I'll get them to phone for the doctor.'

'Nonsense.'

'It's not nonsense. You can't be left here alone. This is where even a wife is handy. I'm wondering if you haven't cracked a rib or two the way your breath is catching you. I'll be off, and don't you move.' And off Angie went, full of concern.

Sandy groaned. He had made a proper mess of things now. Not that it would matter who came during the day, if no one was left with him overnight, when Allan would come.

Some hours later the doctor called, a cheerful medium-sized man. 'What's all this I'm hearing about you wrestling with a bull? I thought you would have left that to your cow.' His grey eyes were assessing Sandy's colour and breathing.

'I did.'

'Tell me what happened.' Presently the doctor nodded. 'She gave you a yank all right. What's the old heart like? Ever give you any bother?'

'In what way?'

The doctor enjoyed laughing. 'Good enough!'

After he had examined Sandy, he remarked, 'You have the heart and arteries of a young man. How did you manage it?'

'By taking great care of myself,' said Sandy.

'I doctored for a while on board ship myself. So you can't tell me much in that line. We must see about getting you to hospital. I'd like a picture of your bones.'

'What's wrong with them?'

'A dislocation – your left shoulder – for one thing.'

'You can put the arm back, surely?'

'I might, but we have an ambulance—'

'No ambulance can get down here—'

'We can take you on a stretcher to the road—'

'The only kind of stretcher that's going to take me out of here is the old black bier, and that's that.'

The doctor looked at him. 'You mean you refuse?'

'I refuse, so you'll just have to do it yourself now.' Sandy smiled. 'It's not one arm I've seen put back and nothing beneath the man but the deck, and not a very steady deck at that.'

'I would have to make sure your ribs are sound first. It's a strong pull?'

'You have already felt my ribs and you know they're sound enough. So go ahead.'

Sandy would not listen to reason. He smiled and began to push himself up. The doctor helped him to the floor where Sandy lay on his back, saying he felt very comfortable, and offered his left hand. 'There it is.'

A light came into the doctor's eyes. 'Come on, then, for the honour of the sea.'

But the doctor was watchful until the final moment; then he put forth his strength expertly and the joint went back with a crack. Sandy paled but breathed on.

'Never a cheep,' said the doctor, fetching the whisky. 'Lie where you are.'

Presently the doctor had the arm bound comfortably and Sandy properly undressed and back in bed.

'You'll need someone to look after you for a while.'

'Don't you worry, Doctor. I've been in worse corners.'

'Maybe. But you're not so young as you were, you'll find out soon enough. You've got a worse shock than you know.'

'I'll get over it.'

'The trouble is getting anyone. But I'll see the nurse. I'm not going to have you left here alone. Besides, you've got to be fed. And what about your cow and your hens? Have you no neighbour who could—' The doctor was interrupted by a figure that passed the window.

'Can I come in?' asked Widow Macleay. 'I saw your car, Doctor, and I wondered.'

'The very woman! Can you deal with a wounded man?'

'I have managed a whole one in my time. What's wrong?' And she turned her head and looked at Sandy.

'Nothing,' said Sandy.

'He was taking his cow to the bull but she was too much for him,' said the doctor.

'That explains it. I saw Angie from Milton taking her home and I couldn't make it out, but I thought maybe she had broken her tether and gone on her own. But when I saw you leaving your car, Doctor, I reckoned there was something far wrong. Is it bad?'

'Bad enough. A dislocation of the left arm; when he has settled a bit I'll see about an X-ray. He is thrawn, Mrs Macleay, so you'll have to deal with him firmly.'

'When you have a man in bed it's not too difficult.' As the doctor laughed her own old eyes glistened. 'If she was as wild as all that,' she added turning to Sandy, 'you should have given her her head.'

'She took it,' replied Sandy.

'It takes even a married man a while to learn what to do with your sex's head,' said the doctor.

'My what?' asked Mrs Macleay.

The doctor laughed. He was pleased with the neat way in which he had dealt with the dislocation and, where so many bothered him about so little, Sandy's stoicism was refreshing. He began talking of food, and when Mrs Macleay said she had just made a pot of broth from boiling beef and could bring the lot in a pail, he said that was excellent and sent her off, adding that he would see her at the car when he would give her some tablets to take back with her and instruct her in her duties. Then he began talking to Sandy about how he must behave.

'You don't mean, Doctor, that you want her to stay here?'

'Certainly. Haven't you another bed?'

'I don't want her staying here,' said Sandy with a grey worried look.

'You're surely not frightened of what people will say?' The doctor's eyes were solemn enough.

'It's not that,' replied Sandy. 'I just like to have the place to myself.'

'She has a way with her,' said the doctor thoughtfully. 'A good managing woman. You might do worse.'

'No,' said Sandy, unable to say more.

'Ah well, when you see *her* taking her head—' He laughed heartily. 'I'll be back to see you soon.' And off he went.

Sandy's eyes closed, his mouth opened, and he let go. He was utterly exhausted and sank away with a strong feeling of death.

But two influences in his recent life gradually came up: one was the desire for that peace he had known in the hills, the desire to die in the hills, literally to pass away from them, and the other was to warn Allan somehow to keep away from the house. Of the two, the first did not matter, the first was vanity, but Allan's need was urgent and he did not want to fail him now. That he would call tonight was almost certain; the more he thought of it, the more certain.

When Widow Macleay arrived she took all her management with her. She had the complete story of his accident out of him before she had heated the broth. His pots and pans, the innermost recess of the dresser, the whisky, the tea caddy, his boots and socks, his trousers, his shirt, vest and pants, not to mention things he had long forgotten, were under her dominion before she began to look about her. He got the awful feeling of an eager woman settling in.

And she was firm, very firm. 'No, no,' she said, 'you need an extra pillow to bolster you up. Wait you.' And through she went to the ben room. He thought of the chest, remembered he hadn't locked it. She would look into the chest, she would look into everything. What would she think when she found the suit tied up? He listened with all the strength he had, trying to gather meaning from the sounds she made, including what were obviously comments of an exclamatory kind. But she came back after no more than a first cursory survey, and sniffing the two pillows she had brought from the bed said, 'It's not yesterday they saw the sun.'

He heaved himself up painfully on his good arm. She caught him as he turned over and getting her forearm behind his shoulders steadied him until she had the pillows where she wanted them.

'Isn't that better now?' she asked.

'It is, thank you.' She wavered before him like a witch.

'You are going to be handless for a while and you may as well reconcile yourself to it.'

'Once I'm on my feet . . . Don't know what I'm lying here for at all.'

'You'll know soon enough when the shock begins to work on you properly as the doctor told me. Have you a tray in the place?'

'A tray?'

'I can see already there's more than one thing you'll need.' She was busy now and soon brought him a plate of steaming broth. 'Take a sup of this. It will rub some of the grey off you.'

'Can't you put it down somewhere?'

'That's what I was wanting the tray for. But it's no trouble for me to hold the plate. Eat up.'

Sandy concentrated on lifting a spoonful, burnt himself and nearly upset the plate.

'Dear me,' she said patiently.

As he wiped his brow with the back of his hand some drops of broth fell from the spoon on his face.

'Tut! tut!' she said. 'Where do you keep your towels?'

'I'm feeling a bit tired,' said Sandy lying back.

'You're the one to be on your feet!' and she gave him a shrewd look. Her concern for him made her manner more abrupt than usual. Firmness, as the doctor had said, was the only thing.

She moved about with remarkable energy as if life had been given a new meaning, and so great was her pleasure in its exercise that obstacles added an invigorating tang. She wiped his face with the only towel she could find and hunted reluctant ears of barley from his beard. 'Have you your specs?' she asked.

He gave a vague wild look at the table and she found them on the mantelpiece. But he had finished with his beard by the time she came back.

However, she tried on his spectacles and said, 'They suit me fine. We're well matched!' And she laughed lightly. But she had a sharper view of his face. 'Perhaps you would like a cup of tea first?'

'I would.'

She was very concerned for him now, so ignored him

altogether, especially after she saw his eyes were closed. It's rest the poor old man needed and, being only seventy-one herself, she thought of a dozen things from beef tea to soap flakes for a washing.

She made sure the tea was not too hot. Sandy was able to drink it himself but he refused to eat and she did not press him.

'You just have a small sleep to yourself,' she said in a firm but kindly voice. 'I'll find where things are myself. Don't you worry.'

Sandy closed his eyes. He could afford to lose the first round but he would have to get pith from somewhere if he was going to shoo her home this night. When she went out he thrust himself slowly down off the pillows, for his left side was painful and must be badly bruised – if not worse. He felt sick, made one or two yawing motions and got some wind up. Then he heard her voice in the distance. Who next? The thought was too much for him and suddenly not caring he gave way and sank into his own weakness.

Once he was conscious of her coming quietly in – and going out. This soothed him in a comfortably hopeless way and he fell into a natural sleep.

'I let you sleep on,' she said later when he asked the time. 'Are you feeling better?'

'I'm a new man. I'm fine.'

'You are a little more like yourself. Now I have everything ready and you need what you're going to get. I found the potatoes—'

'Did anyone call?'

'Angie the cattleman was round, and wee Johnnie, and Duncan from the Clachan, but I turned them away saying you were not to be disturbed and they could pass that on. You didn't know you were so popular, did you?'

'Very kind of them.'

'Wee Johnnie said his grannie would pluck a hen. I told him to thank his grannie, but that you had some hens of your own and I could still pull a feather. And if I know the colour of a hen's comb when I see it there are two of yours that would be more useful in the pot.'

Her conversation was enlivening and while she got the food ready to serve he stealthily and painfully pushed himself up on the pillows.

'Don't blame me for this,' she said putting the lid of a box on his knees for a tray. She got a white cloth under his whiskers and tied it behind his neck. 'You can spill your broth now.'

'It's good broth.'

She supped her own broth at the table and asked him questions between spoonfuls. She was full of business. But the evening was at hand and first she would have to run off home to see to her own cow and hens for they would be wondering what on earth had happened to her. Then she would gather a few things and come back—

'You'll not come back. You have done far too much as it is, and I am deeply indebted to you.'

'What?' she said. 'And leave you alone?'

'Am I not always alone?' replied Sandy.

'Too much alone, if you ask me. But it would be a poor thing if a neighbour couldn't stand by you when you can't stand yourself.'

It was a long intermittent argument and Sandy made more than one tactical mistake, but he hung on to his persistence as to a rope on a sea-washed deck; yet when the meal was over and she had dried the dishes, tidied the kitchen, swept the hearth and built up the fire, he was still not quite sure of her intentions.

Now she had the cow to milk and to feed the scraps

and cold potatoes to the hens. He rested in her absence and let his resources gather. When he heard her voice high and loud in the distance, he groaned. But soon it was clear to him that she was merely giving Nancy a bit of her mind, and even if Nancy had a little milk to let down it's not to strange hands she would condescend now. They were well matched.

When at last she came in, she said, 'I had to tie her tail and then she wanted her hind leg in the pail, and at the end of it there was hardly enough to drown a bluebottle. She's gone her mile. It's started to rain.'

'Hurry off home, then, Mrs Macleay. And thank you a thousand times for what you have done. If you would care to look in in the forenoon sometime—'

'But you'll be on my mind. I could never—'

'Look, now: I only need sleep. I'll take two of the sleeping tablets in a little while and after that, to tell the truth, I would not want to be disturbed. If you promise to do that and not come back through the wet night, it will ease my mind and I'll sleep in peace.'

'It's not right—'

'You'll find an old raincoat of mine hanging in the lobby and you can put it over your head. Hurry now. And good night. And a thousand thanks to you.'

Eventually she went – a little hurt, he thought, but he wasn't quite sure.

He was so relieved when she had gone that he felt he had been uncharitable, for deep in him he knew that what troubled the widow was her kindness, the need to expend herself, and the pleasure she got from it.

He dozed and tried not to move and as the light began to go would have liked to take the sleeping tablets, for a prickly hot restlessness sometimes got the better of him and jerked his legs. But he must not fall into a deep sleep, for a neighbour, coming to call on him, would in the country fashion enter quietly and finding him asleep might sit and wait to see if there was anything he could do. Then Allan might come, scratching at the door.

Even Widow Macleay had seen that the door had to be left unlocked for nurse, doctor . . . it had worried her until he told her that he never locked it, which had astounded her. She would have a lot on her mind this night. Pity he couldn't have given her two of the sleeping tablets!

A flurry of rain beat on the window. So the wind had gone into the south at last. The break had come and the roots in the earth would be stirring, the white shoots stiffening, the buds taking their drenching. To drink and drink . . . many a drunken night he had had himself . . . man never got far from the earth, the soil . . . all the one strange drunkenness . . . that he was getting away from now. He had seen the day when he could rise from the effects of a mauling, know he was going to rise and throw it off . . . The heart and arteries of a young man, said the doctor. That would be helpful flattery, yet not all flattery. But age hadn't the resilience. It could hold on, try to hold on a bit longer, that was all.

He couldn't hold on even to a single thought and see where it went. Thought was difficult. It made his head ache.

But now and then one got beyond thought, into that region where something like thought transcended itself, as in that notion of drunkenness, where man and the earth were caught in the one common impulse, immensely old, a communion rising from creation's root, stirring that which made the sap stir, the buds open . . . not the root and the flower only but also that which stirred them . . . the mystery, that yet was no mystery in the moment of being stirred but something known in the region beyond thought, something that thought could never lay hold of . . . but known, known, when the mind rose to it, and became one with it . . . passing away on the air . . . the scent of creation's flower.

His intromissions with this strange region soothed him, as a memory will often soothe without stirring the emotion attached to it. And oddly enough though he felt it had grown thin, with his belief in it ebbing as his strength ebbed, yet there were moments of what seemed an extra lucidity, a clearness in some still farther region . . . that was there, even while his vision itself fell away from it, and he wondered, and his heavy eyelids fell.

ELEVEN

Queenie's whine brought him to himself. He saw her in the glow from the fire that set the darkness deep in the window. At once he thought of Allan. It seemed far into the night. Then he heard footsteps, the click of the outside door, and presently the inner door moved and a shaft of light from an electric torch came through. Nicol! thought Sandy with a thrust from the heart that hurt him. But it wasn't Nicol, it was the doctor.

He entered quietly. 'Not taken your sleeping tablets yet?'

'No, Doctor. Is it late?'

'Were you asleep?'

'I've been dozing off and on.' He stirred and his breath caught sharply.

'You see, you've got the pain there?'

'It's just – just the muscles.'

'You may beat a widow woman but you won't beat me.' The doctor began to chaff his patient. Two cows, double the hens, and a wife – didn't Sandy know a marriage bargain when he saw one?

The torch lay on the table with its beam on the dresser and the doctor soon had the lamp lit. He was late on his rounds, he explained, because there was a lot of 'flu about, with bowel complications that, he hoped, wouldn't trouble Sandy. He spoke in the homeliest way, stirred the fire up and put on a few clods of peat. He liked the smell of the peat.

'Are your feet wet? You shouldn't have come, Doctor. It's too good of you.'

'Don't know,' said the doctor, warming himself and smiling, 'but somehow you brought back the sea and I thought I would like to see you tied up nicely for the night.'

'I'm at my moorings,' said Sandy, 'safe and sound until the morning.'

'And then?'

'The widow herself is coming back.'

The doctor laughed, chaffed him and began his examination.

'It wasn't the fall so much,' Sandy explained when the doctor had finished, 'as the jerk she gave me and then the dragging on the ground. The folds of the tether got round me.'

'And you a seaman.'

'Isn't that what annoyed me? You would think I had never seen a rope in my life.'

'A cow, too.'

'I know. Like the Cockney who got run over by a cart in the country. Would you like a small taste, Doctor?'

The doctor looked at him brightly and rubbed his hands. 'Do you know, I will. This is my last port of call. And I'm feeling shiverish. The rain, I think.'

'Well, look—'

'That'll teach you to lie still,' said the doctor as Sandy fell back with a smothered groan. 'And let me tell you now; you'll be worse before you're better. And for heaven's sake don't disrupt that shoulder again. One shock to your system is enough. I won't answer for two.'

'Very well, Doctor.'

'Nurse will be in to see you in the morning and make you comfortable. Meanwhile you'll lie there. I don't want you getting up and going giddy and someone finding you stiff on the floor.'

'You'll find a drop of fresh well water in a pail under the shelf behind the front door.'

It was clear the doctor liked the old man, was finding
ease in his company. When he had the two drinks ready,
he shook out a couple of tablets. Sandy said he would take
them later on but the doctor insisted on his taking them
now, saying they wouldn't work for half an hour anyway.
But first he would put his patient right for the night, and
he attended to his needs like a nurse.

If Allan did come, he would hear the voices in the
kitchen and from them he would learn there was something wrong and so keep away. Anyway, he must take the
tablets now, for the doctor had given him a look as if
wondering all the time whether his patient had something
on his mind. So Sandy swallowed the tablets and the doctor
lit a cigarette and made himself comfortable in Sandy's
chair.

Then the doctor came out with it. 'Tell me, is anything
worrying you?'

'Worrying me?' repeated Sandy vaguely. 'She's not
worrying me – only, I'm used to being alone. I have the
greatest respect for Widow Macleay—'

The doctor laughed. 'If that's all, I think you can be
trusted to keep a firm hold on her sheet.'

'She can move close-hauled,' said Sandy.

'To tell the truth, I heard how the police have been
keeping their eye on your place. No real trouble, is there?'

'Not for me. That policeman – Nicol Menzies – has been
out and in, but not for the last day or two, so I'm hoping
it's blown over here.'

'Extraordinary case. No one can talk of anything else.
Remarkable the power of a local murder on the mind. Then
the complete disappearance of the lad who did it. He was
found both in Greenock and Liverpool yesterday.'

'What?'

'The day before, a farm labourer was questioned by the

police somewhere in Essex – or was it Sussex? By tomorrow it will be Plymouth.'

'I see,' said Sandy.

'Black magic. You haven't seen him yourself?'

Sandy lifted his dram. 'I have never felt hidden from the police spy-glass even at my motions.'

The doctor laughed abruptly.

'The night it happened, the policeman went up aloft through the hatch, and under the bed, and then spent the night in the barn, and two or three more nights as well. But you needn't repeat that, for the man had to do his duty. Besides,' added Sandy soberly, 'it was his brother who was killed.'

'I understand now. But – don't let that policeman worry you. I had to give his mother something to calm her last night. Hysteric – more than a bit. He's getting the back-lash. I didn't like the look in his eyes.'

'You mean he's—?'

'He's all right, but when a man gets obsessed there's a certain behaviour – however, there have been rumours and I wondered if he was working anything off on you.'

'No. He's been right enough with me and I gave him the run of the place, though I could see from his set look—'

'That's it. The thing can easily become a mess. The mother's darling was the son who was murdered. Nicol joined the police in spite of her, it seems; and her opinion of the police hasn't been raised. So there's a new kettle of fish cooking there at the moment.' He drank and looked at Sandy. 'Tell me. What brought you here where you haven't a glimpse of the sea?'

It was plain that he was tired of the subject of the murder for, though Sandy did not know it at the time, Dr Drummond had been the first medical to examine Robert's body imme-diately after the crime. The crowd had slowed up his car and, realising an accident of some sort had happened, he had got out. In a small town like Hilton, where everyone knew him, it was not easy to avoid discussion, and among his own friends, particularly lawyers and other professional men, talk ranged intimately from physiological detail to psychological or sexual motive. The thrill of the hunt followed, and fantasy got busy with stories about Allan being seen around Sandy's croft, with Nicol in pursuit, muttering, 'I'll get him.' The doctor had been curious to know just what truth there had been in all this, for a disturbing element of the blood hunt, dark and absurd but oddly persistent, had been gradually gathering force, like some old folk myth. Now he knew enough, and wanted to clear his head with a breath of sea air.

Sandy was also glad to leave the subject of the crime, for though he could maintain his innocent expression and even use Widow Macleay to mislead the doctor it was a strain. To speak of other things openly would at once be a relief and a warning to Allan should he come listening at the window.

Sandy had been brought up on a croft in a neighbouring parish not many miles away and in his last years at sea he thought a lot, as he told the doctor, about his 'young days'. The croft he now occupied had belonged to his mother's people and, as it happened, he was able to get possession, so he bought over what he wanted and settled in; for some men see their fate in the sea but others dream of death on land, and in his own case he knew the very land.

'I am interested to hear you say that, because I remember an extraordinary discussion one night in Alexandria on this very topic. It left me wondering which I myself would prefer for the end, land or sea. So you think it troubles all seamen like that?' asked the doctor.

'I wouldn't say it troubles them. That's not how it

happens. Only now and then, a man here or there, is sure. You wouldn't be sure.'

'Perhaps not,' said the doctor. 'But it's odd that now and then – when things on land get a bit too messy – I have seen a swirl of the clean green water with the tail of my eye. A friend of mine has a small yacht lying at this moment in the canal basin at Inverness and four of us hope to take her north-about through the Pentland Firth this summer. You know it?'

'Only too well,' replied Sandy. 'A dangerous bit of water.'

'Tell me about it,' said the doctor, looking at the old man.

'It's very curious,' said Sandy, 'that you should have raised that subject, for to my old friend Norman it was the sea. He was sixty-two then, a couple of years older than me – an Islesman, from the Hebrides. I liked him well. I had signed off for the last time and was spending the night in Glasgow when I ran into him. He had come through from the east coast to see his owners and we spent the night together. His mate had suddenly taken ill and he tried to persuade me to take his place. I couldn't be persuaded and one drink led to another and from that we got down to whether it's better to pass out in the sea or on the land. It was the clean sea for him. For me, it was the land. And we discussed it in all its bearings as naturally as young people might talk of poaching or girls. It brought us awfully close together. Of all topics, death is the final one, I suppose.' Sandy smiled. 'Your pills are beginning to float me, I think.'

'And you didn't go?'

'Yes, I went. Ach well, he was a grand fellow; besides I thought to myself I might as well have a last look round the Highland coast, for I didn't know this croft was falling vacant then; and, anyway, he said that while his ship was discharging in Stornoway we must take a trip down to see his old home, with the long waves thundering on the sand, the noise his childhood ears knew so well. But that trip we never made. The Pentland Firth – you'll have to watch yourselves.'

'Tell me about it.'

As Sandy described the loading of the vessel with a cargo of coal, the doctor saw the far-sighted seaman's look come into his eyes. The slope of her coamings, the self-trimming, the weight of bunkers distributed on both sides, each detail was still measured in tons or inches before his eyes. In number two hold the coal was close up against the deck, except at the after end where the clearance between cargo and deck was three feet. Then there was a slight clearance in the after end of the forward hold. Altogether she might have taken about twelve tons more, but the Chief had about that much boiler water, and she was down to her draught. She loaded just to the plimsoll marks. Anyway, Norman would take no more; the hatches were battened down, tarpaulins fixed, and they set out in a fresh southerly wind with a following sea.

'Norman knew the Pentlands like the back of his hand, and a slight shift of cargo, taking things as they were, was nothing to bother about – and nothing new to him anyway. She did a good nine knots and, after all, as sea voyages go, it was only a step. As we opened the Moray Firth we saw that we should fetch Duncansby Head around high water and so have the first of the ebb with us through the Pentlands which is just as you should have it. It was a spring tide with high water at Duncansby Head just after three o'clock in the afternoon. At Noss Head there was a strong tide against us, making maybe four knots. The sea was rough for the wind was against the tide. Actually you'll still have the tail end of the flood against you at Noss Head about half an hour later than at Duncansby. Nasty, steep, pitching seas. Norman the skipper went down for a bite of food, because he always took her through the Pentlands himself, always. A born seaman was Norman.'

Sandy paused for a little and his right hand moved slowly over the bedcover in a slight hiss from the rough skin. 'I have sailed many seas in my time in all conditions of storm and tide, but yon north-east corner of Scotland can give you a feeling that nowhere else ever will. It has the thing you cannot foretell, and it rises at you. There's something *under* yon sea. However, we had Noss Head well behind us, on the normal course, with Duncansby bearing nor-nor-west about six to seven miles away. As I say we were hardly making a comfortable passage and when I saw a tide rip on the port bow I altered course a couple of points to get the calmer water. In a little while Norman came back to the wheelhouse. I told him what I had done and he said that was fine. We had been shipping some water over the port side but not a great deal. We weren't exactly anxious but we had a weather eye open for the thing that can come at you yonder. I can remember looking across at Norman from the corner of the wheelhouse. A chap Finlay, from Islay, was at the wheel. Then something made me turn and look aft – and I saw it, a great mass of water, a tidal lump, with the smoke blowing off its top, coming fair at the port quarter. I shouted to Finlay to starboard the wheel so that she wouldn't broach to port when the lump hit us. And she was just beginning to answer her helm when it struck us. It was a sea, that! It lifted us and carried us on its back in a great run and swing, and then we were thrown over on the starboard side and down, with solid water churning over the rail. The unexpectedness of it had something awful about it. She never righted herself and I knew that part of the roar had come from the shifting cargo. I can hear that roar now. The weight and thrust of it kept her from rising and coming back. Already water was pouring in through the stokehold and engine-room doors on the lee side, for they were both open. The two on the port side were closed, but in such a boat you keep the lee doors open for light and ventilation. The sea was pouring in through them and she was settling fast. I cried to Norman, "She'll never come right; too far down." Norman was looking at her. He had the high cheekbones you'll often find on the Islesman and the skin was gathered round his eyes, and he said, "She just might." There was one long moment when you saw him calculating the chances as if she was an animal that just might rise. But she couldn't. The steam steering gear suddenly went, and Finlay said he thought it was time we were making for the raft, and I said it was. For I knew she was through with it, and it could only be a matter of a minute or two. But Norman told Finlay to tell the engine-room to fill the port tank. The engine-room was aft of the bridge, which was amidships, and things were happening very fast now. I think we both told Norman that it was impossible for anyone still to be in the engine-room. Finlay gave the wheel another trial but it was still jammed. Some of the crew had meanwhile got the two lifeboats swung clear, but one was lifted by the swell and smashed against the side. However, there was also a big raft lashed at an angle against the fore end of the engine-room casing on the port side. The more she went over to starboard the more level with the sea came the raft, and the crew made for it.'

As memories crowded upon Sandy he was silent for a little while.

'Was no effort made to shut the door to the engine-room?' the doctor asked.

'The whole thing was over inside five minutes. You have to remember that,' said Sandy. 'However the chief engineer did his level best. But even when he finally tried to get at the emergency stop valve, on top of the boiler casing on the starboard side, he was beaten, for the swell was breaking right over it. The firemen were already up and making for the raft. I remember that last moment well. I was watching the raft and saw it float off all right with all hands on it. I was standing on the ladder to the lower bridge and the only one left to think of now was the skipper. I was actually turning my head to the wheelhouse, when I was swept away.'

Sandy paused, his breathing which had been laboured at times under the stress of recollection began to ease. His eyes were cast up for now he was lying fair on his back and the doctor was staring at his features, thrown into relief by the shadows.

'I hit out for the raft and they got hold of me and hauled me onto it. It was a big raft, with air compartments. No one ever saw the skipper. She turned right over, keel up, then went down by the stern.' After a few moments, he added, 'He could never have come out of the wheelhouse.'

The doctor watched Sandy settling down, saw the wave rise over him, and his breath go heavily from him, and with his breath his conscious mind.

The doctor got up and stood looking at him for a long time as though distant ways and far seas were plotted by the lines of his face. Then he patted Queenie, now on her feet, had a look at the fire, blew out the lamp and followed the beam of his torch to the door.

TWELVE

When he awoke finally in the morning Sandy was conscious of having had a wonderful sleep. Twice during the night he had come to himself, but hazily and knowing that sleep was waiting for him. Extraordinary what two little pills could do! He had always mistrusted drugs of any kind and on occasion bore the morning after as an effect from the night before. He could remember clearly the first man he had ever seen swallowing aspirin, a small man with a pale face, and an old hard-drinking seaman in the fo'c'stle looked at him as at one who would come to no good end.

Sandy luxuriated in the weakness of having given in to drugs, then he stirred and the calm was broken. Stoically he tried to move his body and from the sharp pains a flush mounted. When he wiped his forehead he found it cold and damp and as he brought his right hand down it shook. I'm not in a good way, he thought, thinking ahead, for how was he going to command things from his bed? If only he had finished with Allan before this had happened! He listened to the morning and heard the hiss of rain in the wind.

He would have had a bad night on the Crannock. Everything sodden and not a spark of fire. To lie down would be impossible – and fatal if he tried. He would have to keep on the move. But he couldn't move much in the dark, and it would have been pitch black under the low skies and rain last night. Sandy saw clearly the old beams of timber, little more than dressed trees, and he saw Allan working in the dark like a beaver, levering the beams over an inner end of the trench, blocking the interstices above with stones and soil scraped from underneath in such a way as to channel the rain water into the loch. It would be a job. But it would keep him from perishing.

That might put the night in, but what about today? He could not move about in the broad daylight. And he would need sleep. A time would come anyway when sleep would overtake his young body though it was lying in a pool. After that, a raging pneumonia would soon finish him off.

It might be the best way out. Gloom assailed Sandy and a whelming sense of his own helplessness. God knows why it bothers me so much, he thought. The lad had done his deed and would have to take his gruel. It was the old law, and strong men and the best of men knew it.

But Sandy could not dispel his gloom. Perhaps old age – he had noticed it growing in himself – came to dislike the destroying of life, the deliberate destruction of it. Give it a chance. If age that had had its day could destroy the young human being, then something had gone wrong surely with the warm feeling at life's real core, because that feeling was life itself and the warm surge of life. He felt it now, pure and untouched by thought, and it went, as it were, away from him into a farther region where it was by itself, and in that region . . . what did we know of that region in time or in eternity?

Sandy knew he had not even a glimmer of it . . . though, perhaps, he had had a glimmer . . . though, again, it seemed thin enough now. And suddenly he remembered when in the Far East hearing of a primitive tribe in New Guinea that never punished a man, even a murderer, by taking his life. They simply outlawed him from the community, and that punishment for the man, that banishment, was more than

death, they said. This came over Sandy now with a feeling
of wonder, of enlightenment. Justice was a word that good
men hesitated to use or used with misgiving, but a man
might use it now, fairly enough, and even let it wander with
that solitary outlawed life into the far region. There the life
would have to come to terms with itself and with eternity
or go under. It was given that chance. At the end of everything, death came to all anyhow.

But the gloom was not eased. He could not see through
it. And he had always liked the lad. There had never been
a vicious quirk in him. Even old Lachie, the gamekeeper,
who had once caught him fair and square in a pool on the
river, had only given him a bad telling off – a first and final
warning. After that he had been more careful, for he
respected Lachie.

A few pellets of rain hit the window. The wind would
be funnelled by the hills and sweep over Loch Deoch and
the Crannock in wet sheets. Food could keep the body
going as coal kept up a head of steam, but when the food
ran out . . . The sea water rushed in and condensed the
steam and jammed the steering gear.

Food! His heart's beat quickened. Tonight Allan must
come – if he was able to come – for food. But Widow
Macleay knew every bit of food in the house already. And
what she didn't know she would find out when she came,
any minute now. If he gave Allan food in the night, she
would miss it in the morning. She would ask questions.
And the store was small enough. Even a single loaf. . . . He
got flurried and thought, If I get a loaf into the bed and a
packet of oatcakes, I can tell her she must have miscounted
the night before. Giving vent to his groans for comfort, he
slowly heaved himself on to his seat. After he had let his
swimming head settle, he threw back the bedclothes, and
in the same moment Queenie growled. Sandy heard the

footsteps passing the blinded window and before he had got properly on his back, Widow Macleay's voice called, 'Are you at home?'

Her head came in first, then her stooped shoulders.

'Good morning,' Sandy greeted her.

'You're dark in here.' She pulled up the blind. 'Eh? And how are you today?'

'Fine.'

'I can't say you look it.' She was peering at him from the bedside. 'You're the one to be walking about on your feet! Old Murdo Maclean passed away at three o'clock this morning.'

'Ah, did he? I'm sorry to hear that. He was a fine old man.'

'He was not so much older than yourself.'

'I thought he was getting on for eighty.'

'He was getting on that way, like some more of us. You took the sleeping pills?'

'Two of them.'

'I'm thinking,' she said, looking at the whisky bottle on the dresser, 'that you had more than the pills.'

'I had. The doctor made me.'

'It would be a struggle for you, poor man, though they say he doesn't take a drop himself. He was late with you.' There were two glasses on the dresser.

'He's a good doctor. He thinks I should rest most of the day and try my feet later.'

'He does, does he?' She gave a humoured sniff. 'I suppose you're longing for your tea.'

When the flame was under the kettle she tidied the hearth, got off her knees, and turned to the dresser. 'You won't be wanting everyone to see this bottle.'

'It was on my mind after you left that I hadn't the grace to offer you hospitality.'

'I had all the hospitality I wanted, thank you.'

'Still that doesn't excuse me.'

She put the bottle out of sight in the dresser then lifted the two glasses and sniffed them. He was watching her out of the corner of his eye.

'Ay,' was all she said.

His stomach shook a little in quiet mirth and he felt the pain of it, but her tough satiric ways had a healthy air. He would have to watch her, for her mind was sharp as a needle.

'I'll let your hens out. What do you give them?'

He told her.

'Oats!'

'Only a handful or two. It pays. They lay better,' he justified himself.

'Hm. My hens lay on less.'

'I don't mind betting you give them a feed of oats now and then yourself.'

'If I do, they hear about it,' she said and out she went.

He breathed as if he had been running a small race. Living with her, life would move at a great pace. He expected her back any moment, but when a minute or two had passed he wondered if he would make a desperate sally on the dresser. Then he heard her voice. She was speaking to someone. The hens made a great cackling. The cock almost barked. Feeling very empty and slightly giddy, he resigned himself. She came back with the eggs in an old tin.

'They're laying well enough,' she admitted, making for the dresser.

'Did I hear you speaking to someone?'

'No,' she said, 'unless it was to the dog or that gawky cock.'

'Is it raining?'

'April showers.' She gave the words a mocking shine.

When she had put the eggs into the basket, she began moving his stores about as if she were counting them.

'Three loaves,' she muttered, 'and – what's this, not oat-bread in a shop packet? Bless us, is this what you've come to? Thut! thut!'

I'm sunk now, he thought.

'I'll make you a baking,' she vowed, 'if you have such a thing as a girdle in the place. Where do you keep your oatmeal?'

Her questions were many and he had answers to most of them. When she began to help him to sit up, her own satire made her laugh not unpleasantly. 'You're the one to be trotting about this night!'

'It's just that I can't use this arm and it stings a little when I twist.'

'Ay. And the nurse will be wanting to change your sheets, too. Where do you keep them?'

'The sheets are fine.'

'She'll be thinking they weren't bleached yesterday. Have you ever had a nurse attending to you?'

'Why?' he asked with some misgiving. 'She'll just take my temperature and see I'm all right.'

'She'll do all that,' said Widow Macleay with some enjoyment. 'She'll bathe you and wash your sore parts, and if there's not a bed-pan in the place she'll do her best. She's very capable for so young a woman.'

'Young?'

'In her prime,' said the widow. 'Surely you're not scared at your age?'

'No,' said Sandy vaguely, 'but—'

'But what?'

'I'm fine. I can manage myself.'

'You take some of this tea. It's good strong tea and will put courage in you.'

'It looks as if I was going to need something.' But there was a bleak note in his humour that the widow did not miss.

'There's no need to get upset. I know you men.'

'Perhaps you do,' he said with a touch of dryness in his own voice. There was surely a limit to what a man had to go through needlessly.

'There's one thing I know whatever,' said the widow confidentially.

'I suppose so.'

'It's this: she won't have handled you twice when you'll be looking forward to her next visit.'

It was a shrewd thrust that normally would have shaken Sandy's stomach, but somehow he had become aware inwardly of his own bodily condition and confidence was oozing from him.

'We'll see,' he said. 'Did it rain heavy last night?'

'Solid. The burns are in spate. It will do a lot of good. The ground was crying out for it.'

Now she began chattering to him in a normal friendly way. 'I got drenched before I reached old Murdo's. They have two Glasgow orphans boarded out on them. Decent bairns. Mairag – old Murdo's wife – sent one of them for me.'

'In the early morning?'

'Three o'clock. He had been keeping well enough, but yesterday, she said, he took a bit of a turn, nothing much and he seemed to rally all right. She wondered about sending for the doctor, and then she thought the doctor is that busy, and you can't expect much from a man of Murdo's age, so she thought she would just wait to see how he was in the morning. He was always quiet in trouble, never of the complaining kind. He died in his sleep without her knowing. I did my best and managed to lay him out. I was glad

indeed to do that for her, for if Mairag is soft a bit it's true
kindness that's at the root of it. A quiet decent couple they
were and good neighbours. I'll miss the sight of him at the
end of the house.'

'You haven't had much sleep, then.'

'I'm fine.'

'You're very kind.'

'That's one thing no one can accuse me of, I'm glad to
say. Why aren't you eating?'

'I rarely eat with my morning cup.'

She was arguing with him when the nurse arrived.

Nurse Simpson was a brisk cheerful woman of forty-five
with so much to do she wasted no time. Sandy knew when
he was beaten and concentrated on getting his will to
master the usual evidences of pain. But it was not easy, and
her hands, though gentle enough, were strong. Yet he did
manage to conceal a heavy sluggishness in his right leg.
The pain, like the bruises, were on his left side. This troubled him a little, and again he had the sensation of a creeping
paralysis inside his lower regions. His brow was damp by
the time the nurse had finished with him. And then she
said, 'A change of bed linen will freshen you up.'

He heard the two lowered voices in the ben room as the
drawers of the chest were opened and shut. They had him
now. He was in their grip, helpless as a bairn, and they
would deal with him. It was the kind of thing they would
do well.

Into the kitchen they came with the cheerful innocence
and busy ways of conspirators who knew every turn of the
way ahead. While Nurse Simpson began stripping the bed,
Mrs Macleay held the new sheets to the fire.

'I thought,' said Sandy, who was a sailor, 'that they were
clean enough.'

Both women laughed together, for neither had missed

the critical not to say hurt note which Sandy had tried to keep out of his voice.

'Quite clean,' said the nurse briskly. 'But fresh sheets brighten you up, don't you think?'

'Maybe they do,' said Sandy. 'I was bred to the sea and there we learn to keep things shipshape – or so we think.'

They did little more than smile this time.

'That's one thing I will say for you: it's not the usual man's place you keep here,' remarked the widow encouragingly.

'Do you do everything for yourself?' asked the nurse in pleasant wonder.

'I do,' muttered Sandy, helping to let the sheet out from under.

'Marvellous,' said the nurse. 'But a time comes to the best of us when we're better with someone about.'

Sandy smelt the danger now.

'Don't you think so?' she persisted.

'When that time comes,' answered Sandy, trying to control the shake in his hand.

Nurse laughed. 'You don't think that time has come? You're a hardy old man.'

'Not so old either,' muttered Sandy.

'Perhaps I should have said not so young,' replied the nurse, enjoying the patient and her own briskness. 'But I'm afraid you must have someone. Meanwhile Mrs Macleay is going to look after you until the doctor has seen you again and decided just what we are going to do with you. He said he didn't like the idea of you being here all alone at night.'

'Why not?'

'Well, you're not exactly in a position to help yourself, are you?'

'Only need sleep at night, and the doctor gives me that.'

Nurse crossed to the fire and felt the sheets that were

being aired. 'You mustn't forget that we have a responsibility to our patients. And we have a hospital at Hilton, with nurses and everything. You would get better much quicker in hospital.'

Sandy now felt flattened and cornered at the same time. The drift of their conspiracy was only too apparent; the inexorable force of it muddled his head. And the last of his pith was drained from him by the time they had turned him over and pushed him back and tucked the bedclothes under his whiskers.

'Anything you would like?' asked nurse brightly.

'A stick of sugar candy,' replied Sandy.

The nurse actually looked at him with some uncertainty but the widow cackled. Then the nurse laughed.

He thanked her before she left. Widow Macleay went out after her and he saw them pass the window deep in talk. It took ten minutes for the widow to return, so if she wasn't fully armed before she would be now.

'A sensible, clever woman,' she summed up, cleaving the kitchen with her bows. He felt the draught in the bed. But first, the cow. 'I heard her wondering. It's her stomach that will be putting on her today,' she said in the rich local idiom, and out she went.

It was not much a man could do against that. And a remark she made about old Murdo had opened his insight for a moment in a curious way, and it rather haunted him still. When he had the 'turn' Murdo had known quietly but absolutely that the end was near. Sandy had felt with him in a community of interest strangely clear. He had as it were suddenly gone back and been with him.

The body has a knowledge of its own, but a man must be far on the way to death before he can recognise it. He tried his right leg but the bedclothes were heavy. Then he felt the left side of his head onto which he had pitched and was sure the swelling had gone down. Besides, he could use his right hand all right. After such a violent tumble-up, not to mention the dragging, a lethargy, in itself like the onset of death, might easily lay a man low for long enough. And pain was a tap that, turned on, drained vital life away.

It would be easier to deal with the doctor than the two women, and if he could get round the doctor and have the house to himself this one night more, then Allan would be bound to come. He could give him the suit, the little cash he had, and as for a loaf he could tell the widow in the morning he had given it to the dog. Though for that matter, a paper bag of oatmeal and sugar would be better for him than any loaf, far. He could stuff it in his pocket when he set out over the mountains to the west and south.

After that, even the hospital could have its way.

If Allan did not come tonight, he would never come more. But he would come.

Sandy's eyes closed. When Mrs Macleay came back and began talking to him, he answered sleepily. She gave him a steady look and nodded to herself. She knew the signs when age and illness lost interest.

He woke up for his porridge, saying he was feeling much better, then relapsed again. Mrs Macleay had a busy forenoon, for her neighbour Mairag was on her mind, and she was anxious to know if Will Gordon had seen properly to all the arrangements about the funeral, including the time, the minister, the undertaker, the lair in the church-yard, and the notice in the *Hilton Times*. But the minister would question him, and what the minister forgot the undertaker would remember. Between them all she could probably rely on them. The arrangements at the house she could make sure of herself. But there was a lot to think of. Mairag could hardly be left alone, and yet the two orphan bairns . . . though for that matter they were between ten and twelve, and death was something that healthy bairns got round. All the same you had to keep your eye on them at a time like this, even if what they learned early helped them to grow . . . Perhaps she shouldn't have said to the nurse that Sandy had 'plenty', for in public places like hospitals money could be spent like water. He must have a good penny, she thought, or he would hardly have been so generous in his hidden way to folk that maybe hadn't deserved it. Though it was too often the feckless that got.

Some of her thoughts were passed to Sandy and he guessed a few of them, before she fed him again, left the house swept and tidied, and departed, promising to be back before the night once more to feed the cow, the hens, and himself.

He breathed, and listened, and heard the silence. A thrush sang from the rowan tree at the corner of the garden. A powerful song, brought out by the rain. A ringing song that echoed in the far regions. A rope a man could hang onto when all else was slipping. Beautiful and shining.

Gratitude moved him like a weakening, like a farewell; but he was part of the song as well as the weakening . . . going with the song into the mystery – beyond the farewell.

His mind groped about dimly and he saw Widow Macleay hurrying home, her head and shoulders slightly stooped, full of business; gratitude stirred in him again. He saw her down on the earth, moving about the roots of life, going from one custom to another, knowing them all, the fundamental and final acts. Here was what had to be done. And she did it.

A great song the thrush was making.

He began to breathe heavily as if wings were in his

chest lifting him. Beautiful and far ringing, going over the earth. He swallowed. Tears came into his eyes and wet his face. His breathing lessened and he sank away into sleep.

THIRTEEN

When the doctor came in the afternoon Sandy welcomed him and the doctor, smiling but looking at him closely, said, 'Feeling worse today?'

'Better.'

'But weaker?'

'I have had a good rest since the women went.'

'Did they push you about?'

'Very nice woman, the nurse.'

The doctor's eyes began to glimmer. 'You want to stop where you are,' he said.

'I would rather it.'

'We cannot force you. Now tell me honestly. Any pains?'

'This bandaging—'

'We'll see about that. How do you feel in yourself? Confess now.' As he held Sandy's wrist he looked closely at him.

'I feel a bit tired, maybe.'

'As if you'd been through a mincer?'

'Honestly, I don't think I need anything but a little rest. I have been beaten up before now.'

When he had finished his examination and given Sandy a drink, Widow Macleay passed the window.

'I saw your car, Doctor. How is he?'

'How do you think he is yourself?'

'For a bachelor he has patience, whatever else. I'll say that.'

The doctor laughed and, after some more skirmishing,

prepared to go. 'I'll look in to see you again, perhaps tonight yet, but I won't promise.'

'Thank you, Doctor. But please don't bother tonight. You're too busy.'

'I didn't get the end of that story. You fell asleep.'

'Did I? That explains it,' said Sandy smiling. 'I couldn't remember you going.'

The doctor gave a salute and Mrs Macleay followed him to the door.

'As far as I can make out it's shock mostly, and if it was going to upset him to move him, he's perhaps better where he is. But he must have someone for a few days. If he got weaker and his mind gave in to it, he could slip away easily enough.'

'That's what I'm frightened of, Doctor. I said I would stay last night, but he wouldn't let me.'

'You got little enough sleep yourself last night.'

'Plenty.'

The doctor looked as if there was something he couldn't quite understand about his patient. 'There aren't enough nurses even for the hospital. I'll see what I can do.' And after he had talked of food and medicine, he walked hurriedly away.

Mrs Macleay put on the kettle. 'I'll make you a cup of tea,' she said; 'then I must off home for I left the soup on the fire, but I'll be back later and do everything.' Her manner was cheerful but Sandy was not deceived, for he had over- heard most of what they had said.

When she had gone and he relaxed, the sinking feeling was stronger than he had yet experienced. It would be very easy to slip away. It would be a relief. If only he had fixed up Allan . . . but he would do that. 'Damn it,' he muttered, 'I'll do that. They haven't beaten me yet.' Under him he felt the heave of a ship and smelt the sea, and he saw his own forearm at forty, brown with weather, and his fist. Then his head fell back and his mouth opened.

When she returned in the early evening with a pail of lentil soup and the lump of bacon, which she had found in the dresser, boiled in it, Sandy was ready for her.

But she was cunning and in no hurry. The hens, the cow, the arrangements that had been made for Murdo's funeral, the minister, the weather, the bacon and Danny the vanman's favouritism. Thus she worked round to the nurse and the doctor.

'Mrs Macleay,' said Sandy, 'you are not to worry about me. You have been run off your feet. Mairag needs you at this time. I'll be here in the morning, glad to see you if you can manage over. Until then, I'll take the pills and sleep without wakening.'

'The doctor—'

'Ach, the doctor,' he interrupted. 'It's his job and he likes to see it shipshape naturally enough. If I do not know what I can weather at my time of life—'

The argument came and went, and she gave him a few shrewd back-handers. Even when at last she departed he was left with the uneasy feeling that she still had a shot in her locker. However, he had done what he could. The bright light had gone from the window, soon the dusk would be creeping in. He was very tired. Queenie lay before the fire, her nose on her paws, her eyes turning to him whenever he moved.

Presently he was aware of the light dimming in the window. As he stared at it, a profound sensation of desolation and sadness beset him. It was more than the light going away, more than the nothingness it was fading into. Toothless the wind gnawed at the edge of the roof, bounded away on invisible paws. It had no body. The dark and the bodiless.

He sweated so easily, a weak thin sweat. The skin on his brow was cold and his feet had the coldness of sea water.

Behind the dimming light there were watching eyes, waiting.

Eyes that were no eyes, that weren't there, that couldn't be seen.

He shut his eyes and turned his face away.

He hadn't the energy to call on the weakest thought, to evoke the faintest memory of a vision, yet he knew, somewhere beyond volition, that the opposite to this nothingness was the experience of sitting among the hills and becoming part of everything, with that rare outgoing of the spirit in happiness and peace.

Nothingness . . . participation. The twins.

But, ah, in the moment of nothingness, participation was the illusion, the mockery that was sadder than the dim light; the final crown, whose thorns found no blood.

His eyes opened on the fire; a flame flickered now and then. He met Queenie's eyes and at once she got up and came towards him, her body twisting in shy welcome, soft sounds in her throat.

'Well?' he said to her. The dog and the fire; the oasis.

After that he dozed through a dullness vaguely cramped and irked, in which time seemed at once endless and lost. When Queenie spoke to him, his eyes opened on the window and saw with astonishment and unease that it was night.

Queenie was uncertain. The fire was no more than a red core. He could hear nothing, not even the wind.

Queenie's whine grew firmer, almost a growl.

The footsteps would come now. But there were no footsteps. It could only be Allan, wondering why the lamp was not lit, approaching stealthily. His heartbeats grew too strong so he controlled himself, letting his quickened breathing have its way, and waited. When Queenie's voice became abrupt he hissed at her to lie down. Then he heard a quiet tapping on the door.

'Come in!' he called, bewildered, but realising it might be a timid neighbour, a boy sent to ask for him, someone small. Though it could be Allan, asking for a response.

The outside door was opened quietly . . . a slow groping . . . the kitchen door was moving. 'Lie down!' he said to Queenie sharply, and a figure was standing there, between him and the window, and he decided it was a woman.

'Who is it?'

There was a short silence. 'I heard – you needed someone.' The voice was quiet, husky with doubt.

'Who are you?' Sandy asked.

'Liz Murison,' she answered.

Sandy stared as he would in a dream. She had the stillness of a dream figure.

He repeated her name, his voice more husky than hers. 'What – who sent you?'

'I heard you were ill and needed someone.'

'Did someone – did someone send you?'

'No.'

He was lost.

She put out a hand for support.

'Sit down,' he said and moved so abruptly that he gasped. When he could see more clearly, she was sitting near the fire, a dim figure with pallor for a face.

'How did you come?'

'I walked.'

He could not get used to the reality of her presence. Of all beings on earth, she was the one who should not be near his house now. He must send her away at once.

'What time is it?' he asked in a startled way.

'Must be about ten.'

He gathered himself to deal with her. Allan would be on his way ever since the light went. Any time now – within the hour, certain – he would be listening by the window.

'I don't need anyone, thank you,' he said. 'Mrs Macleay – over by the road – she comes and does what's necessary.'

She did not speak.

She's heavy with child, he thought. Her hand had gone out for support. He took a look at her but could make nothing of her face. Her voice had been husky with dumb misery, but warm . . . her nature warm . . . that kind. Lord, had she run away from home, her parents turned her out?

'What made you think of coming here?' he asked.

'I heard you needed someone.' It was what she must have made up her mind to say and it just kept coming out of her.

'Do you mean you want to stay here and work? Have you left your home?'

'Yes.'

She could not say much, just felt; would break down any time.

'Well, I'm sorry, but – but I don't – I can't – I don't need anyone.' He must be firm.

Then he saw her move. She got up, her hand holding on to the back of the chair.

'Don't hurry, take a rest.' The words came out of him, but he was still being firm. Unless she went soon it would be too late. It was awful not to offer her a cup of tea. But she had to go.

She took a step away.

'Sit down,' he said.

She walked slowly towards the door.

'Wait till you get your breath. There's no hurry,' he said. 'Take a rest for a little while. You're tired, aren't you?'

She did not answer.

'Wait!' he called. 'Where are you going?'

'Don't know,' she said.

'Sit down for a few minutes.' The cold sweat was prickling his brow. 'Sit down now. Take your time.' He heard his own voice, quiet and hospitable, and the irony of this astonished him.

She went back to the chair and he heard the soft thump of her body.

'Poke the fire up,' he said. 'Warm yourself.' Then he was caught by the window and fancied he saw a pale glimmer beyond. 'Wait, draw the blind,' and the command in his voice sent her to the window. She fumbled for a little while, then the small roller creaked as the blind ran down.

'Did anyone see you coming?'

'No.' She got back into the chair; her shoulders gave a spasmodic heave.

'Are you cold? Is it wet?'

He heard her swallow.

'You'll find kindling in the off corner, on top.'

She got to her knees. Her movements were slow. The poker went into the fire, the dull glow broke up as ashes trickled away, and a few sparks shot out. She pushed a piece of stick into the glow and in no time a flame rushed up greedily, for the old bog pine, which he had gathered for kindling, was not only dry but warm. Her head was bare, her body covered in a grey-brown raincoat. She pushed the hot coals about the flame, stirred away the ash from underneath carefully, then found the tongs and slowly but surely built up the fire.

Having conquered the first panic, Sandy was trying to think hard but finding it difficult. She would have to go, but also she would have to go somewhere. He couldn't just send her into the night. He thought of Widow Macleay.

'Any water in the kettle?' he asked.

She was sitting before the fire; she hadn't looked round. Now she got on her knees, lifted the kettle and shook it. 'Yes,' she said in her low voice.

'Put it on. You'll make a cup of tea and then we'll see.' His mouth was sticking with dryness. He wiped his brow and stretched for the jug of water the doctor had left for him. The table was by the head of the bed, the jug, the lamp, his sleeping tablets, and a box of matches within reach. The water had a salty taste and as he tilted the jug for a second mouthful it came in a gulp and ran down his chin. As he coughed, the jug shook but he put it back on the table. He saw her face looking at him.

She had sandy brown hair and her fair skin had a pallor behind the fairness that turned it almost white, like ivory. There was no curl or wave in her hair; it was straight and lank. Her bones were not small; she was strongly made, the bone in her face smoothly covered but clear; not stout but loose-jointed, untidy, warm as her voice. Wondering whether she should come to help him she did not come, and somehow in an instant he liked that restraint in her, saw its tragic look in her eyes. She had taken her beating and did not expect much.

'When did you have anything to eat?'

'Earlier,' she said. 'I'm not hungry.'

'I'll tell you what we'll do.' He was going to tell her about Widow Macleay, but his cunning went against him for she had not yet eaten. 'You'll find food in the dresser. I could do with a cup myself.' On its own, his voice added, 'Light the lamp.'

He saw her features above the light. The eyes were not blue but brown, her nostrils were finely made, her mouth large but not loose, the pale lips parted with the tips of the upper teeth showing; her brow was smooth and wide. It was not a girl's face but a woman's, with the immaturity of the girl in it. If ever he had thought of her as a wanton or a trollop he now got another impression. As his eyes fell, he saw the coat hang loosely about her.

She was dumb, but dumb in the region of feeling, beyond thought, and this he understood and it affected him.

He told her what to find in the dresser and did not forget the boiled ham. Her movements were slow because she was weary and weak, but they were sure. She did not fumble. She was used to doing things in a house; she pulled out the drawer in the kitchen table expecting to find the cutlery.

While waiting for the kettle to boil, she sat down in his chair.

'Will your people be looking for you?'

She took a moment. 'No.'

'Did you tell them you were leaving?'

'I told my father I would never go back.'

Sandy felt the night and the far world coming at him and he let go for a little time. When he relaxed completely he knew his resources trickled slowly back, even if he felt they were trickling away.

She brought the teapot to the table and poured out two cups of tea, then returned it to the fireplace, leaving it on the spot where he always placed it himself.

She cut some bread, two slices of ham, and found the salt. He told her he could not eat ham, wanted nothing but the tea as he had already had a big meal. 'Eat it up your-self,' he said in a kindly voice; 'that's what it's for.'

She stopped dead still looking down at her hands. He began thrusting himself up. 'Could you push them behind me?' he asked.

The table moved under the pressure of her hip as she held his shoulders with an arm and got three pillows behind him.

'Would you like to sit right up?' Her voice was toneless, as if it would not intrude on him. Again this moved him and he smiled.

'No, that's fine. I haven't – a lot of pith – at the moment.'

She brought his tea and waited. He lifted the cup, took a mouthful, and returned it to the saucer which she held in her hand. After a glance at him, she put it back on the table.

'Good tea. Now eat. I'll take another drink in a minute.'

She sat down at the table and buttered some bread, but before eating she began drinking her tea. He did not look at her, but was aware that she must have nearly emptied her cup. Then she was standing beside him again.

'Never mind me,' he said.

But she waited until he had drunk.

'Will you not eat something?' she asked in the same voice.

'No. It's just dry I am. If you want to please me you'll eat yourself.'

She sat down, but when he looked sideways at her he saw she was making a poor job of the eating.

'Take the ham. You're young, lassie; you need it. Don't be afraid. We'll do what we can for you.' Sandy had a way of speaking quietly, kindly, that went very near the bone. Again all her movements stopped, her head went down, as if someone were saying grace at a table. Then her shoulders heaved and he heard the draw of breath in her nostrils. She did her best, she trembled, her features became contorted above her pressed lips, but the sob broke through. She struggled desperately, but the internal pressure was too much for her. 'I'm sorry,' she said. And that did not help, it only made things worse. 'I did not mean—' The flood broke through.

It was the last thing she meant to do, poor girl. She

would have wanted to be cool and capable. Sandy had a profound intuition of the pitiful nature of the human condition. It was at his board, all of it. It went into the far night, carried beyond the choked animal sounds she made, and he saw Allan coming in the night. Here it was, the whole tragedy and pity of it to the last terrible shred.

I'm weak, he thought, feeling the tears on his face. When a man got old and done he grew weak as a bairn. He made no sound.

She gradually grew still, her emotion ebbing like any other elementary force, like the sea. She wiped her eyes as she went to the fire, then came back with the teapot. He glanced at her and saw she was ashamed to look at him, but she would do what she had to do, beyond all hope though she was. She poured some hot tea into his cup.

'Thank you,' he said as she stood beside him.

Her eyes shot a look at him and met the glisten in his, saw the tears on his cheeks. An extraordinary expression came into her face, startled, almost stupid. Then her eyelids fell and the cup trembled in the saucer.

He lifted the cup and drank. He held onto it and drank again. Then he put it back on the saucer. 'That will do me,' he said.

After a time he asked, 'You're not finished?'

'Yes.'

'Very well,' he said calmly. 'You have nowhere to go?'

'No.'

'I'm not going to ask you any questions now. Pour some tea into your cup for I am going to give you something to take.'

She obeyed.

'The doctor said he might call on me tonight yet. Others may come too. Widow Macleay may send someone. I don't want them to find you here.'

She waited.

'It would be too much for you and for me now.' He stretched out an arm. 'That, give me that . . . Thank you. You need sleep. You'll take two. I take two myself. Take them now; swallow them down with your tea.'

She never hesitated.

'They'll take a while to work on you. There's a bed in the ben room. I don't want you to show a light in the window for long. There's a blind on the window and I hope it's working. If you put the lamp on the floor over there and left the door open you would see your way in – first – to draw the blind. Do that.'

She did it and came back.

'There should be a candle on the top shelf of the dresser.'

She fetched it down, began clearing the table, and soon had the kitchen exactly as she had found it on entering.

'That's fine,' he said. 'I hope you won't be disturbed, but if you hear voices pay no attention. Light your candle now. I don't know what your bed is like and maybe you'd better sleep in the blankets.'

She lit the candle, half a candle in an old-fashioned tall brass candlestick, and hesitated by the table. 'Can I do anything for you?' she asked, not looking at him.

He saw her heart was full.

'Yes,' he said, smiling. 'We haven't shaken hands yet.'

She shifted the candlestick to her left hand and in her right took the hand he put out to her.

'Liz Murison,' he said. 'You're safe here. Put fear from you, and sleep in peace.'

She could not speak and went away quietly.

FOURTEEN

He rested for a while, the lamp lit on the table beside him. It's not one thing that happened when things got going! he thought with a dry remote humour. Her parents . . . tomorrow they could not hide that Liz had disappeared. The mother would go running to a neighbour . . . the father would gloom like Satan . . . the police would ask questions. Another search.

To be found at his croft, where they had searched for Allan, as if the girl was running after the lad she had betrayed, the murderer of the man who was the father of her bairn. Gossip's mouth would be everywhere now. A new sensation for Hilton.

Nicol would be sniffing from a distance, getting ready for a new attack.

Sweat broke out all over Sandy. He smelt it as he moved the bedclothes away to let the air in and wiped where he could with the flat of his hand.

She had come because she would have heard stories about him from the lads in past years, how he lived beyond the edge of the ordinary world, in that region into which they escaped, and found life, and made, no doubt, wild stories about it, full of laughter. She had come out of some obscure impulse which only a woman knew . . . he felt this now but could not think about it, it was so beyond him, beyond any man. The story that he had been hurt and needed someone to nurse him would have been enough to set her feet going. Not to mention her father, who would hate her

now the more he had been fond of her before . . . That kind
of father, looking at his daughter. She was soft and warm . . .

Sandy's head lay over and the sensation of life was a
faint obliterating buzz inside.

She was not what he expected. Trinketty girls with drug-
bright eyes, dance halls and cafés, down streets of foreign
ports . . . the calculating look beneath the welcome . . .

His head rolled back. She had kept her coat on and it
was difficult to see how far gone she was. But she must be
all right for a month or two or surely she wouldn't have
come. Thought went from him and he sank.

Queenie's whine . . . the startled wonder about time . . .
who now? His eyes roved. Queenie whined again. He looked
at her, standing on the floor. 'Hist!' he quietened her and
listened. There were no footsteps. It was Allan.

It had come now!

He heard the fingers on the door, the scratching of his
nails.

'Come in!' he called huskily, keeping his voice from
breaking into hard sound.

He called again and waited. At last he heard the faint
click of the latch. It was a long time before Allan stood
looking at him.

The face shocked Sandy, it seemed shrunken. The beard
had grown, the skin was pale and drawn, the eyes glanced
here and there, shifting with fear; the mouth was slightly
open; listening, ready to bolt. It could not look more like
a criminal's face.

Sandy raised his hand, cautioning him to silence.

Allan's eyes switched and Sandy saw the whites. He was
afraid of the passage.

'Come here,' Sandy whispered.

Allan listened for a moment more, then stepped warily
to the bed.

Sandy nodded sideways towards the ben room. 'Hsh! I have had an accident. All right – don't be afraid.'

Allan had started away.

'She's asleep. Quite safe.'

Allan hesitated, breathing strongly.

Sandy beckoned him.

'I had an accident, won't be up for a couple of days. Doctor sent woman to look after me. I told her I expected a neighbour to call.' The whispering made him cough. Allan took a step back, started to cough, a racking cough he did his best to smother.

Sandy smiled to show there was no need for worry and beckoned him close. 'Take a loaf, packet oatcakes, tin meat, out of dresser. At once. Go on.'

Allan's tongue came between his dry lips, then he went to the dresser and pulled open its double door, took out the loaf, the oatcakes, a tin of meat.

Sandy whispered, 'Three eggs.' And after that, 'Open drawer – right.'

From this drawer Allan took a grey woollen shirt, vest and pants.

Sandy nodded. 'Pull blanket off my bed, second one.'

Allan listened a moment, then quickly throwing back the coverlet and the top blanket, drew out the next, a dull army grey, and threw it on the floor, then re-dressed the bed.

'Keep you going for a couple of days.'

Allan nodded, more reassured now.

'You had it very wet?'

Allan nodded. He was looking ill, feverish.

'How are you doing?'

'Sodden, yonder.'

'Was thinking that. Blanket will help. I have your suit ready, but it's in the other room. Get it next time – and any cash I can scrape.'

'Thanks.' Something of the old Allan was showing through now, but not much.

'I'll try to get up soon as I can, but not sure when.'

'What happened?'

Sandy's account of Nancy's behaviour brought a gleam to Allan's eye and started another short spasm of coughing, but even as he coughed he saw the box of matches.

Sandy nodded. 'But don't show a light on the Crannock whatever you do.'

'I've roofed in a bit.'

'A wood fire smells.'

'Any tea?'

His movements were quick now. He had plainly been thinking things out. He half emptied the caddy into part of a paper bag, and scooped some sugar into the other part.

Tea and sugar, but no milk this time. Allan understood at once, for Sandy kept the milk in the stone-floored closet facing the front door and separating the two rooms of the cottage.

Allan gripped the edges of the blanket, gave them a twist, and carefully swung the bundle over his left shoulder.

'Give me three days if you can,' whispered Sandy.

Allan nodded. 'I can boil food now.'

'Be very careful.'

Then Allan smiled, a warm strange gleam it was, as if his personality had fused or melted, as if the old Allan far back in him looked through at Sandy. With his right hand he saluted and turned away. There was no more than a slight click from the outside door.

Sandy listened for a long time, but all was quiet.

The lad had got away once more.

No sound had come from the other room, and none came now.

In his exhaustion the night was about him, coming from

distance and swarming slowly round inside his head. He would take the sleeping pills in a minute.

And presently he took them. As they began to affect him he had a brief interlude of ease and vision.

Why had she come? What was the motive in the deep undersea of her mind? What set her feet wandering – to his place?

Something he could hardly look at moved him with a sense of terrible mystery.

There was a knowledge beyond reason. It was not to be looked at, questions had no meaning. Things happened.

Human beings moved from one place to another, one day to another. They went on doing this, beyond creeds and massacres, desperation and death.

So long as life was left, it moved. That was about as far as thought could go. He saw patterns of the movement, figures walking on blind feet. He saw the girl coming through the night to his croft.

Between Allan and herself was the burden she bore. Blind and fatal.

Nothing was left but happenings, tomorrow and the next day.

He saw her situation with a lucidity that emotion hardly touched, as though emotion itself were transcended. As his brow smoothed, the wave of sleep rose and took him.

FIFTEEN

She came in quietly and stood looking towards his bed. He greeted her. 'Had you a good sleep?'

'Yes.'

'That's fine. Pull up the blind and we'll have a cup of tea.'

He watched her as she moved about in the morning light. The sun was shining outside and the kitchen was suddenly bright and raw as though caught in its sleep. She wore a skirt and unbuttoned coat of a greenish tweed, and looked like a woman half ready for a journey. Her figure was full, but he would hardly have noticed it, and indeed with the coat-ends hanging loose, she seemed, for a woman of her build, normal enough. Her hair, combed firmly back, fell forward a little as she attended to the fire.

He was feeling wonderfully refreshed after his sleep and confidence was in the daylight. The greater the depression and anxiety of the night, the less real they often seemed in the morning.

'A neighbour called last night. I hope you weren't disturbed?'

'No.' The fire was out and she stood up to look for matches on the mantelpiece. Her face was grey and sick-looking.

'A match is it? Well, now . . . let me see.' He remembered giving the box to Allan. 'Look! Up on the off corner of the top shelf of the dresser. That's it. You'll soon find where things are.' And in a few moments he complimented her, saying, 'That's not the first fire you have put a match to. You'll find fresh water behind the front door.'

Without asking questions, she found the coal bucket, picked out the few pieces left in it, and charged it with ashes. By the time she had the hearth all tidily swept and ready for the day's work, the kettle was giving its first thoughtful sigh.

'Don't be frightened to ask me questions,' he said.

'Is there anything I can do for you?' Her shoulder was to him, her eyes on the dresser.

'No, thank you. The nurse will be here soon and it's washed and pushed over I'll be till I'm near dead. We'll have our cup of tea first.'

She left the kitchen and, listening, he knew she was doing up her own room and making the bed. She would be afraid of the nurse. It would be another kind of battle with a woman. Poor girl, she could do nothing so far but keep inside herself. Then Sandy thought of the imminence of the widow.

The thought shook him. Widow Macleay's eyes wouldn't miss much!

At that moment the widow passed the window, moving fast. In no time her head was round the bed. 'I saw your smoke.' She must have been trotting and still looked scared.

'Wasn't I clever?' he suggested from his sick bed.

'You were never up?'

'Why not?'

'God forgive you,' she said, 'you weren't?'

'It's not my leg that was out at the joint, as I told you.'

She looked at him, at the table, the swept fireplace, the emptied ashpit, and heaved a deep breath. 'If you make a fool of me, Sandy Ross, you'll be the first.'

'Nonsense. A woman with a heart as kind as yours must have been fooled many a time.'

'Who's been in?'

When he spoke jestingly of a new housekeeper, she turned away with knit brows, went to the front door, then into the ben room. Sandy heard the way her feet stopped, and his waking confidence began to ooze from him. Then he heard the questions: Where did you come from? Who sent you? It wasn't the doctor sent you? What's your name?

'Liz Murison.'

There was a pause then. Sandy wiped his brow. Women had no mercy.

'Are you . . . ? Yes, I – can – see.' The widow's last words came so slowly, Sandy saw her looking. Her voice was drier than bog pine.

It's coming now! thought Sandy, holding on by gripping the coverlet with his working hand, yet lifting his ear at the same time for the storm's first impact. All his ear heard was the closing of the door. The widow had shut the ben room door. Battened down!

Well, well! thought Sandy, listening harder than ever, but all he heard was the widow's voice, a scrawl of indecipherable sound beyond the bulkhead. His good hand flapped the coverlet. It was neither a high voice nor a low voice. It went on and stopped and went on like an auger in difficult wood. Sandy wiped his weakness and listened, but from Liz he could hear nothing, though once he fancied he caught a soft run of sound like water leaking from a dislodged tank.

There! The voice had stopped at last. It started again.

Sandy looked wildly around for help and saw the kettle. The steam was beginning to curl from its spout lazily.

'The kettle!' But his voice was no more than a shadow of itself. Behind his well-meant intention the cry had hidden, afraid.

Oh Lord, he thought, she won't leave a stitch on the

lassie! He moved and hurt himself and was helped by the painful diversion.

The steam was gathering its woolly head.

'The kettle!' he distinctly called, if still in a weak voice. After all, it was his house. He was far from well. He was very weak. They just shouldn't take advantage of him. After all, he was the only one of them near death, and damn near it enough.

The steam was volleying forth. The lid of the kettle loosened itself in a preliminary tap or two.

'The kettle!' he shouted so loudly that his voice went hoarse.

He hearkened amid his constrictions and pains, tried to ease his shoulder out if its bandaging and nearly fainted.

The voice had stopped. Thank God! The voice started again.

The kettle lid went daft on toes that tap-danced in a hurricane.

Sandy let his body flatten out in a passive endurance akin to meditation or trance. In a few moments his own voice startled him by shouting fiercely, 'The kettle!'

Nothing happened. As if she would be put off by a kettle! Suddenly the widow entered.

'The kettle,' he explained weakly.

'I heard you,' she replied succinctly not even pausing to throw him a glance. She dealt with the kettle firmly. She took down the tea-caddy, with its frieze of dancing girls, flung legs and eastern instruments, slapped open the lid and paused.

'What's happened to the tea? It's scarcely half.'

'Wh-what?' asked Sandy.

'The tea?'

'Yes, we had tea – last night—' He was hardly interested. How could she expect him to be? In his condition?

'Hm!' she said, and was actually on the point of scooping tea into the cold unswilled teapot before she recollected herself. So great was the shock, she said no more.

May God keep her from finding the lost loaf, prayed Sandy as she turned to the dresser. Don't let her count the eggs.

She had other things on her mind.

Never a word did she utter as she took cups and saucers from the dresser, milk and the glass bowl of sugar. Her eyes measured the quantity of sugar.

'It was late before she came last night,' said Sandy.

'How late?' She pushed the kitchen door shut.

'The clock is stopped, and where my watch is I don't know, unless it's in my waistcoat pocket.'

'Ten o'clock, was it?'

'It was that anyway. What could I do?'

'Hm. You did a lot.'

'She did it all herself,' said Sandy.

'You're telling me,' said the widow.

'I thought of sending her on to you, but I didn't want to give you more trouble,' said Sandy. 'I hardly knew what to do. You had had a hard day as it was.'

'You were thinking a lot about me,' said the widow as she brought the teapot and filled his cup.

'I was,' said Sandy. 'How is Mairag bearing up?'

'As well as could be expected,' replied the widow, putting the teapot back by the fire. Then she returned to the bedside and asked, 'Will you sit up?'

Her arm was so purposeful that he felt its sharp elbow in his spine. He heaved himself up a little more and groaned like a man far through.

'And me thinking you were trotting to your death when I saw your smoke!'

'I'll trot yet,' he said encouragingly, wiping his brow and breathing like a sprinter.

'Ay,' she said. 'You're the fast one.'

'Aren't you taking a cup yourself?'

'Presently.' She pushed the table nearer him. 'Can you reach that?'

'Fine,' he said. 'I'm coming on.'

'You sure are,' said the widow, who picked up many a pithy comment between Danny's van and the Hilton cinema. 'And what now?' she asked.

'What?' asked Sandy.

'What are you going to do with her?'

'I was wondering,' murmured Sandy reaching for his cup. His arm lifted the cup like a derrick and swung it slowly to his mouth, but it shook and she had filled it too full. When she had got the cup back in the saucer, she wiped the coverlet with a towel and stuck the end of the towel up under his whiskers.

'Thank you,' he said, looking down the enormous bib, 'I'll manage now.'

'Well?' she asked.

'Well, I thought of sending her on to you, as I say, but it was that dark.'

'She might lose her way – after finding your house,' commented the widow. 'Ay. And she would be that tired.'

'She was,' said Sandy.

'Just that,' said the widow. 'I hope you gave her some of your sleeping pills.'

From his eye corners Sandy threw her a glance and decided that the reference to the pills was a shot in the dark. For she was moved, he could see, in a curious if not astonishing manner. It was exactly as if the advent of Liz Murison had created a new and grimly exciting world for her, and her talk with him now, even the half-emptied tea caddy and sugar basin, were affairs of secondary interest.

'Would you have me turn her from my door?' he asked.

'You didn't,' she said. 'One would have thought,' she added, 'from what you said to the doctor, not to mention myself, that having anyone to sleep here was the last thing in this world you could abide. Even the doctor wondered about it, not to mention the nurse. They thought it queer.'

'Why? Surely that was to save you all any trouble, especially yourself?'

She looked at his expression, its astonishment, its concern, its almost hurt innocence. But all she said was 'Hm,' as though she could not completely break even for an instant her preoccupation with the new world which had opened out before her with such shattering unexpectedness.

'My first thought was to send her to you. But why, I thought, put her on you? What could I do? If I turned her from my door and anything happened to her, what would anyone think of me, and what would I think of myself?'

'Don't distress yourself.'

'I'm not distressing myself. I'm only trying to show you.'

'What brought her to this house?'

Sandy found the widow's eyes on him and felt his moorings slacken.

'Because,' he said, 'because she heard of my accident and the doctor trying to get someone.'

'It wasn't the doctor she heard of you from. And it's strange, whoever it was.'

'I don't understand you. She was turned out of her home.'

'She wasn't. She went.'

'But her father—'

'Her father, that deacon in the kirk! Yon pretty man with the soft smile on his fat face! A sanctimonious humbug.'

'I didn't know about her people.'

'You live at the back of beyond,' said the widow, plainly

not thinking of space only. 'Are you going to keep her or what?'

'Keep her?'

'Don't you realise what talk there will be about this? Have you no notion at all how the news will hit Hilton? Can't you think of her home this morning and her mother, a decent woman, running around like the poor trodden hen she is, and the great Farquhar himself, with the smile gone off him, and his vanity collapsed like a pig's bladder that a bairn has kicked against thorns? What do you think they'll be saying between the town council and the auction marts? What do you think the police are doing? Sucking their sore thumbs? Who is going to give them the news, and when they get it, will Farquhar Murison come to take his daughter home, with the newspaper taking photographs of them? If your own photograph hasn't been taken before now, you can thank me—'

But at that moment the nurse passed the window. Widow Macleay nimbly intercepted her at the front door and their voices receded towards the barn.

Sandy's eyes roved in a bewildered manner. He was in the midst of it now, skirts all about, with hems on. The swish of them was purposeful around all the corners of his eyes. Outside the cock crew. Lucky cock.

The nurse and the widow and the question of questions: what brought her here? He saw their four round eyes.

The cock had another go. He was doing well.

Sandy turned over and paid for it. Let him calm himself for they must be coming now. Neither sound nor sign of them reached him. His eye landed on the teapot.

'Liz,' he said indistinctly and coughed for his throat was husky.

After all it was still his own house and hadn't she come to be employed by him?

The cock crew for the third time.

'Lizzie!' he called.

For still a few moments there was no sound and he wondered if she had fainted; then he heard her quiet feet coming. His heart melted at sight of her.

'What about your tea?' he asked sensibly.

But just then she heard something and was gone.

The nurse breezed in. 'And how is my patient this morning?'

'Och, not so bad,' said Sandy bravely.

'That's good. Took your tablets, did you? That's fine. And how about your pulse now?' Nurse appeared pleased with her patient. 'You're going to be a credit to us.'

'I hope so.'

'My word, you've been sweating, haven't you? Poof! We'll just have to strip you and wash you from top to bottom. After that you'll not know yourself.'

Sandy looked as if he mightn't.

The nurse laughed. She was brisk and bright on an ordinary day, but now clearly she had caught some of the widow's infection.

When Sandy heard voices in the ben room and knew that all three women were there together he achieved a resignation that realised even listening was of no more use. Drawers were being pulled open and pushed shut. Not much of his private possessions would remain hidden from them now! In extremity, as in a nightmare, a man will remember embarrassing things, and Sandy, when the nurse exclaimed brightly, remembered the white nightshirts he had inherited along with the chest of drawers. Once upon a time they must have belonged to his uncle-by-marriage and he himself had worn them when his pyjamas were out of commission and particularly when the weather was very hot. When he heard the widow's cackle, all he could do was fall back on a still-deeper resignation. The nurse would be capable of opening the nightshirt out, even of measuring it against the widow, at a time like this! . . . with that girl standing by them, and death itself hovering over the house for all they cared. When he heard the lid of his chest fall shut with a clop, he knew they must have seen the suit he had tied up.

Their humour was veiled, their excitement contained, as the widow got the basin of hot water and the nurse set to work, poking the sponge up under his armpits and else-where with firm efficiency. But an end came even to the wipings and dryings and other bodily matters and Sandy lay at rest, relieved in more ways than one, for all they could do to him now was just leave him. Not but that he felt the better of the nurse's capable attentions. Indeed he even wondered dimly about a little present for her when he didn't need her any more.

However, the next thing Sandy realised was that the widow was putting on the porridge pot and the nurse was alone with Liz in the ben room.

Even though he did not mean to groan aloud, the widow heard him.

'Are you all right?' she asked.

'Yes,' he said solemnly. 'What's happening now?'

'Nurse is questioning her.'

'What about?'

'Her time. Do you want her to have her bairn here?'

Widow Macleay saw how that silenced him, and turned to her pot not without some satisfaction.

The nurse seemed to be longer with Liz even than the widow had been, but presently in she came, saying, 'It's high time I was off.' She turned to Sandy. 'Well, do you think you can still manage alone – or are you keeping her on?'

A strange paralysis came upon him.

'He wouldn't like to turn her from his door,' said the widow.

'It's whatever you say,' muttered Sandy.

'In that case it's settled,' said the nurse.

Sandy lost his bearings.

They went back to the ben room. Presently the nurse departed, but she had hardly passed the window when the widow called 'Nurse!' and went waddling off after her.

There was a great silence.

Liz Murison came quietly in.

'Are they off?' asked Sandy.

'I don't know,' replied Liz.

'Make the porridge,' said Sandy, and his voice sounded a little stronger.

SIXTEEN

By the time the doctor came Sandy was able to assure him that he was lying on a more even keel.

'Making old women jealous at your time of life!' The doctor shook his head.

Sandy cast him a glance.

'Your pulse is standing up to it wonderfully,' continued the doctor. 'But I don't want a relapse. I told the widow – and nurse – that what you need is quiet.'

'Thank you,' said Sandy.

The doctor chuckled. 'Tell me, so that I may get it off my mind: what happened after you were adrift on the raft?'

'A Swede picked us up, far west.'

'I'm coming in some evening soon to have a real yarn with you. Just now – take it easy. Don't let anything worry you. Where's the new housekeeper?'

'Through there.'

'Want to keep her?' The doctor was watching him.

'What can I do?' asked Sandy.

'I can do anything you want.'

'It was dark night. I could not turn her from my doorstep.' He paused. 'If I had turned her away then, I had the feeling she would have walked on to her death.'

The doctor nodded.

'If, at my time of life, I couldn't give a night's rest to one so hard pressed, what – what am I for?'

'A profound question.'

'It's not that,' said Sandy. 'I just gave her two of your

sleeping pills and sent her to bed. Tomorrow . . . I'll confess to you, Doctor, that once or twice tomorrow did not feel like something that would bother me.'

'You could have slipped your cable?'

'Easily enough.'

'I was afraid of it. I would like to help you. If you want her to stay on for a few days, I'll see there's no trouble from the Hilton end.'

'Well, all right,' said Sandy, but the doctor saw he was suddenly wearied.

'If you hold on for a bit,' said the doctor, 'we'll see this through between us.'

'Very well.'

'So keep your pecker up. I'm a doctor. My job is to keep life going. Judgment is for other people.'

'Yes,' said Sandy. 'Thank you.' The light of interest began to seep back into his eyes. 'That's it.'

'You don't feel like doing a lot of judging yourself, do you?' asked the doctor with a smile.

'No.' Sandy's head shook slightly. 'Let me say it.'

'Do.'

'I have had my life. I can go. If I cannot now help—' But words eluded him.

The doctor gripped Sandy's hand. 'Never mind these women: they'll fuss whatever you do. And, my word, haven't they got something to fuss about now?'

'Ay,' said Sandy. 'But—'

'But what?'

'Women *are* life.'

The doctor's smile steadied. 'My lord!' he said, and laughed. 'I'll go through and have a word with her.'

Sandy had been hit with depression at the moment when they had agreed Liz Murison could stay on, but now he felt easier, and as he listened to the vague rumble of the doctor's voice or to the silence he was untouched by concern. All at once tears were trickling down his face. They could only come out of weakness but he did not care. To be ashamed of them now was a vanity that was beyond him. The new burden was something he did not want ... and then he thought of Allan. And he knew, in a moment's inner clarity like a last helpless honesty, that it was not Allan himself, not the old friendliness between them, that moved him now, though they were in him, but the thought of the lad being tried and hanged. Somehow *that* he could not stomach. It tied life's tap-root in a knot. It was an obstacle in front of him, between him and death.

All this loomed before him in the region beyond thought, beyond words. It was the region he had slowly been drawing nearer to, but now it was obscure, with enigmas like rocks, and an air above it like a dim light.

After the doctor had gone Liz did not come back into the kitchen. She would be getting her bearings outside. Widow Macleay had returned, after accompanying the nurse halfway to the main road, and been a considerable time with Liz, instructing her in her duties.

'The lassie can milk, that's one thing,' she had said to Sandy, and added, as she was taking her leave, 'so you won't be needing me.'

'Don't desert me,' Sandy had replied gallantly.

Now he heard the silence around the croft and should have been at ease, but to his dismay depression came at him again. So long as he had been fighting for the girl his mind had been occupied, but now that the fight was over somehow the pith was gone from him. But it was more than that and he knew it. Profoundly in him what he wanted was to be left alone. The occasional visit of Widow Macleay was all he had needed, and her tart tongue and capable handling of affairs kept him going in spite of himself.

It was a misfortune that the arrangement had been interfered with.

Depression settled heavily upon him. Even the girl's quietness, the way she had of not intruding, was a weight. His head turned over on the pillow and he had a revulsion against her. Her wantonness had been too much. Too much had come out of it.

He was too far away from young people to feel for them or to care. The widow and the brisk nurse would have put him on his feet and then he could have wandered around his croft and up into his Chair overlooking the loch of the water lilies, and into the hills, where he had his own business. This girl was dragging him back and down.

Presently Liz entered, paused on her way to the fire and looked at him. 'Would you like anything?'

'No,' he answered. 'Later.'

She tidied the hearth, dusted the mantelshelf, lifting and replacing things quietly, and after a little while went out again.

She's not going to be much bother, he thought. That was something. But even her short visit had drained some energy out of him and he felt wearier than ever. He might as well try to sleep, even if he stuck in the bottom of the pit.

He slept for half an hour, and awoke with a curious light feeling of reprieve. He could not understand this, then suddenly realised that he had almost three days, three clear days, before Allan returned. They were like a holiday.

Liz came in on her toes, looked round the end of the bed, and asked him what he would like to eat.

When it came to heaving himself up, she helped him firmly, building the cushions into a steep slope.

'Where did you get that?' He gaped at a red lacquered tray.

'Mrs Macleay brought it.'

'Did she?' He was astonished and felt its smooth surface when Liz placed it on his legs. 'It's the colour of a holiday.'

She smiled and cut the top off his egg.

'How did you get on with her?' he asked, still looking at the remarkable tray.

'All right.'

The sun had moved round to the front of the house and he saw her features in its clear light. She had been weeping and the skin on her face was so fair and wan it looked naked. This impression of a loose nakedness was very strong, with all the softness of youth behind it. She was wearing a print overall.

'Has she been giving you things?'

'I brought some things myself,' she answered.

'Did you?' he said, astonished more than ever. He had thought of her having a row with her father and then walking out with no more than she stood up in, as he would have done himself.

She held the egg in its cup while he scooped out a spoonful then set it down on the tray. He pressed her to eat because she needed food far more than he did, lying on his back as he was.

'Has anyone called?' he asked.

'I heard Mrs Macleay talking to two people. She sent them away.'

'Quite right. And if any more come, I'll deal with them.'

When the meal was over and Liz gone out, he tried to listen to what she was doing but heard only the singing of a chaffinch and the sawing of a great tit. He thought of their nests, the colour of their eggs. If one thing brought back boyhood more than any other it was the unexpectedness of a bird's nest with the coloured eggs lying magically there. How vivid the moment! Lying in his bed, Sandy went with his memory through the birches, up the robin's ditch, over the heather and into sleep.

When he awoke, sleep hung about him, heavy as a drug. It held no responsibility, no anxiety. It was comforting, and lying quite still his body hadn't an ache. He dozed off.

He became aware of voices and at once the sinking dragging feeling of anxiety was back round his heart. What was reaching out its grasping fist now?

It was the widow. 'And how are you feeling?'

'Full of sleep.'

'You'll be going one way or the other in that case,' she said confidently. 'I have brought you a present.'

'For me?'

'Who else? Don't you think it's a good one?' and she exhibited a brand new bed-pan.

'Well! well!' said Sandy. 'God bless me!'

'A companion for your bed,' she said and gave a small cackle as she pushed it under the blankets. 'What don't they make nowadays?'

'Say it!' he said.

'If they made more of that and less of the atom bombs life would be more convenient.'

'Never did you say a truer word,' said Sandy keeping his end up valiantly.

'You can thank the nurse.'

'I will,' he promised.

She cackled. 'You won't have to reach so far whatever. How's the lassie doing?'

'Fine,' said Sandy, wide awake now. 'She's no bother in the house. I'll say that.'

'A poor weak thing. Weak, weak.' She shook her head at the fire. 'But she keeps a tidy enough house.'

'Any news?'

'So you're wanting the news next? Ay. I'm afraid there's

no chance of the great Farquhar storming your bed. A pity, because I would have liked to have said to him what I couldn't to the lassie. He's washed his hands of her.'

'Has he?'

'And if so, as I said to Will Gordon who told me, there's a chance his hands may be clean for once.'

Sandy chuckled softly.

It took her all of fifteen minutes to give him an outline of the news which included verbatim remarks by Hilton's more important persons from the provost to the foreman scavenger, with a banker, two grocers, an ironmonger, a lawyer and the convener of the Education Committee added for convincing measure. The Chief Constable had a poultice on his thumb and Nicol the bobby a death's head on his neck. 'He's in a bad way that fellow,' and she stopped.

'Nicol?'

'Ay. They say his mother is going off her head.'

'Surely not?'

'Dr Drummond was called to see her last night. I'll get the truth out of him when next I see his car by the road, and if by any chance I miss him, you'll put a word to him yourself?'

'Yes,' murmured Sandy staring at the window.

'Will says they think Nicol himself is going a bit queer. In his off hours he sneaks away into the hills.'

'What for?'

'He thinks he'll find the body of Allan Innes lying dead. It seems he said to someone that he saw himself looking at the body, but he can't find the place, though he'll know it when he sees it. And if that wasn't just in a dream, it's queer.'

Sandy was silent.

'A young man asked me the way to your place. Nicely dressed he was and very pleasant. I asked him where he was from and he said he was from a newspaper in the south. He said he wanted to feature you, but I told him you weren't fit to have your features taken.' She was sitting in his chair and the shrewd look she gave him sent Sandy's hand to his whiskers. 'They'll do fine till you're up and about. You can clip them then,' she added sensibly.

'He went away?'

'Not him! He said he wanted to make a story of crofting life because in the south they didn't know what a croft was. If it's a croft you want, I said to him, there's plenty without bothering a poor, old, done, sick man.'

'Ay indeed,' said Sandy.

'Hmf!' said the widow. 'He engaged me in conversation, and if he did it wasn't all on his side. At least I can say that.'

'I'm sure,' said Sandy.

'Then he took my photograph.'

'Never!'

The grey wing of hair that was inclined to straggle over her left temple she smoothed back into place rather primly while the sinews in her neck tautened pertly. 'He did.' She looked at him. 'And why not?'

'Why not indeed?'

'But I didn't let him off with it. If you're going to take a photograph of me it won't be like this, I said. He laughed at that and a merry laugh it was. Do you know what he said then? "Would you like a comb?" And he produced a comb from his breast pocket!'

'A comb?'

'A comb! What do you think men are coming to? Maybe a man in his position has to be ready for every eventuality. You never know. However, I told him I had a comb of my own, and off I went, but if I did, he came with me. He had such a beautiful voice and nice manners I made sure he was English, so I asked him. You'll never guess?'

'No.'

'Born in Portree in Skye.'

'You spruced yourself up then!'

'He took a photograph of me standing in the door, though he nearly ruined it by saying, just before he clicked the thingmejig, "Down south they think a croft is either a cross between a Shorthorn and a hummel stag or a thing you wear in your hat".'

A tremor shook Sandy.

'How he enjoyed the fresh eggs with his tea after that!'

'Oh he would!' said Sandy and his wet eyes shone. 'Wh-when was this?'

'On the way home from your house this very forenoon.'

By the time she left him he was exhausted and would have been happy if only she hadn't referred to Nicol. Like a drugged toothache, this would lie in wait for him.

And it did. He had never been so affected by sleep. He awoke and dozed off and was generally in such a state of lethargy that the simplest thought hadn't the energy to find a shape. But now and then he caught a glimpse of Nicol's face, his sharp searching features vanishing into a landscape, towards the shores of Loch Deoch, with the Crannock lying off the upper end.

And he saw Allan's face, its scrubby pallor, its hunted criminal look, the hacking cough.

As in lenses that opened and shut these two figures came and went over glimpses of country . . . After Allan had appeared with the fever on him and the cough he had gone back – to swim the cold waters of Loch Deoch, wintry cold.

Even the widow had been queerly touched by the story of Nicol looking at Allan's dead body in a place he could not find. She had known it was not the kind of story that anyone would make up. It had the awful compelling power of second sight. In whatever bodily condition or state of mind, Nicol had seen himself looking at the body beforehand.

In Sandy's weakened condition this vision haunted him through moments of extreme lucidity.

It would be as good an end as any. He realised that and was not ashamed of it. And when he thought: I am trying to make it easy for myself, he knew also there was some condition or place far beyond himself where such an end was an apt finish, a fitting conclusion. In the long run the sum is added up, the balance squared.

If anything, it was too apt. Too apt, thought Sandy, turning his head. Not quite right. Not altogether. Because he was obsessed by his deadly hunt for Allan, Nicol was forcing even his vision. Yet it was near it, it was terribly near it. O God, it was terribly like the thing.

Liz came in with eggs in a basin and he was aware of her standing on the floor as though she had news for him.

'What is it?' he asked.

But already she was moving to the dresser, where she paused. 'It's just that I found a nest with nine eggs in it,' she said in that voice of hers which had no edge or sharpness at all; not that it was diffident, though there was diffidence in it; it was natural, warm, a little remote, without the edge that intrudes. There was something in it that seemed to wait without expecting much.

'Where?'

'Under the old harrows and things, over from the midden.'

'Clever! You'll have a few more for Danny now.' Then his eyes opened, even his mouth. 'The van – I forgot – when?—'

'Tomorrow. Mrs Macleay told me.'

'Tomorrow! God bless me, a lot has happened since last time!' He was trying to gain time. 'Someone must go.'

'If you tell me what to bring—'

'Yes – surely – we'll think about it. We'll need a lot. Yes. That'll be fine. We'll see.'

She put the eggs in the basket and went out.

He would have to get extra food for Allan. How on earth could he give food to Allan now without her finding out? The eye that had found the eggs would hardly make a mistake in the number of loaves, the quantity of tea, sugar . . . His old heart started up again thickly, sickeningly. When he began groping for a story, an invention, that might deceive her, he could find none. Suspicion would enter her . . . she would hear him . . . they might come face to face. His thought went blind as if his eyes had been hit.

An awful premonition of a second disaster, another fatality, came upon him.

Unless he took her into his confidence, made her lie low when Allan came . . . He realised that he knew nothing about her, had no idea how she would react, what she might do, driven beyond herself, where she might go, what she might say in a wild distress beyond reason.

Quiet women – it came back like an infernal story, a joke from women-troubled days – were the worst when they broke loose. He had not been able to speak to her about Allan, about what she had done. He couldn't. And what would she say even if he did? What could she? The thing was done. The rest was a horrible curiosity.

And now the true nature of the dreadful situation began to come at him, all the thoughts he had avoided, by using his prostration and the trick of going from one happening to the next, rising starkly before him.

If she had any feelings for Allan still, if some blind instinct had pushed her towards the croft even to be in Allan's wake, how utterly inconceivable that anything could come of it but some sort of horror! It would have been bad enough and impossible enough if she had simply betrayed Allan, because Allan was the kind of fellow whose very nature would not let him forgive. He could never have taken her as she was even had there been no crime. Men and women had been known to overlook, to forgive, though with what ultimate results heaven knew. But Allan was not of that kind. He had always been too swift, too sheer, like the otter in the pool . . .

But it was no such simple case. She was carrying the bairn of the man he had murdered. This rose as a stark, dreadful cry in the hollow of Sandy's mind.

When darkness fell she lit the lamp and drew down the blind. Quietly she went about preparing the kitchen for the night, pushing the table towards the head of his bed, placing within reach of his arm the lamp, the box of matches, the sleeping tablets, the drinking jug.

He had wondered what she would do when night fell. Would she sit at the fire mending or reading through one quiet hour and another?

But he could see she was not going to do that. Some instinct made her avoid it. The day's work was done and she was going to her room.

There was a rightness, a delicacy, in this that touched him.

'Good night,' she said.

'Are you off already?'

'Yes.'

'Very well. Good night.'

And now the kitchen was empty of her and he could listen to its quiet space and to the quiet spaces of the night outside.

He had better get rid of her before anything terrible happened. That was going to be difficult now, he thought. Why had he kept her? He could have got rid of her today easily enough. The doctor or nurse might have had some reasonable idea of what to do with her, of some place or other where she could have been sent . . . What place?

The instinct or faculty beneath rational thought asked the question bitterly. 'She is an outcast,' it said, and he saw its sharp eyes as those of an alien being inside him. 'She is an outcast, and she knew you would take her in.'

It was true. He realised that his sort of kindness was nothing but a terrible weakness, nothing but an indulgence. Bitterness pricked at him until his legs would not lie still. He reached out for the small round carton of sleeping tablets and swallowed two and drank and wiped his mouth.

It was shortly after that, when he was in sleep's borderland, that he had a particularly horrible vision with much of the sharpness of a pure hypnagogic illusion. She got to know that Allan was alive. She had a hankering after him. Then out in the barn she had her child, and in order to put herself on Allan's level she murdered it.

SEVENTEEN

'You would think it was the New Year,' said the widow as she and Liz Murison laden with goods from Danny's van entered the kitchen the following forenoon. 'Are you throwing a party or what?'

'Is it yourself?' said Sandy.

'Who's going to eat all this bread?'

'You remind me of the time long ago when the Campbells were up in Caithness raiding Wick. They brought back hundreds of bottles of whisky and one loaf. "Who's going to eat all that bread?" asked their chief.'

Sandy could see she was in good fettle. More than that: Liz Murison was in her tail. For whatever reason, she had taken her stand with regard to the girl. She had arranged her own kind of battle in the wide sweep of personal and public affairs. 'Have you your specs?' she asked.

Liz brought them from the dresser.

'Go out and see to the hens,' said the widow, dismissing her shortly, and without a word Liz went.

She fixed the spectacles on Sandy and then handed him a folded newspaper. 'Do you know anyone there?'

Sandy looked at the photograph of Widow Macleay standing in her own door with a merry laugh on her face. 'If it isn't you to the life!'

'Don't you think the laugh spoils it?' Her tone was off-hand but he caught the undernote of anxiety.

'Spoils it! It's the making of it.'

'I'm not so sure.'

'Hah!' said Sandy. 'You might like to think of yourself as a hard woman, but the camera has found you out, not to mention the newspaper man.'

'That fellow!' declared the widow. 'Wait till I get my hands on him!'

'Why?'

'Look at what he said.'

Sandy's eyes glanced over more than two half-columns with the photograph nestling in their midst. 'Not all this?'

'Read it!'

Sandy twisted his head to get the light better on the print and began to read. The opening paragraph had its reference to the countryside where a notorious crime had so recently been committed and the alleged criminal had so mysteriously disappeared, but after that direct link-up with public interest the writer had gone on to his interview with Mrs Jemima Macleay, who not only was a crofter but as the interview, with question and answer, showed in no mean manner was also a satirist and a wit. After the first paragraph Sandy's brows smoothed and then his cheeks wrinkled and then his mouth laughed.

'Well, well, you had him there!' he declared and tried to get the light still more directly on the print.

'I never said half of it,' declared the widow.

'You said far more,' Sandy reckoned, 'only he would have to go canny for libel.'

'I'll admit I was in a dither till I finished it,' said the widow. 'I have had a narrow escape. And him egging me on.'

'And eating your eggs at the same time.'

'The young rascal! I'll never live it down.'

'They'll have you on the Agricultural Executive next.'

'Oh, be quiet!'

'"Hilton folk like other city folk are good at the cackling,"' read Sandy aloud, '"so are our hens, but the hens lay eggs for-bye."' Sandy nodded. 'Tersely put.' He put down the paper to wipe one eye, then resumed. '"They think,"' read Sandy, '"that a hen crosses the road to get to the other side. Farther than that their intelligence doesn't go."' Sandy nodded again. 'Shrewdly expressed. "Even a hen that lays away lays an egg."'

'Oh stop it!' she said and her body gave a small twist as if it would tie a knot in itself.

And Sandy had to stop for laughter hurt him. 'You have upheld the crofters' end whatever. So many of them think the heather grows between our toes.'

She smoothed back the wing of hair in a modish way.

'And he has done it well,' declared Sandy. 'You can see he is on your side. Did you give him two eggs?'

'Three,' she said, 'and a dozen away with him. He wanted to pay for the dozen, but I told him I wasn't selling. After he had gone I found five shillings on the table.'

'Good lad!'

'You think it's not too awful?'

'It's splendid. And the photograph is beautiful.'

She borrowed his spectacles and had a tenth look at the photograph herself.

'You should send a copy to your brother and his family in America and your daughter in New Zealand,' said Sandy.

'Danny said he would get me two or three more.'

'What did Danny say about it?'

'It's a wonder you didn't hear him laughing here. I was watching for him because I was wanting to be at the van at the same time as Liz Murison so that whoever was there would have me to reckon with. I thought it would make it easy for the lassie.'

'That was thoughtful of you.'

'Hach!' said the widow. 'I might have saved my pains, for foolish as the paper may be it banished all else.'

It would,' said Sandy. 'So Liz managed fine?'

'Danny was waving the paper at me like a flag and indeed to tell the truth when I saw it I got such a shock I forgot all else. While I was trying to make head or tail of it, the lassie was getting her messages. Then she came down with me and my messages till I could get my specs and see it right and read it. And then I came back with her. And here I am, and I can well believe now the world is going round as the old geography book said.'

'When I get on my feet tomorrow I'll put you up for the County Council.'

'Tomorrow! And here I am forgetting even to ask how you are.'

'You're my best tonic. I'll be about in a day or so, and the thought of the lassie's condition has been bothering me a bit. To tell the truth I was wondering if you couldn't take her now – or find some place where – where—'

'Where what?'

'At a time like this she needs a woman near her. She can't know much about – about what she should do and that. I would feel better if she had someone like yourself beside her just now.'

'I'm looking at you,' said the widow. 'I don't mind telling you that once or twice I saw the grey look in your face. I think now good nursing will see you round the corner. The lassie will be fine for a month or so. The sickness has left her and she's strong and able. Nurse and myself talked it all over, and it seemed more than strange that she should have come here in her need to help you in yours. As the minister says: the ways of Providence are inscrutable.'

Sandy's hand groped about the coverlet, and his mouth groped for a word.

'Your arm itself will be slung for three weeks,' continued

the widow, smoothing the paper on her lap with an involuntary caressing gesture. 'How could you milk Nancy for one thing? But apart from what you can't do, you won't have the pith to do what you can, not for a time.' Her voice caught a lighter note as she added, 'We're not going to have the hens coming in and laying in your whiskers. So compose yourself and be grateful. When it comes near her time I'll see the lassie through even if – if it means another newspaper.' She got up. 'I have an awful feeling I left the front door open and I have two hens yonder that would find a sweetie-biscuit supposing you left it under your pillow.'

The more Sandy thought it over through the long afternoon the more clearly he saw there was no possible way of countering the widow, short of simply dismissing Liz, sending her away now. And even if he screwed himself up to doing that – which he knew he could not do – it would appear so inconsiderate even brutal an act that the widow, the nurse, the doctor, everyone, Nicol the policeman, would be bound to wonder just what was behind it. Either the old man is going wrong in the head, they would say, or he's hiding something. And the notion of 'hiding' would at once evoke the mysterious disappearance of Allan.

I could not have tied myself up more completely if I had tried, thought Sandy bleakly.

Depression settled down on him grey as a mist on a bleak moor. Was it today they were burying old Murdo? He saw the scene in the graveyard and thought that at least Murdo was through with his troubles and at rest. Death had that justice. It was the final act of kindness. The irrevocable movement of the invisible hands.

So far away in his mind that he could not get near it was his vision of passing away in the hills. Illusion. Illusion. As the light dimmed in the window, the thrush began singing on the rowan tree. Never had he heard such an urgency of song. The world rang with it, but he could neither go with it nor leave it, neither be moved by it nor yet not be moved. So near mockery that it was heavy and sad with despair.

Was it the song of some glory that had been intended? he wondered. Intended, but somewhere lost. And as he wondered he got lost, and the song took him and he asked the blind powers that did not hear him why the song should be, and the glory behind the song, and its outpouring in such urgency.

Mystery. That was the last word, the word you came to at the end. No corner of its coverlet could you lift. Man's stoicism was not a creed, only his last attitude. He went without finding out. He went into the darkness.

Far away indeed was the glimmer he had seen among the hills, the lifting of the mystery in the experiencing moment, the mist lifting before the sun, the world revealed.

That evening as they ate their supper he thought of asking her about Allan, asking what had gone wrong. But he could not bring himself to do it, hadn't the energy, did not perhaps care enough. Besides, he hardly knew the lassie yet. She would break down.

But the thought remained with him and the following morning after the nurse had gone and Widow Macleay remained behind to give him all the news about the funeral, he found an opening after the widow had said that Mr Davidson was coming to see him soon.

'To see me?'

'And put up a prayer for you, though according to the doctor you're past praying for now.'

'How that?'

'Because you're on the mend. All that sleep and dozing of the last day or two was the bottom of the depression.

You're pulling out, though you may well feel weaker than ever, he says. The nurse is pleased with you.'

'Mr Davidson may pray notwithstanding,' said Sandy. 'And that makes me wonder: will he want to pray also for the lassie?'

'What? . . . He might! And I've seen that face of his set like sour milk. Men! That poor weak thing.'

Weak? She seems strong enough to me.'

'She's a hefty lump of a woman, but soft as putty. When I think of the way that fellow who fathered her bairn got round her . . . but what's the good of talking now?'

'You asked her?'

'What do you think I have a tongue in me for? A quarrel! Allan and herself had a quarrel! Could you better it? God bless me! He turned on her because the fellow Robert had seen her home from a dance that Allan couldn't get to at the last minute and it seems there were tongues that wagged. As if tongues ever did anything else! And one thing led to another and Allan got flaming mad and blistered her, and she didn't take it from him either, and they broke off. Shortly after that he left the garage in Hilton and Robert had her on the rebound in a clear field. Don't talk to me,' concluded the widow, 'it makes me tired.'

'What sort of fellow was this Robert?'

'His mother's pet. Never stuck to one job for more than six months, nothing good enough for him, full of airs and smiles, seemingly, with new clothes bought out of the pound he made now and then playing the big melodeon in the local dance band. Danny said he had a taking way with him!'

The smile rose to Sandy's face despite him.

'Did he offer to marry her?' he asked.

'Offer! He would offer her the world – next month, or the month after – when the grand job he was expecting came round the corner. Then his mother took a hand. She was bitterly against him marrying her and then – but why should I dirty my mouth? – then his mother asked if he was the only one who had been there, if he was sure he was the father.'

Sandy's head fell back.

'I may be easily misled,' said the widow, 'but I know that lassie and I saw the look she gave me, poor thing. If Robert's mother is needing the doctor now, it's no wonder.'

Silence fell between them for a little while. The widow had closed the kitchen door and Sandy heard no sounds from outside.

'I have sometimes wondered,' said Sandy, 'why she came here.'

'You're not the only one,' replied the widow. 'The talk there's been about Allan coming here, poaching – I need not begin on that. You'll have heard it from Nicol the bobby – who has the same mother as the murdered Robert. If the boys ever got anything from field or river they shared it, as you and I know. There are some who forget that. Of anything they ever caught, there was never sold as much as a rabbit's scut.' She was restless and her head turned to the window. 'There's no doubt she has a hankering after Allan.'

'Still, you think?'

'Still. It's not the kind of thing that's killed by a quarrel, more's the pity.'

'I wondered.'

'There was all that talk about Allan coming here not only in past days but after he had committed the crime. The kind of man *you* are is known. You had your accident and she was drawn.'

'But surely she wouldn't have come if she thought there was any chance of meeting Allan face to face?'

'Don't ask me,' said the widow. 'A woman can become so doited and throughother that she hardly knows what she's doing, I'm sorry to say. She might run a mile to avoid him – and hope she would meet him at the end of it.'

'But how could she expect to meet Allan here? Surely the police have searched every—'

'Yes, yes. She doesn't expect to meet him. Yet it's like meeting him all the same – or as near as comforts her a little in the awful burden she has to bear. But you won't understand that and I don't blame you.'

'I can't see how she could expect Allan to do anything but hate her, considering what she brought him to. Surely—'

'Ay, ay,' interrupted the widow with some impatience. 'But that's not the way things work.' She looked at Sandy. 'Why do you think Allan killed Robert?'

'Well,' said Sandy, 'he would be angry with Robert—'

'Angry my old shoe,' said the widow. 'If he had not cared for the lassie he would have been glad to be rid of her, and would have laughed at her being caught. Served her right! he would have thought. You should know what men are like.'

'You mean Allan still cared for her?'

'Ah me!' and the widow breathed heavily over man's elementary obtuseness. Then she said flatly, 'Yes.' But after a moment she thought she might as well try to make the deeper implication clear. 'He cared for her *and she knew it*.'

'How? I understand he never even saw her when he came.'

'No.' But she could forgive the old man; she could have great forbearance with such as he. 'Liz Murison is a kind quiet girl, the sort that endures. I could never maybe have much patience with her myself, but I know her sort. They say still waters run deep. They say many a thing. Hmf! But down in the depth of that lassie the desperate deed Allan did was like a great cry to her. She knew then.'

The invisible hand, that touched Sandy's thought sometimes, touched the house now.

'You would think I had nothing to do,' said the widow, breaking the silence and briskly getting up. But she lingered as if what she had said was still upon them.

'You make me wonder,' said Sandy vaguely, 'what would happen if two such people ever did meet.'

'He would probably kill her, too,' said the widow. 'But we should be thankful we haven't that to worry about,' and with a firm grip of her newspaper she took her departure.

EIGHTEEN

The widow's words remained with Sandy through the afternoon. Allan would come in the early part of the night, if he was able to come. Sandy remembered the cough, the pallor of the unshaven face, the suggestion of fever. If only he didn't come for a night or two, Sandy might well be on his feet, and then it would be easier to deal with him, to let him in with caution and see him out. But he knew Allan would come tonight, though on his hands and knees.

When Liz was out attending to the day's last chores, including the milking of the cow, Sandy made his effort to get up. He was not going to be beaten easily. It was a slow deliberate process, full of pauses, but when at last he was on his feet and his left side gave way altogether, he fought back slowly into bed like a blinded warrior, the spark of will sheltering itself cunningly, refusing to be blown out. Once more on his back, he let go and sank a mile.

He came to himself in a stillness and saw Liz standing between him and the faded daylight. Shadows were in the kitchen, the quietness of early evening on the world.

'What is it?' he asked.

'I saw someone – up on the edge of the trees.'

It seemed to him that his heart stopped in the hollow where all was stopped. 'Who?'

'I think it was Nicol the policeman.'

His heart began thudding. Allan had come into his head.

That it should be Nicol was bad enough, but at least it wasn't Allan seeing Liz.

'Nicol,' he said. 'He'll be spying again.'

She neither answered nor moved.

'Never mind,' muttered Sandy. 'If he comes, you stick to your own room. I won't let him bother you.'

She went to the fire and began making it up. His own simple words remained in his mind, for he suddenly saw where they led. Even at that moment it seemed very remarkable to him, confirming what had happened more than once before, with its strange suggestion of mystery or magic: the opening of the unexpected door. He could use her sight of Nicol to cover the coming of Allan.

'Nicol has come here before in the darkening, creeping in quietly and whispering,' he said, gaining strength. 'Don't come out of your room whatever you do. I'll fix him.'

Her movements had stopped while she listened.

'I think he's going a bit wrong in the head that fellow,' Sandy added with a husky sarcasm. 'Though maybe it's only his stomach, for I doubt if he gets fed properly. Now and then I've given him some food to take away with him. I think he just likes to have a talk with me. Everyone has a burden of some kind.'

She did not answer and he looked at her on her knees before the fire. Sometimes he was tired of her and of everyone, longing to see the last of them, if only to lie in complete peace with the silence about him and the extension of space into which his spirit could wander. But sometimes an emotion rose in him with a poignancy sharp as it had been in his youth or boyhood, as though the intervening period of full manhood, whose egoism obscured the sharpness, had never been. As he looked at Liz Murison, he was suddenly moved by some essential picture of life too deep for him to comprehend, yet in some measure comprehended, too. There was more compassion than cunning in the simple question that asked her if she slept well.

'Yes,' she answered.

'I'm glad of that. Go you to sleep and don't be frightened that anyone will be let into your room. I'll see to that.'

'Thank you,' she murmured.

His heart was moved. 'I don't know what I would have done without you. And I haven't even talked to you yet about paying you for your work, but we can settle that once I'm on my feet.'

She got up. She made a curious impulsive turn, an almost animal movement, towards the window. 'I don't want anything.'

'We'll see about that. Don't you distress yourself, like a good girl. And look, when I'm at it – if Nicol does come quietly tonight I wouldn't say anything to anyone. What happens here is our own concern. Rumours and gossip weary me sometimes. That's all, and I won't say it again. You can sleep in peace.'

'You're very good to me.'

'Nonsense! It's you who are good to me.'

'Oh no!' she said, and fought hard to keep her emotion back. Quickly she left the kitchen.

As he listened for her weeping he heard footsteps. 'Is there anyone in?' called the high voice of Mr Davidson the minister.

'Come in!' cried Sandy.

'Well, well, well,' said Mr Davidson, stooping as he shook the extended hand. 'The Milton bull was one too many for you, I hear, but you *will* argue. How are you now?'

'Ready for another argument. Please take that chair.'

'Impenitent. The leopard and his spots.' Mr Davidson

got the chair where he wanted it and sat down, putting his hat inadvertently on Queenie's head instead of on the floor. 'Tut! tut!' he said, and put his hat on the table. 'News of your accident was late in reaching me, and what with presbytery meetings, births, marriages, funerals, and education meetings, I have been delayed, though, as I sometimes said to my conscience, I could hardly look upon you as one of my flock.'

'Perhaps I have you there,' replied Sandy, 'for there is no one I would sooner have as my shepherd.'

'You always had the word. I'll say that,' said the minister with his dry but not ill-pleased smile. 'Did you feel as near your latter end as that, then?'

'Near enough,' said Sandy, and added, 'near enough for the thought that if I was worth having a final word said over me, you would be the one to say it.'

Their eyes held for a moment, then the minister nodded. 'Very well,' he said simply.

'Thank you,' said Sandy.

'And now,' said Mr Davidson, 'begin at the beginning.'

As Nancy charged through the gate and laid Sandy low, the minister shook his head. 'Sex. That's the word they use nowadays. A powerful dynamo, they say.'

'It pulled the arm out of me, bruised my right side, and left me incapable of biting my thumb,' Sandy admitted.

'The outward manifestations of the inward riot,' said the minister with a grim satisfaction. 'They wouldn't believe me. They think I'm old-fashioned and don't see their smiles. But I see them all right. Oh yes. Sex and blood and brutality: that's what you want to introduce, gentlemen, to the young, I told them.'

'Who?'

'The worthy members who administer education nowadays. Films for the schools! You'll start showing them how

Blood Hunt

a bee sucks honey, I told them, but will you end by showing them how the drones are murdered and the working bees flail themselves to death in three weeks, and if so with what object?'

'Ah!' said Sandy.

'I translated the parable for them,' said the minister. 'Moreover, I told them I had made it my business to see films when I was last at the Assembly in Edinburgh. I saw one and it made the hair stand on my neck, and my teeth gnashed, and the poison of violence ran about my gums. If it had that effect on me, what will it have on our godless youth! for I have that to which it can be related, but they have nothing.' He shook his head. 'We should know the truth, they answered me. Truth! I said to them; even Pilate asked: What is truth? Perhaps you can answer that question where Another was silent. That's what happens in the world, they said to me. And I answered them in their own doggerel: You're telling me.'

'Was that in Edinburgh or before the local Education Committee?'

'Both,' answered the minister.

'I wonder, Mr Davidson, if it would be too much trouble to you, but there seems to be no one in at the moment and if you opened the kitchen dresser there you should find a bottle of cordial. It's the doctor's orders that I must fortify myself occasionally.'

'Hm. I hope you are not overtaxing your strength.'

'On the contrary.'

The shelves of the dresser were so laden that Mr Davidson had to get to his knees. 'You don't,' he said at last, hauling forth the whisky bottle, 'mean this?'

'That's exactly what I mean,' answered Sandy. 'And if you accompanied me it would be an honour. Illness has its trials.'

Under Sandy's direction the minister found two tumblers and presently he was in a position to hope for Sandy's early and complete recovery. Sandy reciprocated the compliment, and in this spirit they toasted a mutual good health, using the Gaelic *Slainte mhath* which gave a fulness to the flavour.

'As I was saying,' began Mr Davidson – and paused.

'Go on,' said Sandy respectfully.

'I thought I heard someone.'

As they listened, Sandy threw the minister a look.

'I may have been mistaken.' Then Mr Davidson looked at Sandy. 'Is it true that the woman Liz Murison is staying here with you?'

'You didn't meet her on your way?'

'No.'

'She may have gone to Mrs Macleay's, otherwise she might have made you a cup of tea.'

Mr Davidson looked at Sandy for several seconds. 'How did you come to have her in your house?'

'She just arrived,' replied Sandy. 'It was late one night, too late to turn her from my door.'

'Did it not occur to you that you could send her home?'

'It's the last place she wanted to go to.'

'And you countenanced that? Had she not been the cause of enough sin and crime already? Sex and sin and murder. If we cannot deal with it on our own doorstep, how can we expect to cleanse the stables of the world?'

The minister's pulpit voice had the carrying power of a corncrake's and Sandy thought of Liz in the next room.

'It would need more than one broom indeed,' Sandy replied in a light voice that was meant to be serious but hopeful.

'You treat the matter without the deep consideration it demands, my friend. I am sorry to say I am disappointed in you. When her father spoke to me I said I could hardly believe it of you, and would not until I spoke to yourself. So you are keeping her here instead of sending her back to her father, a worthy man and a deacon in the church, who is anxiously waiting to receive her?'

'If he is as anxious as all that, he is better able to come for her than I to go with her,' replied Sandy, with a firm mildness.

'Did you order her back?'

'When she came I was at a low ebb, and she nursed me, and fed me. Any orders going were the doctor's orders. I can but refer you to my worthy neighbour, Mrs Macleay, who helped me so much, a kind woman whose discourse is often edifying and always to the point, and I earnestly hope you will call upon her before going home.'

'Hm.' Mr Davidson stretched for his glass, as Sandy had done. They finished their drams simultaneously. 'Ha-a-a! The rigour of the true argument is not in you. You sometimes move like a serpent in the heather, my friend. I have noticed it before now.'

'I was born in the heather. What could you expect?'

'I cannot emulate your tone in so desperate a matter. Its implications extend too far. We have to take a stand, and that on the most difficult of all places, our own doorstep. I must talk to this unfortunate young woman. Someone must show her her duty – such duty as is still left to her. When will she be back?'

'It's not easy to say,' replied Sandy.

'Hm. Time is getting on. My housekeeper has a strong sense of duty when it comes to meal times.'

'Women are often difficult,' murmured Sandy.

'Difficult enough. But if man does not take a stand on the great moral issues, woman never will. It's not in her nature. There are times when a woman has no more moral sense than a fly on the window pane.' His lips met grimly. 'We had a meeting, a particularly difficult meeting, no later than last night, when I fought over this very issue of sin and violence issuing from a godless vacuum, and when I got home, still greatly moved. I was informed – I was informed,' repeated the minister, 'that the potatoes were spoiled!'

'Potatoes!' breathed Sandy. It really was too much. He looked at the bottle.

'No,' said Mr Davidson firmly. 'I never taste when I am visiting.'

'But surely you don't look upon this as a visit.'

'You distract me,' said Mr Davidson. 'If they must have violence and blood and brutality, I said to them, if they must have fear in their picture houses to curdle their blood with satisfaction, then, I said, give them the fear of God.'

Sandy nodded. 'Either that or the love of Christ.'

With battle in his eye, the minister buttoned his coat and glared at Sandy.

'If you must go,' said Sandy, 'make it a small one for the road.'

Before Mr Davidson had finished, the inner meaning of his discourse attacked Sandy insidiously. For finally the whole social structure was based on the family, and if the whole Christian structure had a similar foundation, then so long as the sanctity of the family could be maintained by an overt act, that act should be performed. This young woman, who had wreaked such havoc, should be returned forthwith to the parents who were waiting to receive her and ready to fulfil their responsibilities before man and God.

'Do you mean – now?' muttered Sandy.

'Now!' said the minister. 'My car is at the roadside and I will deliver her to her parents.'

The cold sweat came pricking at Sandy's brow. He had only to call the girl from the next room. The temptation was so strong that his whole body gave a slow writhe, but in the desperate need for a little more time, for further thought, the writhe found direction towards the bottle which was beyond his reach. 'Wait a little – perhaps—' he muttered weakly.

'I can see you have been overtaxed,' said the minister, his voice falling to a human level. 'Let me assist you. If I have spoken strongly it is because I feel strongly.'

'Believe me, you have never uttered your deepest thought but it has moved me, and remained with me.'

'More than once you have said what has remained with myself, and, perhaps, in the silent watches – I hope I may do more than forgive you for your reference to the love of Christ, over-ready as it was. My fight is often a solitary one, and sometimes I have wondered if I have been moved more by the fight than the substance.'

'Never,' said Sandy. 'No, no. Someone must see man's duty and be prepared to act. I wish I had your strength and your firmness.'

He spoke with such sad sincerity that the minister was moved. They were both moved. The minister poured two small drops, more by way of token or communion than anything else. They looked upon the spirit in the glass, they looked at each other, and into their eyes came a remote gleam, a far recognition of their poor common humanity, of Sandy's pitiful weakness and of the minister's hopeless strength, and they nodded to each other with a politeness that was the foam of grace, and they drank all the spirit in one mouthful, quietly, as though it were wine.

'Let us pray,' said Mr Davidson.

It was a simple and noble intercession, and Sandy's vision travelled through the little window. Within his weakness his spirit was touched to wonder and to disquiet. The mystery had come to his bedside, strange as it was astonishing. For it had never truly been within his belief that the words could reach a listening ear. He was troubled, too, by his own duplicity, by that vague movement of an easy sympathy within him which could only bring disaster. Yet as he listened on, and even while he felt not a partaker in the higher communion, something of the minister himself was revealed, and Sandy looked at him and was with him, and was with him in far times and places, and he saw the toils in the human face as it struggled for beatitude. The old human story, but with this added now, as though it were revealed to him for the first time, that the communion was between man and man, that here the veils had first to be removed, the husks shed, the cocoon broken, before the spirit could take wings. 'I bring you this new commandment,' said the minister, and paused, as though somehow words that Sandy had dropped so lightly stole now upon him unawares and troubled him. There was a short silent travail of the spirit, then humbly, yet not too humbly, the minister repeated the most revolutionary saying the world had yet heard: 'I bring you this new commandment: love one another.'

Their manners were now quietly distant, like men who had met in another place, and the minister seemed taller than he had been as he looked down on Sandy and shook his hand.

'You need all the nursing you can get. I will think things over,' he said.

'Thank you,' said Sandy.

'You have humbled me sometimes, my friend, but if so you are the only one.' As the minister smiled his features caught an oddly fighting twist as though he had been strengthened for future combats with the heathen.

'You heap coals on my head,' murmured Sandy.

'A few may do you no harm,' said the minister with a humour drier than good peat. 'God be with you.'

'And with you,' responded Sandy.

NINETEEN

That was the last chance, Sandy thought after the minister had departed. I could have called her and she wouldn't have dared not to go with him. I could then have had the house to myself, Allan would have come, I could have given him the suit, all the clothes he needed, all the money we could find, a bag of food, warned him about Nicol's search of the hills, told him to take his way to whatever was waiting for him in this life.

The inner ironic spirit with the alien eyes glanced at him: you would then have been free of him.

Yes, I would then have been free of him, replied Sandy, and felt profoundly depressed.

What – what's wrong with me? he cried silently, and wiped his brow.

We don't want to love one another, he cried. Words! Words! I only want to be left alone.

He thought of the girl in the next room who must have heard every word the minister had said, and he did not care. He had no desire to speak to her now. He hoped she would not come in.

In a little time she came in to make the evening meal, but he was heavy and tired and did not pay much attention to her. Then it seemed to him that she moved through the faint dusk with the dumb fatal preoccupation of one whose mind is made up. It was very quiet in the kitchen. Outside the thrush started his evening song. As she drew the fire under the kettle she stared at the flame.

He had nothing to say to her and would say nothing. 'The minister was in,' he said.

'Yes,' she replied very quietly.

'I suppose you heard him,' and his tone could hardly be less interested.

'Yes.'

She hadn't a lot to say! He threw her a glance and saw Queenie's eyes upon her with the bright expectancy that has the notion of food behind it. The dog seemed to have taken to her.

'Is Queenie behaving herself?'

'She's very good,' she answered. As she looked at Queenie, a faint warmth touched her face, a recognition, like colour running deep into a flower. But it was hedged about, contained far down, by some element of being that had had to live inwardly a long time.

'That thrush is a strong singer,' he said in a factual way that didn't exactly blame the bird.

As her face turned to the window he saw the distinct glisten, the reflection, of light in her eyes. She had good features. Each bone had finished its own sweep in its slow smooth way as though the nature she had been given could not interfere with it. So many girls had taut pert features. She obviously had combed her hair for the minister. All at once he saw that she was beautiful, and yet in some way that moved him obscurely it was not her own beauty but the beauty that belonged to her as a young woman, as youth. It belonged to a region he had known, it went over the world. Generously it gave itself, moved by its very nature to give, and the world, being the world it was, landed it.

Now she had lifted a dish of scraps and was going out. The dog came behind her, went to her right side, her left side, did everything but get between her legs, for Queenie was a sensible enough bitch mostly.

I'm weak, thought Sandy. I have no more sense than a fly on the window pane. A useless futile kind of man if ever there was one, and now more than ever. It was enough to make him angry. It was. Angrily he muttered, 'Lord if I cannot be kind to a lassie like that, what am I here for?' And his eyes glared at the bloody phantoms around him.

The outburst made him feel hungrier than he had been for some time. And then he saw she was off her food, pretend as she would.

'Sometimes Mr Davidson rides a high horse.' This sudden remark of his struck even himself as almost amusing. 'It's a white horse,' he added, rather crisply laconic. 'A charger.' The vision of Mr Davidson on horseback seemed to inspire him. 'One of the horsemen of the Apocalypse,' he said: 'though I can hardly remember who they were. Do you?'

'No.'

'He should have been in the cavalry anyway,' Sandy concluded and lifted a spoonful of chicken broth with a firm hand. 'Very good,' he said of the broth. 'Was it Widow Macleay or yourself who thought I should have it instead of my tea?'

'You can have a cup of tea after.'

'Very good,' he said. 'A high horse and he sits it well, but a kind man and a good man, though I don't always let him off with it.' He was surprised to find how strong was the impulse within him to have a sharp thrust at the minister, and at more than the minister. He took two or three spoonfuls, then, while chewing a piece of bread, remembered: 'The man on the white horse was called Faithful. The very name!' He gave a husky chuckle, for now he remembered the next thing: 'He had a sword, and do you know where the sword came out of?'

'His mouth,' replied Liz.

'Exactly,' he said, more than pleased. 'Had you to read your bible, too, even Revelations?'

'Yes, when I was younger.'

Sandy's mouth opened on its own: 'You would have measles, too, and chickenpox.'

'Not chickenpox.' Her colour was rising.

'I had chickenpox,' he said, 'or was it whooping cough? The only thing I do remember was colliewoggles, for I thought I was going to die in a ditch. It was after eating green apples from the tree in the blacksmith's garden. The blacksmith was terribly proud of that tree. After our visit they say he sat under it every night with his big hammer.'

The smile welled up in Liz's face.

Sandy had a feeling of gaiety, of fighting gaiety, and it came to him from a world he hadn't been in for a long time.

'Do you know, Lizzie,' he said, 'I have the feeling that I'm round the corner.' His tone was surprised and confidential. 'It couldn't have been the minister?' Then he remembered and his voice fell a tone. 'Ah, it must be the dram!' He nodded, but with little diminution of the gleam in his eye. 'Eat up,' he said to her encouragingly. 'We mustn't let Faithful on his white horse be too much for us.'

His friendly words and manner troubled her and he saw she wanted to leave the table.

'What's on your mind now?' he asked sensibly.

Her fingers broke the crust of bread, then she lifted her head and looked at the dresser. 'I can go away.'

'Of course you can. I would never ask you to stay longer than you want.'

Her eyes came back to the fingers that nervously crumbled the crust. She couldn't add a word.

'When would you like to go?' he asked.

'I could go now.'

Silence held him despite himself. Between them all they were determined to give him his own way, to do what should be done, to send her off.

'Where would you go?'

After a moment she said, 'Somewhere.'

'Back to your home?'

'No,' she muttered.

'In that case aren't you as well here?' When she did not answer, he added quietly, 'I suppose you could not help overhearing the minister. But you're not staying with the minister, you're staying with me.'

'Don't want – to be – a trouble.'

'If that's all, lassie, you're none. Indeed you have been a very great help to me. What would I have done without you?'

'You're too kind.'

He saw the working of her features, the pressed lips, the wet blinking eyelids.

'Don't distress yourself, now. Stay if you would like to.'

'I don't know,' she said. 'I don't know what to do.' The last words rose nearly to a cry but she left the kitchen with the sob still choked down.

It was then that for the first time he entered into her world of desperation. He had realised her position clearly enough before but always against his own feelings, his own concern for himself and the quiet days he desired, for Allan and the queer need within him to set Allan on his way. Ultimately to see them all on the way – and out of his way; a selfishness almost pure because it was beyond even the stage of asking anything from anyone. But now he entered into her world and it was quick with the emotions of desperation, and he saw her turn this way and that, with no opening anywhere, with the awful past behind her, the closed doors, the door that forever swung shut upon her, face how she would, and the future that was no door but a terror. He heard a choked sound and knew she had smothered her mouth.

Life was a trap. She was caught. The jaws had got her. She was young and the fibres quivered. In her mind torment sat and hit blind hands against the nearest door.

He found suddenly that the face he was looking at was the face of Maria. Her dark eyes came close in the bloom of her young face and he saw the expression in their depths. Her recognition of him had an ineffable intimacy.

His head moved because he could hardly bear it. Normally he could remember her at odd times without any stress, for the past was awake behind the horizon. Often its most intense, most vivid moments could vanish altogether. Even the worst storms were forgotten – or recalled for the sake of a story, like the story he had told the doctor.

Now he could see Maria's eyes when he wasn't looking at them, as if she were standing in the shadow to his right, though he was staring through the window.

Presently he realised it was dark and he wondered if Liz was still in her room or if she had gone quietly out while his thought had been on its travels. It must be getting late; the days were lengthening. She could not have gone away altogether! He hearkened for a while, then he called her name.

She came in from the next room.

'It's dark,' he said.

'I thought you were asleep.' It was her excuse, but she was composed again, with the earlier blind drag upon her.

After lighting the lamp, she cleared the table and washed up, then tidied the kitchen for the night.

'We have had a disturbed evening,' he said at last, 'and we could both do with a good sleep, but I may be troubled yet. You didn't see that fellow Nicol again?'

'No.'

'He'll wait for a bit, I expect.' His voice did not relish the prospect of the visit, though prepared to accept it. 'So I'll not take my sleeping pills just yet.'

When she had the table ready for the night, she asked if there was anything more she could do.

'There is,' he said. 'I wish you could have a good sleep.'

'I'm fine.'

'You'll worry over that man on the white horse. I know you.' He turned his eyes to the table. 'Open that wee boxie and take out two. That's right. Leave them there. Now take out other two and drink them down with a drop of water.'

She hesitated.

'Do as I tell you,' he said kindly but firmly. 'While you are under my roof I am looking after you, and no one will dare to interfere with you. Go ahead now.'

She swallowed the two sleeping tablets.

'That's more like the thing.' He nodded, satisfied with her. 'Put everything out of your mind and let sleep take you. I hope you will stand by me till I am on my feet anyway. After that – we'll see. Goodnight, sleep well, and thank you for your kindness to an old man.'

'Goodnight,' she said.

Something soft in her voice, warm with unspoken gratitude, touched him, and as she left the kitchen, carrying the lit candle before her, a warmth of gentleness welled up behind his own eyes. That such emotion should touch him so easily made him realise once again how weak and foolish he was, but he said to himself, 'Well, well, what does it matter?'

Men traded in vanity very easily, but when life came down to rock bottom there did not seem to be an awful lot to be vain about. Not a great deal, thought Sandy, his mind beginning to lift from Liz Murison to what might be happening outside the croft, to eyes that might now be watching the light in the girl's room.

That Allan and Nicol could come into collision was not so very unlikely, at any rate until Allan knew of Nicol's latest obsession about finding the body. From a hill-top anywhere near the lily loch, a good pair of eyes could cover a vast stretch of country, and as the days went by Allan would tend to take chances. It was the off season for the hill: no fishing, no shooting or stalking. Even the ewes would be down on the low ground and the heather-burning over. A fellow would find it hard to lie up all day like a dog in a kennel, with nothing but his dark thoughts for company, particularly as the dusk began to fall and he knew that no one would then be on his way into that wild country. He could swim ashore and get into the cover of the small birches that bordered the burn which entered the loch. He would probably guddle trout there to boil in his tin. If the cold water hadn't killed him by this time.

However, things tended to take their own shape if you gave them the chance. If he got Allan safely away tonight, then by the time he would return in three or four days, he himself would be on his feet, and once on his feet it would be easy to get the tweed suit and other things that had occurred to him – soap, the old hollow-ground razor which must be somewhere . . .

In the midst of his contrivances came a lull and this lull was invaded by a horrible thought. A flush of heat went over his body and the blood-beat thudded in his ears. In his vision, Nicol's face was thinner and darker, the face of the obsessed hunter, the remorseless face that would find its prey. He had come out from the trees to get a proper look at the croft. Why? He must be off duty. Should he appear now while Allan was in the kitchen, Allan would fight him, both would fight to the death . . .

The night was silent. From far down by the river came the thin screech of an owl. Queenie's head was on her paws and did not move.

As turmoil ebbed, his mind wandered vaguely, then paused upon a brightly lit scene in a hollow near the loch of the lilies. It was his first autumn in the croft and as he walked across the strip of grass he saw a rabbit stirring sleepily on the edge of the heather. In his astonishment he stood still and realised there was something wrong with the beast. It looked drunk. As he approached, it turned from him and he saw a round red spot behind its head about the size of a florin. It tumbled stupidly. Out from the heather came a stoat and sat up, no more than four yards away, sniffing wickedly. Sandy lifted the rabbit, examined the round spot which was all raw flesh, without a trace of fur, not even bleeding. Then he killed the beast and thought, Well that's an easy way of catching a rabbit! But even while he grinned the complex of the wild had been so vividly in him that he had suddenly spat savagely at the stoat.

The time came when Queenie's head lifted, when she got up and looked at the window and looked at Sandy. She was uncertain, and Sandy quietened her with a frown and a low hiss.

He heard the scratch on the outside door. It was Allan.

'Come in!' he whispered, and Allan was there with the lamplight on his face. Queenie was sniffing at him, excited. He put down his hand and she licked it, the whine breaking through. Allan smiled, his pale face with its scrubby beard looking worn and desperate. He swayed slightly and Sandy motioned him to the bedside.

'I don't want you to stay long,' whispered Sandy. 'The housekeeper saw Nicol up by the birch wood today. He thinks you may have perished and is looking for your body.

So for God's sake be careful. Now listen. You'll get what food you need in the dresser. I'll be up in a couple of days or so. If you come back the fourth night from now, I'll have the suit for you and a razor, soap, and other things in a bundle behind the barn door under rubbish. It's not safe coming in here—'

Allan was suddenly assailed by a hacking cough which he tried to smother. He leaned against the bed, then stuck his face into the bedclothes. The spasm passed.

'The warm room,' he explained while his ears listened and his eyes roved. No hunted beast ever had that look.

'The cough is not settling on you?'

Allan shook his head. 'Thought I was done for. Water terribly cold.'

'Fever bad?'

'Burning – but not so bad now. Made a raft and paddled ashore.'

'What if someone sees it?'

'I'll paddle back in dark and take it to bits.'

'Had you a fire?'

Allan nodded. 'Old dried wood. No smoke. It was good!'

But all the time he was on the alert and now he glanced at the dresser. Unbuttoning his jacket, he unwound one of Sandy's potato sacks from his body.

Sandy motioned him to the dresser.

As he brought out each item of food he glanced at Sandy who kept up a whispered commentary lest by any chance Liz might be awake when to her listening ear silence would be more disturbing than quiet talk. There were no eggs because the housekeeper had been to the van in the forenoon, and no milk except what was in the milk jug. Take a drink of it,' said Sandy.

Allan hesitated. 'Anything to hold it?'

Sandy thought hard then shook his head.

But Allan was now probing into deep corners and produced one of the empty bottles which Sandy had brought from the barn and swilled out. He withdrew the cork and sniffed. A smile came into his eyes as he nodded. When he had half emptied the jug, he paused, but Sandy whispered, 'In with it!' When Allan held the bottle to the light it showed nearly half full. After that he fished out a tin of salt. This was clearly a find of importance and soon he had two or three tablespoonfuls in a screw of paper. His eyes were now very bright, and Sandy remembered the humoured brightness of past poaching nights. A touch of the old vivid reckless spirit rose in the lad as he swayed, yet noiselessly and with a sensitive hand stowed each item away.

'Any potatoes left in the pit?'

'Yes, but—'

'I won't leave a trace.'

Sandy swallowed. A premonition that they were now going too far, that disaster was being invited, came upon him.

'Better be off,' he whispered.

Allan gave the neck of the sack a twist and slung it quietly over his shoulder. 'What will you say to her?' he asked, coming to the bedside.

'That's all right. Don't worry.'

Allan nodded. Always the old man could be trusted to see beyond the event. 'I'll remember about the barn. Goodnight – and thanks.'

As he turned away Queenie was in front of him. He patted her head. 'Not tonight.' He threw a smiling glance at Sandy then gathered himself for a quiet exit.

Long after the outside door had closed, Sandy listened intently to the night. But no sudden riot broke the silence, no sound came from Liz's room. The lad had won away again.

It was like a miracle, like a hidden pattern of events happening quite simply within the large pattern that touched it everywhere yet remained unaware of it; like the dream that in its experience was everything, yet to the daylight was nothing.

As the whine broke in Queenie's nostrils he glanced at her, but saw at once that she was merely restless. Twice she turned after her tail on the rug before flattening with a distinct thump, the thump of disappointment, of discontent. And suddenly he realised that there was still another pattern: Queenie's exciting nights after the rabbits, the vivid scents, the moonlight, the hunting world of pure animal grace. To her, Allan meant that.

He swallowed his two sleeping tablets, screwed the wick of the lamp down until the flame flickered and went out, then pulled the bedclothes up to his neck. The sigh that went from him was heavy with exhaustion and he was soon fast asleep.

TWENTY

The following afternoon the doctor called and Sandy got up for half an hour. The day after he was up for two hours. On the third day he went to look at the world and found it good.

'I seem to have developed rheumatics all over,' he said to Liz.

'It will be the sore parts,' she suggested.

'May be so. Aren't the birds busy? Ah, look, yonder's two of the shepherd's sheep! A new hole in the fence somewhere. There's Williamina and she's laying.' He pointed his staff at an elderly fat tidy hen. 'She's one that lays away.'

'I don't think she's laying away.'

'Have you ever noticed how very innocent a hen looks that lays away?'

On the fourth day he was able to move around without too great an effort in hiding his discomfort. In the barn he got Liz to examine a tether which he used on Nancy for certain strips of open pasture, particularly a low ditch in the far east corner near the river where the grass came away early. When Liz was gone thither, he went into her room, took the suit from the chest and even found the old cut-throat razor among forgotten odds and ends of a past life that looked up at him from the chest's bottom. For a little time he looked back at them, then he searched the pockets of his best suit for cash and altogether managed to collect nearly five pounds. He had already walloped the dust out of a sack and presently stowed its bulging hemp under his own bed. He could add food after Liz had gone to rest.

No one called that day, not even Widow Macleay, but when supper was over and the kitchen tidied up a figure passed the window. Liz went hurriedly to her room and presently a voice called, 'How are you?' It was Angie, the cattleman from Milton. Sandy welcomed him and for a little while courtesies were on the wing.

'Ay, you're tough,' said Angie, sitting opposite Sandy, with his bonnet on his knee. 'The boss is always asking for you. Indeed everyone is always enquiring. But you have a watchdog yonder!'

'Who?'

'Widow Macleay. You'll have to be minding your step there!' Angie laughed.

'Do you think so?'

'Everyone had to go to her for the news. And they got more than the news often!' His head tilted and the laugh hit the roof. 'What a bar! I thought I must come and tell you.'

Sandy waited.

'The boss, as you know, is a hell of a man sometimes. Well, himself and Achdunie were on the way home from the sales with a fair shot in, for prices were good. You'll have seen the great article on the widow in the paper with her photograph an' all? Ay. Well, they had been talking about this and the boss decided, by God, they would call on her. So they worked out what they would say and then, solemn as judges, they drew up and went down to her door. The boss knocked and asked after her health and said they had called on important business and she invited them in. They spoke of the article in the newspaper and the great honour it was to the whole farming community. Then he said they had called as a deputation on behalf of all the farmers and crofters in the parish to ask her to stand for the County Council!'

'No!' Sandy laughed with Angie. 'Did she take the broom to them?'

'She did, but by this time both the boss and Achdunie had worked themselves up into believing what they said. By God, they said to her, they meant it. And the more she told them they ought to be ashamed of themselves to let whisky talk the way it did trying to make a fool of an old woman, the more they swore their intentions were honest. One outdid the other in telling how useless half the members on the Council were, until at last, whatever the widow may have suddenly thought in her own mind, she thanked them and said she would sleep on it!'

'Good for her!' cried Sandy.

'By God, she turned the tables on them!' Every time Angie hit his knee his bonnet fell to the floor and when he had exhausted his topic, he asked, 'Has Nicol the policeman been at you again?'

'He's been around, yes.'

'He's going queer, yon fellow. They say it's his mother. But, anyway, they're giving him holidays. And do you know how he's going to spend them? Looking for Allan's body!'

It was dark before the cattleman left. Liz had gone to bed. Half an hour later, Sandy hid the sack behind the barn door.

In the morning, after his cup of tea, he wandered down to the barn. The sack was gone.

At that moment some of his lost world came back upon Sandy in a swirl of freedom. Allan was away! Over the hills! He looked up the slope to the birch trees and westward to where the crest tumbled over into the loch of the water lilies. Beyond were mountain ridges sweeping round southward against a clean sky. The air was clean with a cool nip in it. Through the air went spring crying its own news that an ear could almost catch. How invigorating, the invisible that the eye could all but see! The peewits tumbled after it in hot chase. A gorgeous chaffinch on the rowan tree finished his remarks with characteristic abruptness and was off. Geordie, the cock, suddenly crew. What a wild and laughable bird! The neck stretched up and over until the feathers stood on it and the red wattles shook. Fantastic and valiant – with a dying fall into the abyss beyond the world, mournful beyond belief; a heraldic sound if ever there was one. Yet none was less impressed than Williamina the hen, a bird that with ardent eye and inquisitive beak would peck at rubies on the golden streets and know when she was cheated. Even when Geordie's wing came down and he siddled like a griffin, she only pecked harder than ever as if her time was short now. Which indeed it was.

Sandy lost his last ache. In the moment of freedom he saw life and the world as a blessed gift and stood at the heart of what seemed the creative intention. He knew the feeling quite well. It came back to him, like a memorable scent suddenly encountered, peat smoke or wild thyme, but, where the scent was tethered, it took wing. As his eyes lifted with it, they set Allan on his course over the hills and in that moment Sandy wished the lad well, through time and chance. No man gets away from his reckoning, but with luck he may learn how to face it.

Liz came out with a bucket of dirty water. As she stooped, pouring it into the drain, he looked at her and wondered if she was nearer her time than she had let on. A faint anxiety touched his blessed mood, and for the first time touched it not on his own account but entirely on hers. He turned away round the corner of the barn and stood looking up the slope in the direction of Milton. He liked the girl. She was quiet and sensible in her ways. In the last day or two she had spoken more naturally. However tight the knot in her mind, she kept it there. Never a complaint had she uttered so far, but on the contrary had appeared grateful for the roof over her head. Right enough, it would be a relief for her to be free of her father Farquhar's look, of the things he didn't say, and he would have said a few. And there was never a wife to a man like Farquhar but she got beaten down in the long run. Even if her mother had a mother's sympathy for Liz, putting it at the best, it would be mournful and hopeless. As a boy he had known one or two old women who could sit and sigh. In the end they perhaps got to like it.

There was something soft in Liz that touched the heart. That was the truth of the matter. And if he had helped Allan on his way there was no reason why he shouldn't help Liz on hers. Indeed it would give him considerable satisfaction. And the woman who would know just what to do for her in her trouble, where to put her or send her or what not, would be the widow.

At the thought of Widow Macleay, Angie's jocular words of warning came back and Sandy's stomach began to shake with mirth. She'll have to be wilier than she is if she's going to land me, he thought, and his regard for the widow in the midst of the thought never stood higher. Let her marry the County Council! Liz appeared and said, 'Your porridge is ready.'

Turning too quickly he stumbled. In a moment she had taken a step or two towards him and he saw the concern on her face. 'This old knee will take a day or two to jump a dyke,' he declared.

But as she went towards the house, she glanced back over her shoulder. She's making sure I'm able to follow, he thought, amusement in his eyes.

Sandy did not like his porridge too well boiled and he did not like it too hot. When it was firm on the spoon he

could dip it in the bowl of milk, and if the milk was laced
with cream, just enough to leave a skin on the spoon, then
the mouth knew that the porridge was not only palatable
but also a good food. In the old days when a poverty-
stricken crofter got this food morning and evening, he could
make do with what chanced between from a rabbit's haunch
to a hen's leg, mutton to mealy puddings, with kail and
leeks in the Sunday broth, an egg now and then, oatcakes,
flour scones and butter, and potatoes always in the pit. If
such iron rations, backed by a barrel of cured herring, with
the richer flavour of venison and salmon at an odd exciting
time, did not give the poor fellow enough energy to turn
the wolf from the door, then a drop of smuggled whisky
was a great and inspiring help.

All this and more, Sandy knew well. What he had
forgotten was what now came upon him, and what came
upon him this blessed morning was the porridge all ready
in the plate, with the bowl and spoon beside it upon a
clean cloth. By God, as Angie might well have said, he had
only to sit down to it. No wonder it was the man who had
always said grace before food. Trust him to take the credit,
before God.

But there was one thing more, and after the first spoonful
Sandy acknowledged it to himself not for the first time: Liz
could make better than he the kind of porridge he liked,
with the absolute certainty added that there would be no
lumps in it. If she erred at all it was perhaps in making the
milk just a shade too creamy. Though there again it was
the kind of fault that grew on one. As the porridge slid
past his tonsils on its creamy way, he said, 'I think I know
where the two sheep got in, and if you come up with me
we might tie the hole with a strand of wire.'

'Queenie and me found the place yesterday. They're
getting under the bottom wire of the fence.'

'Ah! Is that the place? Down from the gate?'

'Yes. I stuck a bit of stick in it – but it may not hold.'

'You'll soon know the place better than myself. You like working with the beasts and fowls?'

'Yes, I like it fine,' she said naturally.

A day or two ago she would have stopped at 'yes'.

'It's a quiet place here, and that's what I like it myself for.' He supped his porridge. 'You're teaching me bad habits.'

She glanced at him.

'It's this porridge,' he said. 'I have never tasted better. What on earth will I do when you leave me?'

The lashes fell over her eyes.

'Now, you listen to me, Lizzie. This is my house and this is my croft. While you need them you will look upon them as your home. You have your difficult time ahead of you, and your mind may not be easy often, but however desperate you may feel from one thing or another, always remember you have me and this place behind you. I won't say it again. But I would like you to remember it.'

Her fair skin had slowly flushed, and now a tear rolled down one cheek and then the other. She got up to attend to the kettle.

'We'll go and have a look at the fence,' he said, 'for you'll have to be my other arm till this one's out of the sling. Though indeed I don't think it needs the sling. It's just the doctor's way of tethering me.'

'Nurse said it, too,' murmured Liz to the fire.

'She would,' said Sandy to the plate he scraped clean.

As he stood in the barn with a piece of wire in his hand, his eyelids lowered calculatingly. He had only one last awkward bend to get round and the way to peace would be clear before him. There had been something in the lassie's face when she had turned away with the tears on her cheeks. Of course she would be easily moved just now and the tears were natural enough. But there had been something else, some glint of the wild tragic in her mind. God knows what she might do when it came to the birth, what strange hate or terror might boil up then. She was too quiet often. Ordinary human decency to her now might make all the difference in her time of trial or temptation.

Anyway it was a nice day. It was really a beautiful day. Queenie did more than renew her youth, she almost gambolled.

'She can hardly believe it,' said Sandy to Liz as they went on their way. 'Sticking round a croft door is enough to make a barker of any dog.' His eyes lit up. 'We're late with the seed, but it would have done no good in cold ground.' He was full of observations. When he paused to get his breath and ease his left leg, his eyes got a better chance to rove. At the second stop, his voice caught a fond note. 'Do you think there's a bonnier spot in the whole wide world?'

'I think it's beautiful.'

'Do you now?' He was delighted and gave a cheerful flourish with his stick as he tackled the slope again.

But before the mended hole in the fence he stopped, this time in solemn wonder. 'You didn't do that?'

'No.'

His head nodded slowly as he looked at the three slim sticks of hazel that went in and out the fence wires before disappearing into the earth. He caught one of them. A firm neat job. 'The shepherd,' he said. 'A neat-handed man if ever there was one.' He marvelled for a little time. 'Let us sit down.'

'Do you think you should?' she asked, for the earth was cold if not damp.

'I'll tell you what it is, Lizzie,' he said in the confidential tone of one revealing a business secret. He stretched out his legs and his toes fell sideways. 'The world has quiet decent people everywhere.' He nodded. 'The salt of the earth. And the earth needs its salt. I'll tell you a queer thing the shepherd told me no later than last month. We came on one of his sheep all by itself and pining away. It looks a queer mysterious disease, almost human, you would say. But what was wrong was nothing in the sheep, but the lack of a certain salt in the soil. When the right salt isn't there, life withers and dies. People can shout and spout and make all the fuss they like, but that's the simple truth at the heel of the day. The quiet decent people. The salt of the earth.' His eyes crinkled in humour, for he was talking a lot, but she was easy to talk to. 'Bless me, it's damp right enough!' he declared suddenly, pressing his palms on the ground.

He hadn't taken more than a few paces when he stopped. 'And if yon isn't Jimmy coming with the tractor! It's full steam ahead now! Come.'

For the next three days, Sandy was on the move most of the time. At night sleep overcame his aches without benefit of tablets. The doctor warned him, the nurse paid her last visit, and the widow flung more than a few pithy rejoinders at the tractor man who was inclined to provoke her. And it wasn't easy for the widow, for Jimmy, who hadn't a hundredth part of her wit, had only to say, 'You can tell that to the County Council.' Once, when he deliberately doubted the quality of the seed, she was goaded to a retort on his potential manhood that, far from silencing him, only shook him to a fundamental mirth. But to Liz Murison, Jimmy was as off-hand and natural as though she belonged to the place.

It was on the fourth night after Allan had taken the sack from behind the barn door that Queenie drew him back from the edge of sleep. His head lifted from the pillow.

'I saw your light going out.' Nicol's figure was scarcely discernible in the fire's smouldering eye.

'It's you, is it?' breathed Sandy. 'Light the lamp.'

As Nicol replaced the glass funnel, his face seemed not only thinner but darker in a disturbing avid way. He had taken the night in with him; and then Sandy realised that it was not the dark night outside, but the dark inner world in which the fellow now lived.

This impression grew stronger all through the exchanges of conversation and silence, for it was clear that Nicol had something on his mind, something secretive that he was nursing, some evidence about Allan that was ominous.

As apprehension touched Sandy he became more hospitable. Nicol stirred up the fire and placed the kettle on top of the glowing coals. All his actions were slow and deliberate.

At last Sandy asked, 'And what's taking you out here at this time of night?'

'I have been looking for his body.' As Nicol turned his eyes from the fire, Sandy met their dark gleam.

'His body!'

'In the darkening tonight I thought I recognised the place, but—' He was sitting on Sandy's chair.

'What place?'

'Beyond the loch where—' Again he did not finish his sentence, and the silence became monstrously charged.

'But surely you have something – something to go on?'

'I have,' said Nicol.

'Well, I suppose it's your business,' said Sandy after waiting for him to go on.

The note from the kettle grew higher and Sandy told him where to empty the teapot swill. Not until he had drunk some tea did Nicol come away with his 'conviction' that he would find Allan's body. 'I saw it quite clearly.'

'Did you?' said Sandy, accepting the 'vision'.

'The body was quite fresh.'

'It's a long time now.'

Nicol's expression narrowed in a sarcastic, sinister way. 'I might have thought that myself, but – I came on something.' The gleaming eyes were back on Sandy. 'You haven't seen him?'

'Seen him?' repeated Sandy, staring at Nicol. 'Surely you know I have been on my back for a long time?'

'I know that.'

'Well?' challenged Sandy.

'He got something out of this house.'

'This house? Are you talking in your senses or what?'

'I'm talking in my senses all right. You're not the only one in this house.'

'No,' said Sandy. 'But if you have anything to say against anyone in this house you better say it now.'

'I have only the evidence of what I found. How it came there I don't know, but it points to this house.'

'What did you find?'

Nicol hesitated, like a miser who could not bring himself to expose his treasure lest it be filched from him or transmogrified in some way.

'Listen to me,' said Sandy in a low firm voice. 'I have no wish to poke my nose into your business, but as an old man I would warn you for your own good to be very careful of what you say or do in the way of accusing anyone. How it happened that the girl in the ben room came to this house I can tell you exactly. She has suffered enough, and though I have helped you in every way I could, as you know, I cannot – and will not – have any vague accusations made against her now. I am completely satisfied in my own mind that whatever you may have found – and that's your business – she had nothing to do with.'

'Do you always leave your outside door unlocked at night?'

'Since my accident, yes, lest the doctor or a neighbour should call. The doctor has visited me late, and Mrs Macleay and others. Then I can call to them to come in, as I called to you.'

'But since – the girl – came here, couldn't she lock it?'

'Yes.'

Nicol's smile caught a slightly awkward scepticism that made it more sinister.

'You cannot imagine why I did not ask her to lock it?' asked Sandy.

'You could have,' said Nicol.

'Certainly.'

Nicol smiled again.

Sandy said to him, 'If the door had been locked when you tapped on it, she would have had to get up and open it *to you*. My God, cannot you understand that she is shy of meeting anyone?' He stopped for his voice had been rising, and his anxiety lest she might be overhearing what they now said suddenly stood in his face.

Nicol finished drinking his tea. He did not eat anything.

'Is that sleeping tablets?' he asked indicating the small round carton.

'Yes.'

Nicol rose. 'If they made you sleep deep, with an open door—' He smiled again as he stretched himself. 'Thank you for your tea. It was never anything against you. I know what I know.'

'That's about all any of us can know,' replied Sandy with the first touch of dry sarcasm in his own voice.

Nicol stood awkwardly for a moment, then he said 'Goodnight' and went out.

TWENTY-ONE

That night Sandy had to take his sleeping tablets but not before his mind had run ahead like a chess player's. It was quite possible, indeed it could be taken as certain, that Allan on his long trek to the Crannock would rest and open his sack and eat some of the fresh food. Even a piece of paper wrapping left behind on the heather would show up from a long distance. And with bad luck in the dark night he might have left more than a piece of paper. But when Sandy had gone over the total contents of the sack, he was satisfied that whatever Nicol had found could not be directly related to his croft. Every household had food, most of it bought from the same grocer's van. But even if there was something he could not think of, then it was still true, as Nicol had implied, that Allan or indeed anyone else might conceivably have come into the kitchen when he, Sandy, was sunk in his drugged sleep. What Nicol did not know was that Liz Murison had also taken sleeping tablets. Thus the case for the croft and the girl would be difficult to pierce. In fact, the whole affair would be simple and easy – *if Allan had gone away.*

There was the doubt that for a long time kept sleep from Sandy, and the more he turned it over, the more uneasy he felt. In the mind's last quiet watch on the plane that leads to the brink of sleep, when thought becomes vision and figures move inexorably, he saw Allan so clearly that even the lad's inmost impulse seemed to be laid bare. As its den to a fox so now was the Crannock to Allan. He had got used to it. He was safe there. The worst was over. It would be a couple of months yet before the keepers would think of carting the boat back to Loch Deoch. Indeed it might well be more, for Loch Deoch was in a deer forest and the shooting tenant would not appear before August. Gamekeepers or stalkers did not fish hill lochs for brown trout as a personal hobby.

But at a deeper level still, the lad had got knitted into the background that, as a hunter, he loved so well. It was from this realm of the instinct that Sandy now got his conviction that Allan had not left the Crannock. He would stay there for some time yet. He would stalk the croft for food. Man had been a hunter over a stretch of time so vast that his civilised period was in comparison but an affair of yesterday. Men who went fishing and hunting today were evoking in themselves that vast past, and finding a sustained delight keener and cleaner than any other they knew.

However, the anxiety that overwhelmed Sandy so starkly before he at last fell asleep, lost its edge in the bright daylight. Though there was plenty to do about the croft, he managed on the third day to reach the loch of the lilies. There he fell in with the shepherd and they had a long talk about Nicol's obsession, for the shepherd had seen the policeman that very morning in plain clothes climbing the slope of Carn a Choire. But the talk had given the old friendliness between them an extra pleasure, for the shepherd got all the details of Sandy's accident out of him and they laughed a lot. On the way home Sandy felt life's glow revive within him. There were good men in the world. Out of the purple bloom on the birches would soon blow that green in which the sunlight glows like a magic fire. Moreover it was seven days since Allan had last visited the croft for food, so the lad must really have headed south over the mountains. Let Nicol climb his hills! It was probably the very medicine he needed!

On the following morning early Sandy had gone round the back of the house to take his ease and have a look at a patch of ground which he was going to use for turnips when he heard a scream and another scream from the direction of the barn or byre. Realising an accident of some sort had happened to Liz and half wondering if Nancy had kicked or crushed her, he trotted past the heap of harrows and old junk, round the gable-end of the barn, and saw a stooping figure running down by the garden wall. At the corner of the wall the figure paused and threw a swift glance back. It was Allan, his face white and desperate. For an instant he stared at Sandy, then was gone.

But Sandy had no time to think of him, for Liz's appalling cries from the barn took him on the run in at the door. She was lying on the inner edge of the heap of hay, near the crib or manger, her whole body writhing in a convulsion of agony. At first Sandy thought Allan must have attacked her, must in a sudden mad anger have smashed her to the ground. She was squirming, struggling round half onto her knees, her fists full of hay, her hair over her face, her teeth clenching the wild animal yell back into her throat.

Sandy cried her name and got down on his knees, but not until she made certain motions did he realise that the girl was in labour.

'Lizzie, my lass,' he called to her warmly, 'I'll help you. Wait you now.' He slipped his left arm out of its sling and eased open or off the clothes she had already been tearing at. His friendly words fell upon her encouragingly. 'Many a lamb I've helped into the world. You're safe with old Sandy. I'll look after you, my lass, should the sky itself fall in small bits. That's you! Grip hard now!' and he gave her his hands.

Never had Sandy been at so long a birth, but he was full of knowledge and resource, and when she tried to smother the scream he told her to let it out.

'That's yourself! Take the roof off!'

And she all but did. He wiped the sweat from her brows, and moved the hay, got her body as he wanted it, and told her how to help herself. Then a spasm came upon her that opened her eyes in a wide fearful way, as though the unknown in terror had her at last, and at that instant the wide-open eyes came upon Sandy in a bewilderment that was pure trust – while it waited for the next incredible, excruciating moment.

Sandy knew he had her then. They were beyond the surface and communion was between them. He could feel the surge of her need towards him, her human need, the groping desire to hang on to him even while her hands twisted in the hay.

When the male child was born Sandy thought it was dead. He did what he could to smack life into it, to breathe life into it. From her livid panting face her eyes looked and hardly cared and shut and looked. Then there was a thin cry, new to the world, and it hit her in the heart, so that her gasping increased and her body fell away in exhaustion even while her arms lifted forward before they fell.

Sandy wrapped the child in her underclothes and the underclothes in his arm-sling, then kicking some hay into the manger he laid it there. A new-born lamb didn't manage a drink for a little time, as he knew. He spoke to Liz who was now lying utterly spent, eyes shut.

'He's fine there till I bring some warm water and clothes. Don't you move till I come back.'

Her brown eyes opened and from the far place where agony was absent she smiled to him, and it was a beautiful smile, so pure it was like an offering.

'You did well,' he said, 'my dear lassie.' Then he started off at a trot.

He had a deep movement of gratitude towards her for

having helped him so well, and what he had dreaded was being got round. She would accept the child yet. He had the feeling that she had accepted it already just because he had been kind to her and helped her. But he mustn't be long. She would be better without much time to think. The kettle – thank God, it was full, its edge against the fire, while the porridge pot over the fire was almost boiling, with no meal in it yet. A good housekeeper, a capable girl, if ever there was one. He could not think beyond the sheets on his bed, for they were warm, and the nurse changed them often enough, as heaven knew. So he ripped the two sheets off his bed, stuck the soap in the towel, the towel in the tin basin, and with the heavy iron kettle hanging from his good arm he started back. The child was puling in the crib, and there she was halfway towards it. But he soon stopped her.

'Wait you!' he called. 'I'll soon deal with him. He's in for his first baptism now. And it won't be his last with all that lungs in him, if I know anything. Ay, ay! we're hearing you,' said Sandy as he poured the water into the basin and felt its temperature. 'It's just right,' he declared. 'Luck is with us this morning.'

If Liz was wild-eyed and restless, Sandy paid no attention to her. He knew how tough the newly born animal was, incredibly tough – up to that point where it suddenly and mysteriously gives up the ghost and dies on one's hands. But there was no sign of dying here. He handled the fragile slippery body with an easy confidence, dried it with the towel, rolled it in one end of a sheet and brought it to the arms that were waiting for it. 'He's earned his drink,' said Sandy.

He busied himself until he saw the look in Lizzie's face above the round nuzzling head, then all anxiety fell from him. 'I'll have to make yourself comfortable next, but

that won't take long.' Off he went with the kettle and
into it he emptied the hot water from the porridge pot
and filled up with cold. A good wipe down would do
her fine meanwhile. With new hay and a bed quilt. The
very thing.

'You have enough swaddling clothes here,' said Sandy
lifting the end of the bedsheet in which the child was
wrapped and throwing it from him so that it fell on the
girl's face. Then he set about washing his patient and doing
all that had to be done, until at last the second bedsheet
was round her and the quilt round the sheet and the hay
underneath dry as bone.

'Not much of a bed for you,' he said at last drying his
hands. 'But when you're fit for it we'll have you back in
your own room and if anyone tried to move you from there
without my permission he'll need more than a block and
tackle.'

He smiled to her encouragingly, for at the moment he
was very pleased with himself, and even more pleased with
her for having behaved so well. She hadn't smothered the
child. She hadn't even bled to death. When he saw the tears
starting to run, he merely looked at her face more closely
and observed that her hair was damp and the drained skin
on her face not much better. Both could do with a wipe,
so he went off for some more water.

Of all that happened that morning to Sandy, what
happened next gave him the greatest shock. With the wet
end of the towel he had wiped her brows and was bringing
the cloth down her cheek and under her chin when her
head suddenly, impulsively, moved and she kissed his
hand.

'Well, well,' he said smiling broadly and then, as one
who liked to finish a job when he was at it, he wiped her
eyesockets. 'There's not much noise from *mo laochain* now,'

he observed, getting back on his feet. 'I could do with a drink myself. What about a good strong cup of tea?'

As he went back towards the kitchen he was deeply stirred. It was not only that the poor girl had kissed his hand; it was also something else. Dear Lord, it was a fact, and they could say what they liked, thought Sandy, but there was something in the human soul ready to cry its gratitude, given half a chance. There was. There always had been. The human soul was like that. It was hungry. So it was. Hungry for the kind word, with lips ready to salute it. Something pitiful in it, perhaps, somewhere; but beautiful too. Very beautiful, with hope shut under the hard surface, waiting for the chance to cry its message through any rift.

And then as he stuck the kettle in the fire he remembered Allan. Slowly he went back to the door and stared about the landscape. From the up gable-end his eyes searched the belt of trees that ran with the river. He would have skulked down to the trees to take their cover as far as they went, on his way back into the hills.

Thoughtfully Sandy returned to the kitchen. What had happened? Had Allan's sudden appearance so upset Liz that labour had come upon her? If so, where had he appeared from in the morning, in daylight? There could only be one answer: he must have been in the loft.

Sandy went back to the kettle and attended to the fire. But what had driven him into the loft? Had Nicol – had Nicol got onto his track yesterday? The shepherd had seen Nicol climbing Carn a Choire. From the top of Carn a Choire, could one see Loch Deoch? No, decided Sandy, but one could see a long way west. And Nicol might have climbed more than the Carn.

He poked a piece of stick into the fire. His shoulder was irking him and with his right hand he eased up the elbow.

Surely – surely the lad was not taking mad chances already? The fact remained – he had not gone away. And he was – yes – seven days without getting any food from this house.

The kettle was taking a long time to boil with so small a drop of water in it. Should he heat some milk for her? Nancy gave an impatient roar. She was neither milked nor fed. Liz must have gone to the barn for hay. The kettle began to sing. He swilled the teapot and was soon on his way with a large cup of tea.

Whatever intentions he may have had about cautiously sounding Liz on what had happened – it was just conceivably possible that she might never have seen Allan at all – they were dissipated by the need for action for Liz could not drink the tea over the infant's head. During his absence she had got most of the sheet tucked around the child, and Sandy now made a nest for the small bundle beside her. His movements were gentle but quite firm, for he had no exaggerated fear of hurting the newly born. From bird nestlings to puppies, calves to lambs, he had a wide experience of nature's incredible persistence and strength where the fragile were concerned. Give them food and warmth, and mountains could blow their heads off and bombs shake the earth. But when he saw the cup tremble in Liz's hand it was another story.

'Are you cold?' he asked.

'A little,' she answered.

He had to take the cup from her; but telling her how warm he would have her in five minutes, he put an arm round her shoulder and helped her to drink.

Stripping the blankets off his bed, he warmed them at the fire, then with the warmth bunched inside he returned to the barn. Neat-handed as a sailor, he wrapped them about her, making a tidy job of it, letting slip an odd sentence of comfort or caution, until he came to her feet. They were stone cold.

'When your feet are cold you're all cold,' he said; 'and there's not such a thing, I do believe, as a hot bottle in the whole house.'

'I'm fine now.'

His brows were gathered in thought, even as his hands kept gripping and massaging her feet. 'A chill on you now would be pneumonia before the night.' In a desperate moment invention rarely failed him. His face cleared. Pulling up his blue jersey, he undid his shirt and thick undervest, and in a few moments had the soles of her feet against his chest and his warm clothes back over them. He did this with a naturalness, a lack of self-consciousness, so complete that the pleasant expression on his face was that of one who had unexpectedly won a contest.

'Is that a bit warmer?' he asked.

As her face fell over and her arms drew the child nearer, he saw a faint colour tinge her cheeks. She could not speak, poor girl. She was young. One has to live a long time, perhaps, before all the ways of the flesh are seen for what they are.

When he got life back into her feet he wrapped them in the blankets and said, 'I'm going to warm some milk, for you need nourishment – and maybe I'll switch an egg in it – and a drop of spirit added would do you no harm. And then I'll go for the widow. For I don't know about moving you to your own room, but she'll know.'

Ten minutes after that he was breasting the slope with such earnest speed that Queenie caught the excitement, put up a brown hare, and followed it out of sight. When he saw Widow Macleay among the hens he called 'Ahoy there!' with such resonance that the tin basin fell from her hands as she stared. Up she came at a waddle to meet him.

'She's had her bairn.'

'What?' Her mouth opened and her eyes glared.

'Come on.'

'What? Anyone with her?'

'Me.'

'God help her!' said the widow, getting her wind back, then she left her own world behind her, with its door open, the food on the table and the pot on the fire.

'Is she all right?' gasped the widow.

'Fine,' replied Sandy.

'Did you – where is she?'

'In the barn.'

'The barn!' She almost stopped before she kept going. 'And no one with her?'

'I was.'

'O God,' said the widow to the upward path.

'I sweated more,' said Sandy, short as his wind was, 'over Nancy's last calf but one.'

But the widow had lost her gaiety. She made a harsh guttural dismissive sound as if Sandy was something in her spittle; and if he did not mind that, he was a trifle disappointed with his heart when he had to fall a few paces behind, for she was making a wonderful passage. However, she overshot her wind in that fine first burst and he overhauled her on the crest.

'Wh-what brought it on her?' she demanded.

'Wh-what?' echoed Sandy, suddenly appalled and playing for time.

'Had she an accident? . . . a fright?'

'Lifting hay.'

'And I told her,' said the widow, under way again, 'what not to do.'

My God, thought Sandy, it's the first thing she'll ask Liz. Why hadn't he warned the girl not to mention Allan? He racked his brains for something to say that might divert the widow, send her to the kitchen first, anything; but one glance at the billowing skirts, the streaming wisps of grey hair, the remarkable motion of the hull on the down slope against a small head wind, made him realise that nothing short of a typhoon would carry her past the barn door. I'm sunk, he thought with such bitter concern that when Queenie barked out of a mixture of bewilderment and frustration, for she had got no more of the hare than its smell, he shut her up in a harsh voice.

The widow negotiated the door without a bump and stood panting above Liz and her child with eyes that missed nothing. 'How are you?'

'Fine,' murmured Liz.

'Eh?' Then the widow got down on her knees. 'What happened to you?'

Sandy in the doorway held his breath though it was not easy.

'I was lifting some hay when – when the pain took me,' replied Liz in her quiet voice.

'Didn't I warn you about lifting? God be here, was it wasting my breath I was?' But her hands were busy. 'Where's that man?' She slewed round. 'Bring two hot bottles as fast as you can.'

'There's not – there's not such a thing in the house,' faltered Sandy.

'Not such a thing! and the place stinking with bottles! Though you needn't pour the whisky down the drain. You'll need that for yourself and the minister.'

'Ay, ay,' said Sandy, turning away.

'And listen!'

'Yes?'

'Make a roaring fire and put the kettle on. Then clean out the ben-room grate and put a fire on there. We'll have to get her out of this ice-house somehow.'

'Very good.'

'Have you had your porridge?'

'Yes,' said Sandy. 'No.'

'You better make up your mind about it,' said the widow, and Sandy was reminded of an old skipper out of the kingdom of Fife who used to turn his shoulder in just that way after dropping a sarcastic remark from his bridge.

On the way back to the kitchen he heaved up his weak shoulder to ease the joint and went over to starboard. Whatever moorings he had seemed suddenly to have loosened. He made heavy weather of it into the kitchen where he sat down before the fire. If his movements were slow, they were still reasonably sure and soon the kettle was over the flames. Now for the bottles.

On the dresser at last he placed one empty bottle and one with a good sup of whisky in it. Sandy had long been an abstemious man, and not merely because whisky was difficult to buy. Though the cream jug shone with cleanliness, he smelt it all the same. Something in his nature revolted against pouring the precious spirit into an open container. There it would not only evaporate but slowly lose its strength, its goodness, its life. It was bad enough to have it carrying the price of a king's ransom without pouring it into a gaping milk jug. It was indeed. In this difficult if not distressing position, his eye roved for inspiration and landed on two clean tumblers upended on an inner corner of the dresser.

Why not? Hadn't he done well? He poured out what would have been a very small one if his hand hadn't shaken. 'I did damn well,' he said aloud and nodded and took off his drink while the life was in it. He cleared his throat as if it were a challenge to the widow, and put his empty tumbler on the dresser. 'Not too bad at all,' he added in good heart, nodding to himself again. Many a man might have done worse. And to prove it, there was the girl, cold perhaps but she might have been stiff, and her child was with her—

And then he was hit amidships. Here he was drinking to himself and challenging the widow from Fife, even if it wasn't Fife she came from, when he should have been toasting the poor lass with the child, and them with the world before them and not an easy world. By God no, in Angie's words.

With extreme care he tried to pour out a very small drop, a token drop, and would have succeeded if he hadn't felt so generous towards their young lives. His eyes glimmered; a remarkable beneficence came upon his smiling whiskered face. 'I wish you well,' he said. 'May God prosper you.'

TWENTY-TWO

You did fine – for a bachelor,' said the widow and her voice was so rich with humanity it was nearly lewd.

'Things might have turned out worse,' Sandy agreed.

'Wasn't that what was on my mind?' and she glanced at the kitchen door to make sure it was shut. 'And isn't that why I insisted I should stop the night with her?'

'It's more than kind of you, though I'm sorry it should be a shakedown—'

'Hach!' said the widow. 'Broken sleep is as natural to me as broken water to the river; we have both been running a long time now.'

Sandy smiled.

The widow was on her feet. 'Keep that sling on, for if your shoulder comes out again it will make a habit of it. How you kept it in I don't know.'

'I was very careful with it,' said Sandy.

'I'm sure,' said the widow with a sarcasm drier than old lime. 'I have heard many things about sailors.'

'Indeed.'

'But I will say they have hands on them – whatever else. Good night.'

Two or three hours later, Sandy, startled out of sleep, heard the thin puling of a child and the low voices of two women. At once he was a small boy again listening to those very sounds. The illusion was so remarkably strong that he dwelt in it, even while the real situation seeped into its edges. It had all happened before. He saw his mother with a vivid clarity, nursing her last child in its fatal illness, his father's quiet weather-burnt face, his brothers and two sisters, all older than he. The warmth of their lives, the look in their eyes, the old croft house – the whole came about him, almost tangibly; he breathed its air, his young heart caught its beat, his eyes saw every characteristic movement. They were there solidly yet not solidly but fluidly like water, and yet not like water but illusively like air, essential presences painted on a time-less air.

From everlasting to everlasting. The old words came back to him like an echo from a pulpit or a mountain, concerning what could never be known precisely, potent with mystery beyond the mind's grasp.

They had all passed into that mystery except himself and possibly his brother Daniel, who had gone out to the Argentine with some pedigreed bulls and never came back. They had all scattered widely, as was the way with Highland families, and this very scattering brought upon Sandy now a sense of the ends of the earth and of human beings inhabiting the earth, one with another. Men from the old homeland, and women, going forth and settling in different lands among their own and among strange peoples.

The thin puling voice, there it was again . . . as it had been in times past. Then in a moment it ceased, and there was silence.

Queenie whined and Sandy tried to see the brute on the floor. Then he heard her moving paws and the flop of her body.

Was Allan on the hunt for food? He listened for a while but the dog seemed now at peace and no sound came from outside.

He should have gone away, that lad. He should have cleared out when he had the chance. He had been helped enough. No one could help him further. He was too young to feel a deep love for his own land. Yet in the desperate hunt, the animal made for its den. It felt secure there.

It was difficult to judge, to know. But one thing was certain: Allan would never come to the house in daylight. He must have come in the night, and the only place he could have hidden in was the barn loft. Liz had gone in for hay. Allan might have been dozing, heard the sounds, thought it was Sandy and moved on the sounding boards. Liz would have been gripped by terror – and then seen Allan's face in the opening over the crib. As the pain took her and she screamed he would have leapt down and cleared out. His face by the corner of the garden had been white and scared, with something strange about it . . . As the shaven face now came before Sandy he saw upon its upper lip a neat moustache. Not only the new suit but a mous-tache. That was it. Disguise.

When Sandy got over this wonder he came back to Liz, for if she had seen Allan she had given no sign. Of this he could make nothing at all, unless Liz, like himself, had the instinct to shield the lad, which indeed she more than might. But what a burden for her to carry, what a bomb in her mind!

And then a very odd thought came to Sandy, distilled somehow out of the girl's quietness, her endurance, the move-ments she made, the unobtrusive way she did her work: she accepted what had happened and had made her renunciation.

For she bore the child of the man whom Allan had killed. There was no way out of that situation, whatever her heart may have since told her of her love for Allan. Just no way. It was old as the first tribe. Only perverted people might try to get round that, and then only to lacerate and destroy each other.

This conviction came upon Sandy with an extreme

clarity. Indeed his vision passed between times and places like a flying bird. Back it went seventy years to his first home, when the world beyond it was still a world of strangeness and hearsay. The more remote districts lived humanly then pretty much as they had lived for a thousand years, yes and for two thousand years. The same feelings and customs, the communal warmth at peat-cutting and harvest, at Hallowe'en and the New Year, at marriage and death.

An instinct for friendly behaviour old as the first tribe, for beyond the first tribe was the story of Cain.

Then a still odder notion visited Sandy in the clear place of his sleeplessness. The thin spiring cry of life had come into his house as it had come into his old home, and into homes far back beyond that: it had come in the primitive way, in a barn, on a heap of dry hay, not because there was no room in the house, but for other desperate reasons. At this fundamental level the blood remained the blood, whatever man did about it. Out of it came life's thin cry. Whatever deeds man committed, to whatever lengths he carried the story of Cain, ay, even though with atom bombs he would yet make Cains of us all and universal death his aim, at the end of it there would be the few left here and there, cutting the grass for their beasts and feeding it to them in a manger when winter froze the earth. As it had been in the beginning so was it here in his croft now. And outside and beyond – the remorseless Nicol was hunting Allan, no longer as a policeman, no more as a keeper of the laws of the tribe, but as one man on the track of another with that hidden in his blood which the tell-tale dream or 'sight' saw as a dead body. The manger and the hay and life's new cry; beyond it, that hunt. Of all the stories man had made only two were immortal: the story of Cain and the story of Christ.

In the morning Sandy left the house to the women. When he came to the potato pit he saw that part of its face had been covered over too smoothly; the earth had, beyond doubt, been finger-raked.

His uneasiness increased, and, when he had dealt with Nancy, he set off for the birch wood to gather some rotten branches for kindling and some bog pine from the moor farther on where the old peat banks were. Everywhere he looked for human signs and, when he rested, his eyes kept wandering, but all was dumb and still, and he turned homeward with a bundle of sticks roped over his shoulder and his arm back in its sling. As he rested some little way from the house, the nurse and the widow came out and went up the slope towards the main road. A dry smile crinkled his eyes as he saw the earnestness of their colloquy, for the widow had impressed upon him the excellent idea that what had happened in the barn was no affair for the outside world, and she would now be giving all the details of it to the nurse under the ban of secrecy. The nurse would tell the doctor. The widow had her special cronies. It would be a wonder if the banker wouldn't compliment him when he went to Hilton for the money he now so badly needed! And as for the doctor and the minister, he would have to return their sallies, with a little interest added. Well, he might manage that, if only his mind were more at ease.

As he entered the ben room, he saw Liz's face on the pillow, drained and wan. 'Have they left you?' he asked, turning his eyes to the fire.

'Mrs Macleay said she would be back to cook the dinner.'

'You're feeling tired today?'

'A little.'

'You'll pick up soon,' he said, placing some sticks near the fire, 'and it will be nice when you're about again and we'll have the place to ourselves.'

But she did not respond to the banter in his voice and he knew she was feeling pretty low. Dusting his hands he went deliberately to the bedside. 'You're not letting anything worry you, are you?'

Her eyes came full on him.

He smiled. 'If you had a worry you could trust me to look after it, couldn't you?'

'Yes,' she murmured.

'That's right,' said Sandy. 'What happens here is our affair, and no one else's. I'll see it's no one else's.'

Her face turned away and her body gathered under the clothes. She did her best but soon she was weeping heavily.

He put his hand on her head.

'I'm sorry,' she gulped. 'Oh, I'm sorry.' Her body threshed a little and her hands thrust the tears from her eyes.

'What are you sorry for now?' asked Sandy sensibly, smoothing the hair back from her brows.

'Oh – everything!' she cried, blinded by the wild flood of emotion that broke over her.

The dam is burst at last, thought Sandy. He was moved, looking at her, but not much. The eyes of pity were somewhere and what they saw was not a thing that could be mended. Beyond the emotion, life's purpose, if it had any, seemed thin enough. Bleak, and arid as a far desert, and without any meaning that could be apprehended. His eyes strayed beyond the bed to the cot on the other side where the infant was asleep, then back to the face with the tumbled hair and the emotion racking its way out.

As the last resistance was swept aside, she cried, 'Will they catch him?' Wild as her cry was, instantly her eyes were on him, fearful and waiting.

He smiled. 'I hope not,' he said.

All her body grew still as her eyes searched his face.

'He was up in the loft, was he?' Sandy asked.

'Yes.'

He nodded. 'It was food he was after, but he must have gone up there to rest and fallen asleep. He slipped down to the trees by the river and won back to his hiding place.'

She was panting heavily and her wide eyes now roved here and there as in a strange place.

'If this has been worrying you,' said Sandy, 'I'm glad you told me.'

'I couldn't stand it if he was caught and – and . . . I couldn't stand it!' Her whole body writhed in a dry desperate agony.

'It's worried myself,' said Sandy.

'Oh, I couldn't! No! No!'

And Sandy saw at last that indeed she couldn't – and wouldn't. Allan caught – and tried – and hanged. It would destroy her.

So for the first time, and without any clear thought of it forming in his head, he knew why she was here. For so long as Allan was free, she lived in her quiet fatal world of suspense. She could go on. Between herself and Allan all was ended – but Allan lived. If Allan were caught and tried, she, the woman who cared for him beneath her mad folly, beyond sense and reason, would be his murderer. She had come a long road to that conclusion. Beyond it were deeps of the spirit that no words sounded.

'What we have to do is keep calm. If ever food went missing from the house you know nothing about it. I cannot tell you how relieved I was when you said nothing to the widow to make her wonder.'

Intelligence was back in her eyes, her breathing quickening, her hands gripping at the bedclothes.

'Our idea was, when the hunt died down he would head over the mountains and away. That time has now come. Only yon queer fellow Nicol still comes mooning around occasionally, but I dealt with him when things were more desperate than they are. I told Allan about him, so he's on the alert – and is already, if I am not mistaken, well on his way. Now, what I have told you is between ourselves, for I have breathed no word to another soul, and wouldn't have breathed one to you if you hadn't seen him.'

The expression on her face was exactly as if there had been a veil over it and an invisible hand had torn it off.

The very weight of her thought lessened her breathing. Then her eyes came on his face, bright and hot, in a moment of communion, of understanding, that was not gratitude because it was beyond all things personal, and her face fell over on the pillow.

'Once,' said Sandy, 'I was through a time as bad as your own. Terrible it was, and one day I may tell you about it.' He patted her head in his friendly way, but before he could remove his hand she had caught it and without turning her face she held onto it for a moment as strongly as ever she had done in the barn. Without a word more to her, he went out.

TWENTY-THREE

The devil of it was, for Sandy, that he couldn't understand why Allan had gone into hiding in the loft. To say
that he had been tired and gone up there to rest was
nonsense. He wouldn't have gone there unless he had felt
headed off and was afraid to go back and be trapped in
the Crannock. Short of food, he might have been hunting
trout or rabbits. There were many wild spots he could
now lie up in safely enough as long as he kept to cover
in the daylight. He might even have been after a salmon
in the river in the grey of the morning. But at some point
he had seen Nicol. And perhaps he was uncertain if Nicol
had seen him.

Sandy was very worried. He could think a hundred
things but what was beyond any reasoning or mental
contrivance was the feeling, with its dark burden of fore-
boding, that out there in the hills Allan and Nicol were
playing their desperate game, so divorced from broad sense
that it was queer and maddening to anyone but to them.
To hunter and hunted there was no world beyond the
immediate world of the vivid instinct and the next move.

Somehow he would have to get in touch with Allan and
definitely send him packing, even if it meant covering the
ground with his glass as far as the Crannock itself. If the
lad was weak from lack of food, he would contrive to put
that right; then speak to him straight, and break the tie
that bound him to the Crannock as a fox to its den. He
could not go on living there through the long summer

nights when it was hardly dark at all, with the boat back on Loch Deoch and estate servants and hikers on the hills. Already the days were rapidly lengthening. It was time he was off, or this very queerness that was growing on him, the loneliness, would be spotted in a city crowd.

On his first outing Sandy took in all the country round the loch of the lilies, and though now and then he had his telescope on long vistas he saw nothing. Back in the barn a sudden impulse made him look behind the opened door and there was a brown sack neatly folded, with its mouth open. It took the wind from him for a minute. So he had come back, been hindered or interrupted somehow, gone up into the loft and fallen asleep. Sandy nodded very slowly.

That night he put food in the sack, but next morning it was still there.

One thing only was clear: the lad had not been trapped so far. If Nicol had no more than 'signs', even if he had no more than a doubtful glimpse of a figure in a brown – not a dark – suit, he would say nothing in Hilton now. He would not want to be thought madder than he was; and he *would* want above all to bring in the 'evidence' in fact and in triumph, using his holidays to shuttle between the lonely hills and his mother's black face.

But as one day followed another Sandy's confidence began to grow. Liz got on her feet and the widow went back at night to sleep in her own home. Far from rallying Sandy, Dr Drummond complimented him seriously behind his smile. 'It's when a fore-foot meets you first that it's not so easy,' replied Sandy and the doctor let his laughter go. The widow brought the groceries and Danny's gossip from the van.

Each night he put the food sack behind the barn door and found it untouched in the morning.

Sandy himself now became obsessed by the hunt. At first

he had expected to catch a glimpse of Nicol in some lonely spot, but as he entered into the dark drama he realised that Nicol, with something to go on, a sign or a sight, would not show himself in the daylight. The hunter lies low, by the spoor or the water hole. In these bare regions, a pair of keen eyes could see a long way. And that applied to both of them, Nicol and Allan.

Then Sandy realised that it also applied to himself. For if Nicol, from his hiding hole, saw Sandy quartering the ground with his glass, what would he think?

Liz was quiet and preoccupied but a little more human, more spontaneous in her movements. The lull, the after spell, thought Sandy; the long wonder with the eyes far away over the child's head. She would come round in time, and when she did that, thought Sandy, she would be a fine woman, for the softness in her would firm up but never harden, for if you are born with a generous nature it is almost impossible to get rid of it. At times a smoothness on her brow seemed to widen the space between her eyes and she looked very fair, and in that fairness dwelt the something beyond beauty that is the tragic wonder of the human state. That there was light in it also gave to the beholding eye the far memory of a promise. Poignant it was, and not easy to bear or to forget.

When a few days passed, Sandy began to think that Allan must have really gone. The sight of Liz had been a tremendous shock to him and having left her screaming in the hay he was bound to think that she would tell of what she had seen. His instinct would surely be to put as much distance as possible between himself and this part of the world.

Yet Sandy was not impressed by this thought, indeed it left him uneasier than ever, as though desperation had only the more surely sent the lad to earth. Moreover, he would know that Sandy would not let Liz babble. Indeed on reflection he might well decide that Sandy and Liz were in collusion, especially when no sign of an organised hunt immediately appeared. Of Nicol's obsession he knew.

The day came when Sandy decided to bring Loch Deoch itself within his telescope. It would be a tricky operation for he must not appear to be specially concerned with Loch Deoch, lest Nicol should see him.

He asked Liz to make up sandwiches and not to worry if he was late coming home. She did this while he was eating his porridge, and at the doorstep he said, 'If anyone happens to call you can say that I'd been talking of going to the peat bank.'

'Yes,' she answered.

'I'm just wanting to make sure,' he said with a smile, 'that no traces are left of anyone in our part of the world. No news is good news. You're there, are you?' he addressed Queenie and they set off towards the birch wood, the large packet of sandwiches in his poacher's pocket.

He was in no hurry and it was going to be a good day. The clouds were small and high and gave to the sky a summer blue, the blue of promise. The wind was in the west but not much of it and not cold. When he got the smell of the birches, the promise in the blue was confirmed and he stood for a little time among the slim silvered trunks. Compared with man the earth was very old, but old as it was it was quickening with a youth vivid as boyhood. He got the smell of it, the sharp acrid smell that tingled in the blood, or very nearly for his old flesh would hardly let it in. But it was there, and if he could scrape away the old flesh and the barnacles of time, he might feel the swish and surge of it.

He played with this thought for a while, for it had been evading him altogether lately. It took so little to destroy it completely and leave in its place the disillusion that is the last mockery. And this disillusion a man hangs on to like a drug, like the inner end of a den in which he can curl up in safety. In nothingness, with disillusion in the curl of the lip, he is safe at last.

Using a slim trunk to steady his glass, he covered the peat banks and the country beyond, then bore left through the trees and in time came down on the loch of the water lilies. It was half circled by birches and old heather and he let Queenie tire herself by searching out the thick cover, then he went across to the narrow ravine where the small burn came in and sent her up that.

In time he skirted the foot of the corrie in the hill with the cairn on top of it, Carn a Choire, with Queenie hunting around great boulders and now and then putting up a mountain hare. One sign Sandy didn't like – the absence of deer, for he was heading into the wind and the deer therefore could not get his scent. However, he had often come as far without seeing a beast, for it took little enough to send deer on the move, and at different times of the year they had their own particular feeding places.

All that forenoon he wandered through hollows, keeping off the ridges except for an occasional spy, and if a stalker had been watching him he might well have thought the old boy was after something, with perhaps a small rifle slung under his jacket. As he rested in a sheltered hollow by a burn that ran into the main river miles away, he was overcome by fatigue and fell asleep. He awoke with a shiver and felt stiff, but even as he looked at the rowan in the rock-face, and the salley bush and the elder over-hanging a tiny pool, he was invaded by a freshness in that lonely sunny spot and decided to go on. If only he could have eaten, it might have helped. But how Allan could be getting food, if he was still in the neighbourhood, had gnawed at Sandy like a sore tooth he did his best not to think about.

After leaving the burn, he bore to his right where a hollow ran between two low ridges and opened out a barren scoop of waterlogged moor. As he skirted this, his weariness came heavily upon him, with an occasional sharp pain in the left knee that doubled it under him. But he was making for the shoulder of a hill beyond which he should see, or very nearly see, the upper end of Loch Deoch. Beyond that he would not go.

When at last Sandy flattened in the heather, he lay and rested, with Queenie panting beside him. The hill air and the hard exercise were a drug for his overtaxed body which gave way to the sharp-smelling heath and the earth beneath and sank into it with the pleasant feeling that no sleep in an ordinary bed ever quite gave. For a last sleep it was a good place, as he had occasionally thought.

Queenie's whine by his ear wakened him and before he quite knew where he was he had his hand on the dog's pelt pulling her down. But already his eyes were following her point and presently he saw something dark as an otter and not much bigger running along the next hill shoulder. Quickly he brought his telescope to bear and the figure of Nicol leapt across its lens. The haste, the anxiety, of the man hit Sandy in the heart. When Nicol had disappeared, Sandy's naked eyes roved over all they could see. Then he started off.

It was wild broken country with the hills on his right coming down in shoulders and corries to ground that flattened out broadly, glimmering with blue water holes or 'shivering eyes'. Beyond this flat bog-land, the ground rose again into a background of mountains. This was the upper country that drained into Loch Deoch, which lay, as he knew, beyond the ridge far over on his left.

At his own slow pace Sandy could travel far, but now, when he tried to hurry, his legs had neither the pith to drive him on nor the strength to hold him when he landed heavily. Once he lay for a while, with his heart jumping and fluttering in his breast, then he pulled up the left leg of his trousers and probed the knee-cap. But the bones seemed firm enough. It must be something catching a nerve when the weight came in a certain direction, he decided. But his lack of power, of decisive action, had the effect of draining his own anxiety in a fatal way. I can't do what I can't do, thought Sandy, and he went on calmer and even strengthened a little.

It took him a long time to reach the spot where Nicol had disappeared and when he reached it there was no sign of life anywhere; primeval and barren, without movement of fur or feather. So he followed on where Nicol must have gone, crossed an old water course, climbed over its crumbling bank, and in the end was glad to collapse among broken ground for now he could get a clear view of the bog-land that ran far to the north-west.

Slowly he took his bearings. Loch Deoch was still covered by its high eastern crest, but the crest dipped to the north, and where it flattened out, his telescope picked up trees. He knew that narrow belt of trees well. It ran for a mile or two like a snake against the base of the hills, hiding its stream. If he climbed higher he would open the upper end of Loch Deoch, and perhaps the Crannock. When he had swept the prospect to the north-west and seen nothing, he rested, Queenie beside him.

He was staring past her towards the long hill that covered Loch Deoch when he saw her ears prick. He knew she had heard something, and as he held his breath he fancied he caught the thin remotely distant scream of a golden eagle. He slewed round and faced up-wind. Queenie whined and he harshly quietened her. But he could not hear anything now, and though he was disturbed he swept the air above the mountain ridges on the west and far into the north. But no eagle swam into the lens and he brought it down until the far end of the belt of trees, now little more than straggling small bushes, passed across it. The glass suddenly jerked in his hands, and for a little while so moved was he that he could not find what he had seen – then he found it, found the two diminutive figures and knew them as Allan and Nicol, moving around each other, staggering, in the tail-end of a fight. Now they were mixed up and one of them was down. The glass swung off them in Sandy's shaking hands. He got to his feet and yelled, harsh sounds that tore his throat and wouldn't have carried halfway even had the wind been with him instead of against him. With his naked eye he could not see them. He turned on Queenie and fiercely gestured her to that distant spot. Astonished, Queenie gazed ardently at him then off she went, hunting round the near rocks and tussocks, hunting for the rabbits she couldn't smell, throwing a look back and hunting again, foolishly at a loss.

But Sandy was flat once more and searching with his telescope. Now he could see nothing at all, nothing. They had vanished. Then in a moment Nicol was standing in the field of the lens, looking about him like one who was lost or was taking his bearings; he began walking across the flat ground. Even at that distance he seemed to be hurrying, with humped shoulders, staggering. Sandy kept the glass on him until the slope shut him off. Then back he swung the glass and searched for Allan, but there was no sign of Allan.

For a few moments Sandy lay where he was, his face drained grey, the indrawn breath cold in his mouth. Then he got up and went on, moving round the base of the hills

on his right. Now he had a feeling that he did not want
Nicol to see him, so that if he could still do anything for
Allan . . . But no thought formed completely. By keeping to
the edge of the great bog he might miss getting stuck in a
morass and arrive the more quickly . . . When he had gone
on about half a mile, the base of the hill ground on his
right stood clear for a long way ahead. There was no sign
of Nicol. He had had plenty of time to come back across
the peat bog and disappear up a strath or pass that would
bring him out well north of the loch of the water lilies on
the direct way to Hilton.

Sandy's roving eyes came back to a near water course
that winter torrents had cut through the bog and steadied
on footprints in peat ooze. So this was where Nicol had
crossed the open ground. Stooping, he would have followed
the shallow winding banks, like any stalker after a stag on
the other side. From his lookout on the hill, Nicol must
have seen Allan enter the belt of trees.

Sandy continued by the hill base until at last he came
opposite the place where he had seen them fighting. But
he was still concerned about Nicol and, going on a little
way, carefully opened the hollow that Nicol must have gone
up: a pass or bealach that swung round out of sight to the
left after a few hundred yards. Nicol was gone.

Sandy went across the bog.

At first he followed the belt of trees towards Loch Deoch,
then turned and went the other way. Queenie suddenly gave
a yelp by the burnside and Sandy hurried towards her. She
was tugging at a rabbit not yet dead. The rabbit was caught
in a snare. Sandy automatically killed the rabbit and examined the snare. It was one of his own old snares taken from
the barn. The sickness of expectancy in his breast grew.
'Allan!' he cried and listened. Then he came out a few yards
from the side of the burn and saw heelprints, bruised ground.

He searched around till he heard Queenie whine; with a tremble in his knees he went towards her. He could see nothing. A lip of heathery peat had been broken off and over one side of a bog hole or hag. By the way the dog behaved he knew only too well that here was no bolt hole for any beast. He got down on all fours, heaved away the broken tongue of heathery moss, and saw the body even as he himself slid from the bank to flounder in the bottom of the hag. The body turned over and came down against his knees. The thin face was smeared with soft black peat. The eyes were wide open. He felt the forehead. In a quiet anguished voice he said, 'Allan, *mo laochain.*'

TWENTY-FOUR

Getting Allan's body onto the heather took a lot out of Sandy though he did not rest until he had wiped the face, cleaned the peat ooze from the mouth and tried to close the eyes. Then he stretched himself flat out beside the dead lad.

What he had feared had been accomplished and it drained his mind so that body and mind both gave way and sank into that state where feeling itself gave way. It was all over now; it was finished. What had to be done could be thought about presently.

Sandy came to himself with the cold in his bones and a greyness in his head. He heard a croak in the trees but did not look for the raven. The bird would pick out the eyes first. The sun was falling down the sky. It was a long way home.

Methodically he went to work on the shoulder of the bank where he had found Allan, scooping out the soapy peat until he had formed a flat narrow ledge. He dressed it with grassy turves and got the body lying on it face down. He spoke to Allan several times, for the waste of young life troubled Sandy and he could see little meaning or purpose in it. It would have been more like the thing if he himself had been lying in Allan's place. But the mystery did not work out that way and all thought or sentiment about it was vanity and folly.

Before covering the body, he said goodbye to Allan and a sudden resurgence of feeling moved in that place beyond vanity and folly where is neither challenge nor acceptance, but only the pure feeling itself. In the loneliness and lostness of that moment he loved the lad. Allan, *mo laochain*, my little hero; the boy who had come about his croft and lit it with his eyes.

He covered him well so that neither beak nor teeth would get at him, then in the burn close by he washed himself and scraped his boots and clothes.

On the way over the hill he rested many times and Queenie stayed with him, glancing at him often and gulping, her tongue going in and out over her teeth as if she had been running hard.

He knew he would have to think of what next he had to do but a great reluctance was upon him. All that mattered had been done.

As he crossed the watershed at last and saw the tumbled ground towards the loch of the lilies, he sat down, for now he was coming back to the land of the living and some course of action he must have before him. Something had to be said to Liz Murison when he entered at his door.

As he lay over, a hump caught his side and he remembered the sandwiches.

Queenie took each sandwich from him gently, almost with a look of guilt, then demolished it in a couple of gulps. In his own mouth the bread was dry and he couldn't get enough saliva to wet it. At a burn lower down he drank and ate two sandwiches and was glad to be finished with eating. He would decide what to do when he reached the Chair, for by that time he would know whether he had the pith to scramble home.

But his under mind must have been working, for when he crawled into the shelter of the Chair, Nicol was fast in his thought. What was Nicol going to do? Leave Allan yonder and say nothing about it? That was possible, but unlikely, for it would be neither a justification of his own beliefs and ongoings nor bring an end to his mother's obsession. He would want to produce the body – but not the fresh body. If the fresh body were produced and doctors found evidence of violence upon it, then there might be awkward questions for Nicol. All this, as a policeman, he would think out very carefully. But later on, when the body had rotted – to find it then, that would solve everything. The obvious conclusion would be that Allan, after having kept himself alive in the wilds for some time, had crawled into the shelter of a bog and died there.

Sandy found himself suddenly thinking that that would even relieve Lizzie's mind. To such an ending she would become reconciled.

That was important now. In life and living, that was maybe the only thing left that was important. And if it meant taking judgment into his own hands, that's where it had been most of the time, guilt or no guilt. His expression withered in a dry smile.

His duty . . . his duty was to report what he had seen.

Nicol would then be arrested and tried. He could plead self-defence. But he had been hunting for Allan, neither in his uniform nor on duty. That was known. His bitter vengeful attitude towards Allan was known. Allan was not hunting Nicol, he was trying to escape from him. In their lonely encounter it was Nicol who would force the issue, it was Nicol who would kill. Folk would not only believe that; they would know it. In their blood they would know that Nicol had set out to avenge his brother's death and succeeded.

Then a further thought struck Sandy. It came into a lull in his mind. Supposing he went to the police inspector and described what he had seen, what would the inspector do? He saw the police inspector going to Nicol and saying in that quiet voice with its dry inflection, 'No sign of Allan Innes yet?' It would sound like the usual sarcasm and Nicol would answer, 'No.'

He would have to answer no, unless he himself had already reported what had happened.

Confronted by the body and Sandy's story, what could Nicol say? He could deny it, saying he had never been near the place – and leave it to his footprints to confirm the story. It might be too late then to plead that he had acted in self-defence.

What might happen to Nicol came as ashes into Sandy's mouth. In all conscience, there had been enough violence and his mind called halt. He felt like an old man of the tribe, as the tribe had been, and might be again, with decision in his hands for the living, and the responsibility for that decision.

He would say nothing to Liz, nothing to anyone.

Whatever Nicol was going to do he would leave him to do it. And if Nicol never did anything, perhaps some day he himself would find Allan's bones and the lad's death would be seen as set in the balance of justice against the violence he had committed.

After a little while he got up and went slowly on. Right and wrong. Ay, that was easy. But the new commandment: love one another . . .

The withering on his face caught a hopeless light, but still a light, and when at last he saw the croft house, his last dwelling place on this earth, he sat down, for his very joints had gone dry and joggled at the impact of his weight. He would rest only for a little while and not let them stiffen altogether.

His face cleared, for he loved what he saw, not its beauty but just the place itself. Liz came out of the front door and was halfway to the barn when she stopped and hurried back. He almost heard the child crying. She had her hands full now!

When he got under way again he kept thinking about her and her bairn. After all, he wondered, to whom could he have left his croft anyway and his bit of money? In Scots law, all he had to do was write his will in his own hand and it was legal enough. He might find a way of saying something to her some day soon about doing this, were it only to ease her mind.

This thought lightened his own mind and when he was through the head fence the path was smooth. He was coming down by the end of the barn when fair in front of him he saw Williamina making towards the hen-house with a swarm of new chicks around her. Bringing them home from the nest where she had laid away! And cackling at him, too, righteously! 'Well, I'm blest!' muttered Sandy, and the tired smile sank deep in his eyes.

Before he reached the front door he stopped. Liz Murison was crooning an old Highland lullaby to her child. He had never heard her sing before. The tune seemed to well up from his own roots for it had put him to sleep many a time. Her voice was warm and the lullaby full of a woman's knowledge. He put his hand against the wall for a little while, gathered his resources, and went to the door.